SOWN IN DARK SOIL

SOWN IN DARK SOIL

APPALACHIAN ROOTS – BOOK TWO

JANICE COLE HOPKINS

AMBASSADOR INTERNATIONAL
GREENVILLE, SOUTH CAROLINA & BELFAST, NORTHERN IRELAND

www.ambassador-international.com

Sown in Dark Soil

Appalachian Roots – Book 2

Printed in the United States of America

ISBN: 978-1-62020-535-8
eISBN: 978-1-62020-463-4

All Scripture taken from the King James Version, the Authorized Version.

Cover Design and Page Layout by Hannah Nichols
Ebook Conversion by Anna Riebe Raats

AMBASSADOR INTERNATIONAL
Emerald House
427 Wade Hampton Blvd.
Greenville, SC 29609, USA
www.ambassador-international.com

AMBASSADOR BOOKS
The Mount
2 Woodstock Link
Belfast, BT6 8DD, Northern Ireland, UK
www.ambassadormedia.co.uk

The colophon is a trademark of Ambassador

For, behold, I am for you,
and I will turn unto you,
and ye shall be tilled and sown.

- Ezekiel 36:9 -

CHAPTER ONE

The Family

Gold Leaf Plantation, Anson County, North Carolina, June 1854

"Come on, Leah, promise me you'll do this," Ivy pleaded.

"I'm not going to promise anything, unless I know what I'm agreeing to do, and that's all there is to it."

"You two better be gittin' on down ta breakfast, now, fo' your mama goes and gits all outa sorts." Bertha poked her head out the master's bedroom to warn them and then resumed her cleaning.

"Okay, okay," Ivy threw up her hands as she walked from the doorway of Leah's bedroom. "I'll come back tonight before we go to sleep. We'll talk then."

Leah hoped by "talk," Ivy didn't mean more begging. She needed to know what Ivy wanted. Her older sister perplexed her to no end. Ivy rarely gave her the time of day, and now she wanted Leah's help. What could it be?

Leah followed Ivy down the stairs. Even from the back, her sister looked gorgeous. Her feminine curves swayed rhythmically as she floated down the steps with impeccable posture.

Leah had once been envious of the classic beauty. Ivy had flawless skin, just like the porcelain dolls they'd once owned. Her silky hair glowed like sourwood honey in sunlight, and her eyes were china blue. Her pert nose set on a perfect, oval face, and her lips were full and inviting, even in her usual pouts.

When Papa had guessed Leah felt like the ugly duckling, he'd pulled her onto his lap. She must have been seven or eight at the time. "Darling, I don't want you to be comparing yourself with your sister," he'd said. "God's given us all different gifts. Ivy's gift is physical beauty, but yours goes much deeper. You're beautiful on the inside, too. You have the finest mind and the kindest heart of any child I've ever known. Those are magnificent gifts, Leah. Besides, you are very pretty in your own right. Physical beauty can change and will over time. Beauty of character will last forever." Then he'd hugged her tightly, and Leah felt the truth of his words flow into her.

From that moment on, Leah never felt jealous of Ivy again. Instead, she tried to cultivate the things Papa admired: intelligence and compassion. If those were the traits Papa thought most important, then she did, too.

"Well, it's about time the two of you made an appearance." Mother smiled indulgently at Ivy. "You're looking lovely as usual this morning, Ivy."

"Thank you, Mother, but it's rather early for me, and I'm afraid I detained Leah. I needed to talk with her." Ivy must want something in the worst way if she was taking the blame for being late.

"Yes, well you do need your beauty rest, dear."

"I don't know about that." Papa laughed. "I don't know how much more of her beauty we can manage. She gives every young fellow in Anson County a crick in his neck now."

Ivy flashed him an appreciative smile, but Leah knew Papa hadn't given Ivy the huge compliment her sister thought.

"What are your plans for today, Leah?" Paul, her half-brother, asked.

"I plan to look in on Mattie and check on Lucy and her new baby."

"I don't see why you want to go down to the slave quarters so much," Mother scolded. "Those people need to be taking care of their own."

"It's really the mistress's job to be tending to the sick slaves," Papa reminded her. "Leah's just taking some of the responsibility from you, dear."

"Tssh," Mother hissed, but she didn't belabor the point.

"I wondered if you'd like to ride out to the west fields with me later on," Paul told her. I need to check on some things and wouldn't mind some company."

"I'd like that," she told her brother. Although Paul was just their half-brother, he and Leah looked more alike and had more in common than either of them did with Ivy.

Paul had dull, brown hair and hazel eyes, but Leah's hair was a rich, dark brown, and she had green eyes. From the time they'd spent outdoors, their skin had grown darker than Ivy's. Paul had a strong build, while Leah appeared much more petite. Yet, they resembled each other enough to be picked out as brother and sister. She and Ivy looked nothing like sisters.

Paul's mother had died when he was only five. Later on, Papa had taken a business trip to Maryland, met and married Mother, and brought her home. In less than a year, Ivy had been born. Leah came along two years later.

"You go ahead and take care of the sick in the quarters. I'll come by for you about ten," Paul told her. Leah nodded.

"Benjamin, I do wish you wouldn't encourage Leah to go wandering around the plantation." Mother turned to Papa. "She acts so much like a boy now, we'll never find her a husband."

"Oh, I'm not worried about that, Myra. I'm sure some young buck will come along and carry her away before I'm ready to see her go. You just go ahead and concentrate on making a good match for Ivy. She's the oldest and should marry first, by rights. I'll see to Leah, if need be, when the time comes."

"Ivy needs to quit being quite so choosy," Mother said, "or else she may end up an old maid." She looked pointedly at Ivy. This was the closest Leah had ever heard Mother come to scolding Ivy, and her voice still bore no irritation.

"Whatja doin' dressed like dat, youngin'?" Mattie asked Leah. "Ain't you a sight fo' so' eyes now."

"I'm going for a ride with Paul after I see about you and Lucy."

"Jus' so long as it's no beau you is sneakin' off to see."

"Now, Mattie, you know better than that."

The old lady laughed, which started her coughing. Leah gave her a large spoonful of medicine.

"Dat taste odder dan da las' un."

"This is basil juice and honey. The cabbage juice and honey didn't seem to do the job I wanted. Now you rest and get your strength back. Take a spoonful of the syrup as you need it. I brought you some more food, too. You eat it all now."

"Yes'm, Miss Leah. I's sho' will. 'Spect I's be up in no time."

Mattie seemed tiring already. Leah brought her fresh water and put the cough syrup beside her bed. She also set some food within reach. If the old slave got much weaker, she was going to need someone to stay with her and see to her needs.

Leah left and went to Lucy's cabin but found it empty. Donald Mallory, the overseer, must have her out in the fields already. Leah feared it might be too early for the slave to be working so hard, but Mallory wouldn't care.

"Mallory's as good as they come," Papa had told her.

If Mallory were the best, she sure would hate to see the worst. Slavery had become about the only issue on which she and Papa disagreed. The whole notion of owning someone seemed barbaric to her.

After she'd finished up, she met Paul at the stables. They rode out in a comfortable silence.

"How do you feel about Archibald Biles?" Paul finally asked.

She took a moment to form her answer, so she wouldn't sound too harsh. "I feel sorry for him, I guess. I mean, he is so mean spirited and . . . "

"Ugly," Paul finished for her. "He's going to inherit Magnolia Mansion, the richest plantation around here."

"I don't mind how he looks so much as how he acts. He acts as if he's better and knows more than everyone else, and he isn't nearly as fabulous as he thinks he is. I don't like arrogance, and I don't like cruelty."

"Neither do I, Sis. I heard your mother trying to talk Father into approving a marriage between you two. It seems Archie's interested in Ivy, but Myra won't consider that match. She would like to see our connection with Magnolia Mansion, however, so you're the logical choice."

"Papa will never allow it." Leah felt sure of that.

"I wouldn't be too sure. She managed to snare Father into marrying her. She has a way of wearing Father down and getting what she wants."

"Now Paul, you know Papa's no push-over. He's stood against her on more than one issue."

"That's true, but Papa's quite a bit older than she, and he still hasn't fully recovered from that sick spell he had back in the winter."

"If something ever happened to Papa, then you would be the head of the family." She looked at Paul. "I know you wouldn't listen to such a ridiculous idea."

"It's not the best idea, but I thought you should know."

"Thanks, Paul. I'll watch out and not give Archie any encouragement. I would think Mother would want Ivy to be the first to wed."

"I think that might be in the works, too."

"Who is it?"

"Lawrence Nance, I think."

"He's rich enough and not bad looking, but he's too nice for Ivy."

"Well, I get the feeling Ivy isn't too keen on the idea. I wonder if she hasn't met someone else she likes. Do you know who it might be?"

"No, you know Ivy doesn't confide in me. However, she does want me to do her a favor. She's supposed to talk with me about it tonight, but she hasn't given a hint of what it's about."

"Mister Paul, Miss Leah, come quick," the stable boy shouted, as he came riding up at breakneck speed. "It's yo' papa. He's done took real bad. De missus done sent fo' Doctor Lowder, and I's sent to fetch y'all."

They turned and galloped home. Leah followed Paul into Papa's bedroom.

"What's wrong?" Paul asked.

Mother gave a shrug. "He ate breakfast and went to his study. I heard a thump and ran to see what had happened. He'd fallen as he started up the stairs. I had Obadiah send for the doctor and get help to carry him upstairs."

"Don't talk like I'm not here." Papa's voice sounded weak and lifeless, not like him at all. "I'll be okay." He didn't sound okay, and he looked as if saying those few words had taken all his strength.

"Why don't you two wait downstairs for Doctor Lowder and show him up when he gets here. I'm afraid Benjamin will wear himself out trying to put on a strong front for y'all." Mother walked over and opened the door for them. To keep from causing a scene, they did as she asked.

Doctor Lowder came and went, but the news wasn't good. It seemed there was some malady with Papa's heart. The doctor bled him and left some medicine to make him comfortable, but there wasn't much else he could do.

When the doctor had suggested bloodletting, Leah had tried to veto the idea. Some of the more modern evidence she read questioned the wisdom of such practices, and Papa seemed so weak already that she thought he might need all the blood he had. Since Leah knew about healing, Paul had supported her, but the doctor and Mother had won out.

"I don't guess you are up to discussing my request tonight, are you?" Ivy asked as Leah picked at her food at supper. She shook her head.

Papa slipped away in the night, and grief hit Leah like a cannonball. She couldn't believe it. Papa had held the family together. What would happen to them now? Would Paul and Mother continue to be at odds all the time?

The wake and funeral were horrors. Mother insisted that Leah attend and present herself well. Leah would much rather have hidden in her room. She didn't want to be confronted with the reality of it all, and she wanted to remember Papa full of life and vibrant, not stiff and cold.

"But, Mother," Leah heard Ivy whine on the day of the funeral, "you know black makes me look horrid. Can't I wear my silver dress?"

"Not the silver," Mother told her, "but you may wear the gray trimmed in black piping. It's more somber but looks quite well on you."

Leah hurried away in disgust. How dare Ivy worry about fashion at a time like this! Leah's drab, black dress reflected how she felt.

She knew Papa lived in a much better place now, but that didn't offer the comfort she'd expected. She grieved that she wouldn't see him again on this earth.

Leah went through the motions without really being a part of them. If she became involved in the burial, her grief would be unbearable. She felt numb, but she did what convention required, and she tried to remember Papa as he had been—strong, healthy, and full of life and wisdom. Papa had been her champion and encouraged her to learn and explore. What would happen to her now with him gone?

About a week after the funeral, Ivy slipped into Leah's bedroom after everyone else was in bed. "I've got to talk with you. It can't wait any longer."

"What's this all about?"

"Now that Father's gone, Mother and Paul both want me to marry. I can't believe they agree on this."

"I thought you were ready to be married. You're already nineteen, and you've had about every eligible man in Anson County either offer for your hand or come to court you."

"And none of them suit me, but I have met someone. He's from the West, and he's divine. Wait until you meet him. I've never met anyone so handsome. He's like a Greek god."

"Who is it, and where did you meet him?"

"He's been staying with Lawrence's family."

"Do you mean Lawrence Nance?"

"Yes, the very one. They were at the funeral. Did you see them?"

"No, I didn't really look at anyone. What's your beau's name?"

"Luke Moretz."

"Tell me about him."

"His father is a doctor in Salisbury, but his mother died, and his father remarried. His stepmother was jealous of him, and he went to live with his grandmother in Watauga County."

"That's so far away."

"Yes, it is. That's why I want you to go with me."

"What?"

"Mother and Paul don't approve, but I've got to do this, Leah. I've got to follow my heart. Luke's going to have to leave soon. He's postponed leaving until after Father's funeral, as it is. He'll only let me go with him if I have a companion to keep things proper."

"Why run away? Why not get married here first? You could have that big, fancy wedding you've always wanted."

"I'll still have my wedding. After all, his father is a doctor, so they must have money. It's just Mother will not hear me on this, and she's determined to keep me from marrying him. She wants me to get married to some plantation owner and stay close to her. I might have done that, but I fell in love with Luke. I've got to have my chance at happiness, Leah. I've just got to go. Please say yes."

"I don't know, Ivy. This sounds pretty reckless to me. Have you thought it through?"

"I know I love Luke. What else is there to think about? Luke's smart. I trust him to take care of us. We'll be fine."

"Let me think about it."

"Don't take too long. Luke plans to leave by week's end. Please do this for me, Leah. When have I ever asked you for anything? We are sisters. I know you want what's best for me, but marrying Lawrence Nance is not what's best. I would be miserable, and I'd make him miserable, too. Can you imagine being intimate with someone you didn't want to marry? If you get to the mountains and hate it there, I'll make sure you get back here safely. I promise."

"Lawrence Nance is a very nice man. You could do worse."

"Oh, but Luke is so much better. Wait until you meet him. You know, Mother is determined you'll marry Archibald Biles, and he is horrid. It might be a good idea for you to escape, too." Ivy gave Leah a quick hug, something she never did.

Even after Ivy left, Leah couldn't get to sleep. Could she travel all the way to Watauga County with Ivy and Luke? Just the thought of it left her with an uncomfortable feeling. No, she'd be better off staying home. But would the plantation still be home without Papa?

She ended up doing what she always did when she faced a problem. She prayed. Still, the next morning the answer didn't seem any clearer.

"I've invited Archibald Biles and Lawrence Nance to supper tonight," Mother announced at breakfast. "Lawrence has some friend from the mountains staying with him now, so I invited Pricilla Mullins to even things out."

Ivy gave Leah a look, which said, "I told you." They both knew Archibald had been invited for Leah and Lawrence for Ivy. Pricilla, a shy, plain girl with little to say, had been invited for Luke but would offer no competition to either sister. Mother looked quite pleased with herself.

Leah wondered why Mother would invite the man Ivy wanted to marry along with Lawrence. Of course, she could hardly invite Lawrence and not include his visiting friend, and perhaps she just wanted to see him for herself. Leah found herself curious, as well.

Supper turned out to be even worse than Leah had feared. Archie acted overly solicitous to Leah and almost smothered her with attention. However, Leah couldn't help but notice how often he glanced at Ivy with a wistful look.

Lawrence also worked too hard to woo Ivy. He could be charming, but Ivy didn't seem at all impressed.

To Leah's surprise, Luke was as handsome as Ivy had said. Leah had been sure her sister had exaggerated, but she had to admit, she'd never seen anyone as good-looking. He had a dark tan, black hair, and deep-brown eyes. With his square chin and classic nose, he looked like a model for a handsome stone sculpture, except his hair was straight, not curly. He didn't appear as stocky as Paul or Papa, but he had broad shoulders, and he looked strong. Although not as tall as Paul, his perfect proportions and features were put together in a most pleasing manner. Leah could never have dreamed up someone as handsome as he, and she had an incredible imagination.

Pricilla seemed so stunned by him; she had turned speechless. However, Luke treated the shy girl with a courteous gentleness, and Leah's opinion of him rose. She might not be won by a pretty face, but she treasured pretty actions.

Although Luke went out of his way to be nice to Pricilla and even included Leah in the conversation, he only had eyes for Ivy. Leah didn't think she'd ever seen someone so smitten.

Hester Sue Tucker had also come as a guest. Mother hadn't mentioned her, so Leah assumed she came at Paul's invitation. The attractive redhead had been chasing after Paul for years. Regrettably, her temperament matched her hair. She could be charming when she chose, but she also knew how to get her way. If she didn't have her way, she showed her fiery anger. She and Ivy didn't get along at all, and Mother almost loathed her.

"I have an announcement to make," Paul said after everyone had finished the meal. "I've just had the honor of asking Hester Sue to be my wife, and she consented."

By their expressions, Mother and Ivy were as shocked as Leah. She couldn't believe Paul had done such a thing without a hint to her, and so close to Papa's funeral. Perhaps he would have told her the day of their ride, if they'd not had to rush home to Papa. Leah couldn't have changed his mind, anyway. He'd already turned twenty-seven, and he could do what he wanted.

"This is totally improper," Mother protested. "You need to wait until the mourning period is over to announce an engagement. It's not even been a month since your father's funeral. What are you thinking?"

"I'm thinking I'm master here now, and I need a wife to oversee my household."

"Everyone will think it needs to be a hurry-up affair," Mother said.

"They'll soon see there's no truth in that."

"Well, this does change things, doesn't it?" Ivy said, as she locked her eyes with Leah's. Leah had to agree with her sister this time. Living in a house with Hester Sue as the mistress could become a challenge. Mother would hate it and declare war, and Leah would prefer to avoid those two battling for supremacy.

Maybe Ivy had made a good decision, after all. Putting distance between them by moving to the mountains suddenly didn't look as irresponsible. Leah looked from Archie to Hester Sue. She might consider the trip now.

All of Paul's attention had turned to Hester Sue, and Leah wondered how much assistance he'd be. Leah might have considered marrying Lawrence, but there was no way she would ever consider marrying Archie. Paul looked up and smiled encouragingly at her. "Have you ever seen a triple wedding?" he asked. *Oh no, he wouldn't!*

"What do you think of the new compromise?" Lawrence abruptly asked. Tension hung heavy, and he must have decided to change the subject.

"What are they calling it, the Kansas-Nebraska Act?" Archie answered. "It seems to me Congress is determined to give more and more power to the free states. The Missouri Compromise was bad enough, but this takes things even further."

"You may be right," Lawrence agreed. "Things were pretty evenly balanced by the Missouri Compromise, but this new act has the potential of changing all that. It looks to me like most of the new territories may vote to enter the Union as free states. If that happens, the slave states will be outvoted on every issue."

"What do you think, Luke?" Archie asked.

"I've never understood owning another person. It just doesn't seem right to me."

"Are you an *abolitionist* then?" Archie spit out the word, as if he detested it. "I'll not sit at the table with an abolitionist."

"The slave issue doesn't affect him," Lawrence said before Luke could comment. "There're practically no slaves in the western part of the state. The land is too steep and forested to allow for plantations, and the growing season is too short to plant many field crops."

"I see," Archie said. He turned back to Luke. "Well, you can find slavery all through the Bible. There's nothing wrong with slavery."

"Sin is all through the Bible, too," Luke said, "and there's definitely something wrong with sin."

Leah looked down at her hands in her lap to hide her smile. When she had her face under control she looked up at Luke. The man got more interesting all the time. He didn't act like a man she would expect to appeal to her sister. Ivy had always enjoyed the benefits of slavery. She loved being waited on and having someone at her beck and call.

"You've been quiet, Paul," Archie said.

"I agree with you both. Lawrence and I've talked about it. I don't like slavery, but none of us planters could do without it now. Our whole Southern economic system is based on it, and we'd be paupers if we let the slaves go."

"There may come a time when you'll have to make a stand on one side or the other, Paul," Archie said. "South Carolina is already talking of secession if things continue to be stacked against the South."

"South Carolinians have always been a bunch of hotheads. Thankfully, the other southern states give things more thought," Paul replied.

"Do we have to talk politics? I hate politics," Ivy complained.

"I agree with Ivy," Mother said. "Shall we withdraw from the table, girls? I presume you men want to go to the smoking room. Get all your political talk for the night over with there. We women will await you in the drawing room."

"Oh, Mother, isn't Luke wonderful?" Ivy asked as they sat down. "Isn't he just the most handsome thing you've ever seen?"

"He's blessed with a handsome face, but there is more to a man than appearance. He seems set against slavery. He'd never fit in here."

"Oh, Mother, must you always be so practical? Don't you remember what it's like to be in love?"

Mother's eyes softened. She looked far away. "I just want what's best for you," she finally told Ivy. Her voice had softened, too. "You were made for this way of life, Ivy. You flourish here on the plantation. You would be miserable in a life where you had to do all the chores yourself. Fair Oaks is a fine plantation, and Lawrence is a decent man who'll be kind to you. It really is what's best."

"But, Mother, it's not what's best if it's not what I want." Ivy's mouth turned down in a pretty pout. "I'd be wretched, and Lawrence would know it and feel just awful."

"Few of us get what we want, Ivy. We settle for what we can have, and things turn out okay."

Leah looked at her mother. Had she settled for Papa? Surely not. Papa had adored her, and who else would have put up with her trying to get her own way all the time? Mother and Ivy were indeed much alike. Leah hoped she took more after Papa.

While growing up, Leah had tried her hardest to please Mother, but she'd never succeeded. Pleasing Papa had been much easier. She could just be herself, and Papa would be enormously proud of her.

"Perhaps we should talk about this later," Ivy said. She glanced at Priscilla, as if she'd suddenly remembered they had a guest in the room.

"There's nothing else to talk about," Mother told her. She turned to Leah. "You pleased me by the way you stayed out of the talk about politics tonight, Leah. I hoped you wouldn't express your anti-slavery views and ruin the night."

"What Luke said surprised me, and, besides, Archie did most of the talking. He didn't give me much of a chance to say anything."

"Well, I'm glad. I wouldn't want you to spoil your chances."

"Knowing me, do you really think Archie and I would deal well with each other?"

"I think he's just right for you. You need someone to take a heavy hand and keep you in line. Your father let you run wild and make your own decisions for far too long. Archibald is exactly the kind of husband you need."

CHAPTER TWO

Plans

Ivy came to Leah's room again that night. "Have you made up your mind, Leah? Are you going with me?"

"What are you going to do if I don't?"

"I would go regardless, but Luke won't hear of it. He says my name will suffer enough as it is, and it's almost impossible to repair a shattered reputation. He'll not see me totally ruined, but I am going somewhere. I'll not be married off like a piece of meat."

"Like a slave, sold without a say."

"Exactly." Ivy didn't see the significance of her agreement.

"Are you going to stay and marry Archie? You saw what kind of help you can expect from Paul. Your dear brother isn't going to save you. Between Mother and Hester Sue, he's going to be too busy fighting his own battles to worry about ours."

"He's your brother as much as he's mine."

"Well, he's never been dear to me, and I know you don't care for Archie."

Leah sadly recognized some truth in what Ivy said. "Arrange a meeting with Luke. I'll discuss the possibility, but I'm not ready to promise anything yet."

"Oh, thank you!" Ivy hugged Leah fiercely, and the look on her face told Leah Ivy felt she'd already gotten her way.

Leah and Ivy took the carriage to Wadesboro. Patsy, Ivy's personal maid, went with them, and old Jasper drove. Patsy wouldn't dare tell on Ivy for fear of the consequences, and Jasper cared too much about Leah to chance getting her in trouble. Ivy had sent a message to Luke to meet them at the only inn in town.

When they arrived, Ivy told Patsy to stay with Jasper unless she sent for her. They found Luke waiting for them near the doorway.

"I reserved us a table over there. I came early, so I'd be sure to be here when you arrived. I didn't want you to encounter any problems with the men." He led them to the table and held out Ivy's chair. Leah seated herself instead of waiting. She thought the fact that Luke had thought ahead to consider what was best for Ivy and her a good sign.

"I'm pleased you're considering coming with Ivy, Leah. I've been quite taken by your sister, but I do have some misgivings about her running away. She's assured me her mother and brother will never agree to us marrying here first."

"As things stand now, I think Ivy's assessment is correct. I don't think it's going to be possible for her to marry you here."

Luke nodded. "What do you need to know about me in order to make up your mind?"

"Tell me about your family."

"My father's a physician in Salisbury, but he grew up in the mountains. He left to go to college and returned for only a brief time, when he met and married my mother, and they moved to Salisbury. He needed to be in a larger town to support his family. My mother died with a fever when I was five. My father remarried a year later. My stepmother didn't like me very much, so to keep peace, Father ended up sending me to live with his parents in Watauga County. I was about eight by that time. My grandfather has since died, and there's just my grandmother and me."

"How did you know Lawrence Nance?"

"His grandparents on his mother's side live in Salisbury. He came to visit from time to time, and he and I became good friends before I left there. We ended up in college together at the university in Chapel Hill, so, every time I come down the mountain, I try to visit Lawrence, if at all possible."

"You're a college graduate?"

"I only stayed a year. I went because Father wanted me to go so badly. Too many of the other men there liked to attend wild parties, which I didn't, and I missed the mountains and farm life. I think I would have stayed, if there had been something else I wanted to do, but I knew I preferred farming. I bought some textbooks to study further, and went back home."

"Tell me about your home in the mountains."

"As I've told Ivy, it's primitive by your standards. It's a log structure, but we can clapboard it sometime in the future. Downstairs is a large area that serves as kitchen, dining room, living room, Grandma's bedroom, and a larder, and there are four bedrooms upstairs.

"What we farm we basically use. There're no field crops, although we grow a large garden in the summer. We also raise some extra vegetables or livestock to sell for spending money."

Leah tried to imagine it all. "Are you agreeable to all this?" she asked Ivy. "You do realize this will be a big change from what you're accustomed?"

"It sounds so exciting and romantic, doesn't it?" Ivy sighed. "It'll be like taking a step back in time, don't you think?"

"I guess." Somehow, Leah doubted Ivy would want to step back in time when she saw all the work involved.

"It'll be a huge change for you, too, Leah," Luke said. He sounded concerned about her, and something warmed within her.

"I've learned to do almost every job a woman does on the plantation and a few of the men's, too. I don't mind work." Ivy had never done anything more taxing than changing clothes, and Patsy usually helped with that. Leah would've been bored to distraction.

"Papa allowed her too much freedom," Ivy said. "She's been quite the hoyden at times."

"Papa allowed me to educate myself. Along with his encouragement and help, I have a good education. Ivy and I both had a governess, who taught us reading and arithmetic. I used those skills to read Papa's library and to study. Papa liked to discuss things with me, too."

"Yes, you're so educated and outspoken, you'll scare off any man who might be interested in you."

"I don't know, I think an intelligent, educated wife would be a great asset to a man," Luke said.

If Luke wanted an educated wife, then why did he choose Ivy? She had never been interested in knowledge. The man needed to be honest with himself, because beauty must mean more to him.

"I found your comments on slavery interesting," Leah told Luke.

"I should have kept them to myself at your dinner table." He glanced away. "As your guest, I should have known better, but they came slipping out. I do apologize if I offended you."

"On the contrary, I agree with what you said." Leah looked him in the eye. "I've never seen any justification for slavery."

His eyebrows shot up. "Now you have surprised me. I've never met a child of a slave owner who doesn't defend slavery. Even Lawrence, who is one of the kindest people I know, says slavery is necessary."

"You two talk as if the slaves are people," Ivy said. "They really aren't, you know. They would be incapable of caring for themselves. They need us as much as we need them."

"That's a lie the slave owners have perpetuated to make themselves feel better," Luke told her. "But let's not debate the issue now. It's not going to be a problem where we're going. There are few slaves in Watauga County and no large plantations."

Ivy smiled agreeably. She seemed pleased Luke didn't want to argue with her.

"Well, we'd better head for home before someone becomes worried," Leah said. "Let me think on this some more. When do you need your answer, Mr. Moretz?"

"Call me Luke, and I'm planning to leave early Friday morning. I'll need to make different arrangements if you two are coming, so if you could give me some indication how you are leaning, it would be most helpful."

Leah looked into Luke's dark eyes. They held a warmth she hadn't expected. For some reason, she felt she could trust him.

She turned to Ivy. Her sister's expression seemed pleading again. Leah didn't feel Luke and Ivy were at all suited for each other, except in physical attractiveness. They were two of the most beautiful people she'd ever seen, and they did make a lovely couple. Ivy's fair beauty and Luke's dark handsomeness contrasted to make the couple even more stunning. She gave a deep sigh.

"I'm leaning toward going," Leah told them. They both gave her big smiles. "Go ahead and make your arrangements for us, Luke. I reserve the right to change my mind, however. If that happens, I'll send you word immediately. If you haven't heard differently by Thursday morning, you will know for sure we're coming. What do we need to do?"

"Is there someone you trust to bring a trunk for each of you and meet me before we leave?"

"Yes," Leah said, "I can depend on Jasper."

"Have him meet me here Thursday afternoon about two."

"I'll have them loaded in the wagon when I come to pick you up. Meet me about two o'clock Friday morning at the end of your lane. Only bring a light traveling bag."

"Why so early?" Ivy asked.

"I expect search parties out looking for you when you don't show up for breakfast. We need a head start. Leave a note saying you are going away to be married, but don't tell to whom or where."

"I don't think it'll matter," Leah said. "Ivy's been trying to change Mother's mind, so I'm sure she'll suspect it's you."

"Well, we'll just have to be extra cautious, then. They'll look even harder if they don't get a note and think she's been kidnapped or forced. Do you have any questions?"

Leah shook her head.

"Thank you, Leah. Thank you for helping us. I promise to keep you safe, and you can have a home with us as long as you want."

Leah nodded.

"Thank you, Leah," Ivy said when they were back in the carriage. "You won't regret it."

Leah wondered.

The next few days swept by with the speed of a summer storm. Leah prayed for a sign to let her know what to do, but none came. She even made a list of positives and negatives about leaving or staying. The way she saw it, staying had the potential of wreaking much more havoc for her, not to mention Ivy.

Leah couldn't marry Archibald Biles. The cruel man seemed almost evil. He would use violence to make her obey him and probably enjoy it. No, she guessed she'd have to go. At seventeen, she didn't think she would be able to thwart both Mother and Paul. She couldn't believe that she could no longer count on Paul. How things had changed since Papa's death.

Leah began to plan carefully. Somehow, Ivy had talked her into not dressing in black after they left, but she wanted to take the things she'd need.

She waited until after breakfast Thursday morning to actually pack. First, she put a sheet in the bottom of her trunk and laid one of the thinner quilts on top. She placed a second sheet on top the quilt and added some cloth bags with her most useful dried plants and herbs for medicines. She put a wool blanket on top of the herbs to keep them stationary and safe. Then, she added her other things. There was just enough room for the tray in the top.

Into the tray, she added her Bible, a small portrait of Papa, some toiletry items, and a velvet bag with all her jewelry. Some of the jewelry could be sold should the need arise.

She set her medicine chest beside her trunk. Papa had given her the small wooden chest for her sixteenth birthday. It had wooden slots inside, in which the glass bottles containing her liquid medicine just fit. Papa had always been good at choosing just the right gift for her. Her eyes watered, but she shrugged off the memories and continued.

She took a small tapestry bag and packed only the things she would need during the trip. It had some extra room, so she planned to go to the kitchen and pack some food to eat on their way, but she'd wait until everyone fell asleep.

Jasper and a helper came to carry the trunks down after Paul left. Mother would take a long time getting dressed in her room. Bertha would likely know something, because nothing much escaped her. The chubby slave had nursed Leah when she was a baby, and she and Jasper were close to Leah. Leah knew Bertha would do her best to keep the others from seeing anything suspicious.

The two men took the trunks to the stable to hide them until it was time to go. Leah saw Ivy had packed two large Saratoga trunks.

"I had a hard time narrowing it down to just two trunks," Ivy told Leah when she mentioned it. "I could have easily packed four or five more. After all, we're leaving for good." Leah doubted if Luke would be pleased.

The girls had been aided by Paul's plans. He decided to hold a ball on Saturday evening to announce his engagement and invited all their friends and neighbors. The house had been a beehive of activity all week. Mother reluctantly helped arrange everything. She acted as if she were planning her death sentence.

"You should have the decency to wait a respectable time after your father's burial," Mother had told Paul. "This is disgraceful. The neighbors will think it's scandalous."

"You know Father would have approved," Paul had told her. "You're just concerned you'll no longer be in control."

With all the uproar, however, no one paid much attention to what Leah and Ivy were doing. Ivy ended up helping with the affair more than Leah. Leah spent much of her time in Papa's study. She felt closer to Papa there. "Am I doing what's best, Papa?" she whispered. The walls were silent.

Leah also walked around the plantation and saw all the slaves she'd grown to love. She couldn't really say good-bye, but, in actuality, that's exactly what she did. She would miss them, but she'd come to believe her leaving would be for the best. She couldn't stay here and marry Archie. She'd rather die and be with Papa first.

Leah went to the stable Thursday afternoon to ensure nothing would impede their plans. Jasper already had the trunks stowed in the closed carriage.

"Might be best if you's ride along, Miss Leah," Jasper said. "If I's stopped, I don't know how I'd 'splain havin' a closed carriage out by myself. The pattyrollers'd be sho' to search and fine da trunks."

"That's a good point," she told the old man. He helped her into the carriage. She didn't have much room with the three trunks, but she wedged herself in.

Paul came riding in just as they pulled out. "Where are you off to?" he called out.

"Errands," she yelled back and waved. *Whew, that was close.*

She saw Luke waiting outside the inn when they pulled up. He stood beside a covered wagon.

He and Jasper loaded the trunks from the carriage to the wagon. "I thought I said one trunk each."

"Ivy said she had a hard time limiting it to just two. She's taking only a fraction of her newest clothes."

Luke shook his head in disbelief. "I guess I'm ignorant when it comes to well-brought-up young women. At least you managed with one trunk. You do have just one, don't you?"

"Just one trunk, but I brought my medicine chest, too. I hope that's okay. It's small, and the vials fit in special slots, so they won't break. I hate to leave most of my herbs behind, but I guess I can collect more when we get to your place."

"You'll have different ones there, too. Some of them are really useful, like ginseng. Granny can help you learn the new ones. She's good with herbs and healing. I think she's the reason my father became a doctor."

"That's good to know. I won't feel so bad about leaving my herbs behind, then."

He smiled at her. "I think Granny will really like you."

"Jasper," she turned to the old slave, "I'd like to go by the church, while we're in town."

"Yes'm, Miss Leah."

"You're a church-goer, then?" Luke asked.

"Yes, I am. My faith is an important part of who I am."

"It's that way for me, too. I'm glad Ivy feels the same way." He smiled. "We don't live near enough to a church to attend regularly, although a circuit rider comes through from time to time. We still have our own Bible study every Sunday and devotions every evening.

Leah wasn't sure how committed Ivy was to her faith. She'd never chosen to be baptized, and her church attendance seemed to be more social than anything else.

Luke helped Leah into the carriage. "I'll see you and Ivy in about twelve hours, then."

"We'll be there."

"I'll say good-bye to you now, Jasper," Leah whispered in the old slave's ear after they returned. Alone in the stable, she moved to give him a hug. Jasper wrapped his long, boney arms around her, and she felt secure.

"I's sho' gwine amiss ya." He pushed her back and looked at her face with tears running down his cheeks.

"You know I have to go." She watched him closely. "It's not the same without Papa, and I can't marry Archibald."

"I know dat be de truth. He be uh evil man, dat un. I's be prayin' fo' ya.

"I'll be praying for all of you, too. You tell the others I love them." She didn't have to say which others. Jasper knew.

Leah stood on tiptoes and kissed his wet cheek. Then, she turned and walked away with tears streaming down her own face.

She walked around outside for a time, while her eyes cleared. It wouldn't do to have to answer questions about why she'd been crying. She walked down the front lane to judge how long it would take Ivy and her in the morning. It would take about ten minutes according to her chatelaine watch pin.

She turned and walked back toward the house. She would miss this place. It had been the only home she'd ever known. The house looked beautiful in the thick evening sun. It had been made of strawberry red brick with white mortar holding them together.

The columns and all the trim were white, and the charcoal gray shutters looked so dark they'd pass as black.

As she walked, the sun hit some of the windows at angles and turned them into panes of gold. Maybe this had been why the plantation had been named "Gold Leaf." She'd always fancied some previous owner had probably grown tobacco. Papa had bought the plantation for Mother before Leah was born. It might not be the biggest or most lavish plantation in the area, but it held a special beauty.

Ivy seemed so excited and happy at supper that Leah feared someone would suspect something. She tried to give her sister a hard look, but Ivy paid her no attention.

"You seem to be in high spirits, Ivy," Mother said.

"I am. You know how I love a ball, Mother. Do you think Lawrence will ask me to dance? I remember he's one of the best dancers around."

"I'm sure he will," Mother said, looking quite pleased. "I'm glad you are beginning to come to your senses."

"I'm not promising anything, Mother, but I know Lawrence isn't so bad, and he's considered quite the catch around here. I'm willing to give him a chance, but that's all."

Leah looked at her sister in surprise. She never guessed Ivy could be such a good thespian.

"Well, that's a start," Mother said.

Ivy came to Leah's room at one-thirty. "I think it's getting close to time."

Leah sat up, and they lit a candle. She'd remained fully dressed.

"Is that what you're traveling in?" Ivy's dress looked more suitable for a dinner party than a journey. She even wore her hoops and crinolines, which would make it hard to maneuver in and out of the wagon.

"Yes, I wanted to look my best for Luke."

"Ivy, you could wear a gunny sack, and you would look better than anyone else."

"Well, that would certainly cause quite the scandal, wouldn't it?" she giggled.

"Let's get you out of here before you wake up the whole household." Leah gave Ivy's shoulder a gentle push. She picked up her travel bag and led the way. Ivy's bag looked heavy, but Leah didn't comment.

At least the sky shone clear, and the moon and stars gave more light than she'd expected. Leah saw Ivy hand her bag to someone as they started down the drive. Patsy.

"I didn't know you planned to bring Patsy," she told her sister.

"Well, of course I am going to take Patsy. Who would look after me?"

"I assumed you'd look after yourself."

"No, silly. I'll also have Patsy do my part of the chores. I'm not about to destroy my fair complexion or my smooth hands and nails."

"Are you agreeable to this?" Leah asked Patsy.

"Yes, Miss Leah. I figure you girls need some looking after, and I don't have family here no more."

"I thought you taught her proper English for me, Leah. It doesn't sound like it."

"She isn't using slave dialect. It would've taken longer than you gave me to get into all the grammar."

Leah feared they would have to wait on Luke, since they had left the house early, but he was waiting for them at the end of the lane. Ivy wrinkled her nose at the covered farm wagon.

"Are we going all the way in this thing?" she asked.

"I need to haul some things back," Luke told her, and with all your things and having to leave secretly, this seemed the best option." He looked at Patsy. "Who's this?"

"This is my slave girl, Patsy. Papa gave her to me on my twelfth birthday to be my maid. I brought her papers along, and they're in my name."

"I am not taking a slave along." He said it in a low, stern voice.

"I can't leave her behind," Ivy pleaded.

"Do you want to go with us, Patsy?" he asked.

"Yes, sir. Miss Leah asked me the same thing. I'd be happy to accompany you. I might be put in the fields if I stayed or, worse, sold off."

"On one condition, then. When we get to a town with a lawyer, we'll free Patsy. She can still go with us, but she'll be free. I'll not have a slave as part of my household."

"But, she's worth a whole lot of money," Ivy protested. "Let me sell her if you don't want me to have her."

"No! She can stay here at the plantation, or she can go and be set free. Those are the only two options acceptable to me. If you can't live with one of those, you might want to consider staying, too, Ivy."

"Luke, you don't mean that." Ivy's whine sounded like a little girl's. "You know I'd end up married to someone else within the year."

"It's not what I want, Ivy, but I feel strongly about slavery. I will not own another human being."

"There you go again. They are not human beings. Not like you and me."

Luke chose to ignore her statement. "What's your decision, Ivy?"

"We'll go, and I'll sign Patsy's freedom papers whenever you say."

"Thank you, darling." He kissed her cheek.

Well, Luke had stood his ground on that one. Leah had wondered if Ivy would manipulate him the way she had every other man who'd taken a fancy to her. Maybe it wouldn't be so easy for her to control Luke Moretz.

CHAPTER THREE

The Departure

Luke drove through the rest of the night. Ivy sat beside him on the wagon seat and Leah beside her. Patsy stayed in the back. Ivy leaned her head on Luke's shoulder and fell asleep. Leah couldn't get comfortable enough to sleep.

"You were quiet when Ivy and I were discussing Patsy," Luke said in a loud whisper.

Leah turned to him and smiled. "I thought you handled the situation very well on your own."

He smiled back.

"Where are we headed first?" Leah asked.

"I think we'll probably make Albemarle sometime this morning, although the travel is going to be slower until daylight. At least it's a clear night. The almanac said there would be a full moon, but I prayed it wouldn't be cloudy. We can stop in Albemarle and eat some dinner, then continue on to Salisbury. We should be in Salisbury in time to eat a late supper, and I plan to spend the night with my father."

Ivy woke up when the sun rose. "I'm hungry," she said.

"I'm sorry. I didn't know how to ask for food at Fair Oaks without giving away our plans."

"I have some ham and biscuits and walnut bread in my travel bag," Leah said. "There should be enough for all four of us, but I didn't bring anything to drink."

"I have water, but do you mind drinking from the same canteen? I didn't bring the wagon and team to the plantation, and I haven't had a chance to fill the water barrel."

"That's fine, as long as I get to drink before Patsy," Ivy said. Luke gave her a hard look.

They ate as they rode. Luke allowed Ivy to drink from the canteen first, and he drank last.

"Thank you for bringing the food, Leah," Luke told her. "That was a fine breakfast. I especially enjoyed the walnut bread."

"Thank you. I baked that yesterday morning."

"I'm going to need to get off the wagon and have some privacy," Ivy said.

"I think we all could use a stretch break," Luke agreed. He pulled the wagon off the road beside a stream. "I'll give the mules some water, while you ladies walk behind that thicket over there."

Ivy wisely decided to take off her hoops behind the bushes. She told Patsy to put them in the back of the wagon. It made boarding the wagon much easier and gave them all more room.

The farther west they went, the worse the road seemed to get. Ruts had formed when the roads were muddy, and they'd dried into a washboard. The wagon swayed from side to side and sometimes threatened to tip over as it rolled along the cratered road.

"Why are the roads so rough around here?" Ivy asked after one particularly hard jolt.

"I thought it would be better if we stayed off the main road," Luke said, "at least until we make Albemarle."

They were all tired by the time they reached Albemarle. Leah couldn't wait to get off the bumpy, hard seat and have some tea. Leaving so early had made for a long morning.

"As you can see, Albemarle's a small town," Luke told them. "Not only is it the county seat of the newly formed Stanly County, but it's also located at the crossroads of the Old Turnpike Road, which runs from Fayetteville to Salisbury and the Old Stage Road, which connects Raleigh and Charlotte. The town's not been incorporated, but I feel certain it will be soon."

They passed the courthouse, a white clapboard building sitting in a large town square. Leah saw businesses which read EARNHARDT & MOSS, GENERAL MERCHANDISE; JAMES MCCORKLE, ATTORNEY; and GILLAM AND WOOLY, two physicians.

Luke must have noticed, too. "I thought we'd wait until Salisbury to see an attorney about Patsy."

Leah looked around carefully. She saw a tailor's, a shoe shop, a blacksmith, and several grog shops. She saw only one nice-looking church but thought there must be others in the area. The sign in front of this one read CENTRAL UNITED CHURCH. The square had a large town well. They found a hotel run by Daniel Freeman, and they stopped for dinner.

The hotel looked nice enough. They went to the dining room and ordered some stew and bread. Patsy ate outside in the back. She didn't seem to mind as much as Luke did.

"Don't worry, Master Luke," Patsy told him, "it's just the way things are."

"Well, it shouldn't be," Luke said.

The unfairness of slavery seemed to bother Luke even more than it did Leah. She found she didn't notice the injustices as quickly as he did. Being the daughter of a plantation owner, she guessed she had become accustomed to many of the practices.

Luke had left the wagon and mules at the stable behind the hotel. He'd paid for them to be given some food and water.

"Why didn't you get horses instead of mules?" Ivy asked.

"The mules are cheaper, and they'll be able to pull the mountain better, unless I bought draft horses."

Leah realized for the first time, this trip would be a costly one for Luke. She didn't think he'd planned on taking three females back with him on his return journey. She wondered if she would have the opportunity to sell some of her jewelry in Salisbury to help out. It might be easier there than in Watauga County.

"There are still several gold mines in Stanly County," Luke told them as they finished their meal.

"Wasn't the first gold discovered in the United States found near here?" Leah asked.

"Yes, if I remember my history, that happened in Cabarrus County. A little boy, John Reed, found a big, pretty rock in 1799, and his family used it for a doorstop for about three years. Finally, his father decided to take it to be assayed, and it was gold. North Carolina was considered a gold center until gold was discovered in California in 1848, and now those with gold fever are rushing west." After they'd finished eating, they collected Patsy, and walked to the stable.

"What do you have in the back of the wagon?" Leah asked as Luke helped her into the wagon.

"Just some supplies. Things like sugar, flour, coffee, tea, and a few tools. Staples are cheaper in Anson County. I bought more than usual when I realized I would need the wagon. We aren't heavily loaded, or else we'd have to have a larger team to get up the mountains."

"How far is it to Salisbury?" Ivy asked when Luke climbed into the wagon seat beside her.

"Oh, about the same distance as it's been from the plantation here. I'm going to take the main road from here on out, so we should make better time. I'm counting on the search party stopping along the way to ask if anyone has seen us, and that should slow them down. Since we've had about five or six hours head start, I'm hoping it will be enough."

Leah hoped so, too. She bowed her head and prayed for God's aid in their escape.

The trip to Salisbury seemed long, since they'd already been on the wagon for hours. Leah felt sore and stiff from the bumpy ride and hard seat.

Just outside Salisbury they were stopped by slave hunters. Luke moved his rifle, a modern breech-loading gun that looked brand new, from the floor of the wagon to rest across his knees. Leah knew he'd kept it loaded on the way.

"We're lookin' for eight escaped slaves from Richmond County," one of them said. "Have you seen any sign of them?" Tobacco spittle ran down his scraggly beard as he talked. Leah didn't like the way he and the others leered at Ivy and her.

"No, we came from Albemarle, but I haven't seen anyone who could have been an escaped slave," Luke told them.

"What're you haulin'?"

"Just some supplies and my fiancée's maid."

"Let me see the slave."

"Come here, Patsy."

Patsy stuck her head out of the wagon.

"She's about the age of one of the ones I'm lookin' for. You got her papers?"

"I do," Ivy said. "Hand me my travel bag, Patsy."

"What's a gorgeous woman like you doing in a farm wagon?" one of the men asked Ivy.

Ivy ignored him and dug through her bag. She extracted the papers and handed them to Luke.

When Luke handed them to the spokesman, Leah wondered if the man could read. He looked over the paper quickly and handed them back to Ivy, but Luke took them.

"The escaped slaves are probably staying off the main roads," the man said, "I guess we'll need to backtrack and see if we can pick up a trail. Come on, boys." They rode off, and Luke breathed a sigh of relief.

Not long afterwards, they arrived in Salisbury, one of the biggest towns Leah had ever seen. Luke drove directly to his father's house, a pretty white clapboard with black shutters.

"Come on and bring your travel bags." Luke took Leah's bag and his, because Patsy carried Ivy's bag and her own things tied up in an old shawl.

Luke's father answered the door.

"Can four weary travelers find a place for the night?" Luke asked.

"Luke!" His father hugged him. "It's so good to see you again. Come in, come in. How was your trip?" He ushered them into the sitting room.

"Oh, it had its ups and downs," Luke said with a mischievous glint in his eye. "Let me introduce you. Father, this is Ivy Morgan, my fiancée; Leah, her sister; and Patsy, Ivy's maid. Ladies, this is my father, Clifton Moretz."

"Pleased to meet you, Dr. Moretz," Leah said.

"Likewise," Ivy added.

"Fiancée, huh? My, oh, my. This is a surprise, Luke. Well, welcome, everyone. Have a seat, and I'll get Frances."

Dr. Moretz, a handsome man in his late forties, seemed warm and welcoming. Leah liked him immediately.

Frances came in, and introductions were made. "How long are you staying?" she asked Luke. Leah could tell by her tone she hoped the answer would be "not long." She was a tall, thin woman with a pointed nose and a serious countenance. She looked to be about ten years younger than her husband.

"Not long, madam. We'll leave early Monday morning."

She nodded. "Excuse me, while I go see to supper."

"Is there anything I can do to help?" Leah asked.

"No, I have help." She almost sounded insulted.

Dr. Moretz turned to Leah, "I'm sure you'd like to freshen up. Will you girls be able to share a room? There's a trundle bed for your maid."

"Yes, sir," Leah answered. "That will be fine."

"Will you show them to the guest room, son? You'll still be in your old room."

They followed Luke up the stairs. The guest room turned out to be a large room with a comfortable looking bed, plenty of furniture, and even a settee. An expensive-looking carpet covered most of the open floor. The window opened up on the rear of the house, and, when she looked out, Leah saw a lovely flowering garden.

"I'm going down to take care of the team and talk with Father," Luke said. "You ladies get settled and come down whenever you wish."

"I'm going to freshen up and change this crumpled dress," Ivy said.

"You go ahead, and I'll go for a walk in the garden," Leah told her sister. "When you're finished, I'll come up and change for supper."

"Come, then," Luke said to Leah. "I'll walk you down."

"So what do you think of Salisbury?" he asked.

"The town looks lovely, and I would love to explore it, but it appears to be a little crowded to live here."

"I prefer more open space myself. That's why I'm happy in the mountains."

Luke led her to the garden and opened the gate for her. "If you've not gone upstairs by the time I get through, I'll join you here," he said. "I expect Ivy will take a while."

"I'm sure she will."

Leah walked through the garden paths and enjoyed the late spring flowers. She could tell someone gave the garden a lot of attention, and it had been thoughtfully laid out with benches set at advantageous locations. Leah didn't sit, however. She'd had enough of that today.

A soft breeze rustled through the trees, and she heard voices slowly drawing nearer—Luke and his father. Dr. Moretz seemed to be giving Luke advice about a lawyer, and then he changed the subject.

"I'm so sorry about how Frances treats you, son. I guess she's just jealous and knows you'll inherit the bulk of my estate. She's not a bad woman, you know."

"I don't care nearly as much about your estate as I do being with you. I miss our talks."

"I do, too, son. More than you can imagine, and I know, if Frances wasn't so cold with you, you'd visit more. I hate that for all of us. The Morgan sisters are certainly attractive girls." Dr. Moretz changed the subject again.

"Aren't they though?" It sounded more like a statement than a question. "I've never met anyone who can compare with Ivy's beauty."

"Leah's not lacking in appearance, either, and she seems like a very capable young lady."

"You've barely met them, and you've already sized them up?"

Dr. Moretz laughed. "Not entirely, but they are impressive. I wish you were staying longer, so we could show them off around town. Well, there's always church tomorrow. I guess that will have to do."

"Church will always do," Luke said, and his father laughed again.

"I see you're still here," Luke said as he joined Leah.

"I'm enjoying the garden. Someone has done a lovely job."

"I think Father has a gardener who comes in once a week to trim and weed, but Father enjoys being out here himself. He says it helps relieve some of his stress."

"You seem to get on well with your father. Papa and I were close, too. I miss him."

"I'm sorry about your father," he took her hand, gave it a brief squeeze, and released it. "I know it must be hard. Is that part of the reason you decided to leave the plantation?" His touch had affected Leah more than it should, but she did her best to ignore the sensations.

"Yes, that and the fact that Mother seemed determined I should marry Archibald Biles. I expected Paul to back my refusal, but he's so caught up with marrying Hester Sue Tucker, he isn't paying attention to anything else. When he mentioned a triple wedding, I knew I had to get away."

"So, it wasn't my charm that won you over?"

She smiled at his teasing. "I'm afraid not. I don't think running away is what's best for Ivy, but she'd made up her mind. I wouldn't be here at all, though, if I didn't trust and respect you."

"Thank you, Leah. I realize that's a great compliment. Who did your mother have picked out for Ivy?"

"Didn't you know? It's Lawrence."

"I should have known, shouldn't I? I wondered what was up when we were invited to supper, but I never put it all together. I thought it was just neighbors getting together, and I was happy to be able to see Ivy." They walked in silence for a while. Luke seemed deep in thought. "What do you think of Lawrence?"

"I think he's a nice fellow. He would make some young lady a wonderful husband."

"Might you be interested?"

"No, I have never felt anything but friendship for him, but I'd much rather marry him than Archie. At least Lawrence wouldn't mistreat me."

"Is Archibald that bad? I wasn't impressed with him, but I don't know him."

"A dear, old friend of mine calls him 'evil.' He doesn't just beat his slaves, he tortures them, and there are more mulatto children on his plantation than any I know. He's a cruel man, who'll do whatever it takes to get what he wants."

"I didn't think Southern ladies were supposed to know about such things as mulattoes."

"They know about them. They're just expected not to talk about it. I'm afraid when it comes to saying what I think, I don't always do as expected. I'm sorry if I spoke out of turn."

"You haven't embarrassed me, and I hope you'll always speak what's on your mind. Yes, you and Granny are going to get along just fine."

"The more you mention her, the more I'm looking forward to meeting her."

"Do you think Archibald will cause trouble because you ran away? Is he going to hunt you down? He doesn't sound like a man who gives up easily."

"That would be true if he cared about me, but he doesn't. He would have preferred to marry Ivy, but the family never made her available to him. That, and the fact he'd not spoken for me yet, should make me safe. He wouldn't have allowed me to shame him."

"Shall we go in? We both need to clean up for supper. Frances insists we dress for the evening meal. You won't have to do that at home."

Leah chose to wear one of the dresses she'd brought for church. Patsy had spot ironed the wrinkles from being packed when she did Ivy's.

"I didn't expect Ivy to bring you, Patsy," Leah told the slave, "but I'm glad she did, especially since you'll get your freedom."

"I'm thrilled by the very idea of freedom. Do you think it'll really happen, Miss Leah?"

"Yes, I do. I heard Luke talking with his father about a lawyer just a little while ago. I think you will be free before we leave Salisbury."

"Does that mean I don't have to be a slave no more?"

"Yes, it does, but, if you stay with us, Ivy's probably going to expect you to still wait on her."

"But, I could leave anytime I got ready?"

"Yes, you could, but you need to be careful, Patsy. It's hard out there if you don't have a means of earning a living. If you decide to leave, you let me know, and I'll try to help you. I'm sure Luke would, too."

"Yes, miss. Master Luke's a good man, isn't he?"

"Yes, he is."

"He's too good a man for Miss Ivy, if you ask me. I can say that to you, can't I? After all, I'm going to be free real soon."

"You can say anything to me, Patsy, but you'd better be careful what you say around Ivy."

"Yes, Miss Leah. I know that."

Leah descended the stairs to find Dr. Moretz standing at the bottom waiting for her. "I heard you coming, and I wanted to direct you to the others. They're waiting in the parlor."

"Oh, I'm sorry. Am I late? Have I delayed supper?"

"No, no, dear." He tucked her hand in his arm. "Luke's not down yet, and the food is just now having its finishing touches."

Leah saw Patsy standing at the top of the steps. "Where will Patsy eat?"

"Come Patsy," the doctor beckoned. "I'll direct you to the kitchen. You can eat in there."

"I'd let the girl eat with us, but Frances wouldn't allow it," he whispered to Leah.

"That's fine," she whispered back. "Neither would Ivy."

Ivy and Frances were in the parlor talking like they were old friends. Ivy wore the silver gown she loved. It made her look enchanted, almost magical. She looked every bit the breathtaking princess.

"You look beautiful, my dear," Dr. Moretz said. Leah looked up to find him looking at her, not Ivy.

"Why, thank you, kind sir."

"That's not empty flattery, Leah. You are quite lovely, and I like that dress on you. It suits your hair and skin tone."

"Thank you," she said more seriously. The sincerity in his voice surprised her. She'd never received compliments with Ivy in the same room.

She looked down at her dress. The tailored silk with different widths of ivory, rust, and brown vertical stripes made her appear a bit taller. It also made her waist look even smaller.

Luke entered the parlor. "I'm sorry if I've kept everyone waiting. I found a newspaper and lost track of the time." He looked at Leah, as if he'd heard his father's comment.

"You're fine, son. All of us have just assembled."

"Well, now we can eat," Frances scowled.

They gathered at the table with Dr. Moretz at the head, and Frances at the other end. Two children joined them. Teddy, introduced as Luke's half-brother, sat between Ivy and Frances. Luke's half-sister, Maggie, sat on the other side of Frances.

"How old are you, Maggie?" Leah asked to make conversation.

"I'm seven, and Teddy is five," she answered.

"You look and act older," Leah told her, and the girl gave her an appreciative smile.

"Eat your supper," Frances reprimanded her daughter. "If you and Teddy don't behave, you'll eat in the kitchen from now on. I'd prefer that, anyway. This is your father's idea."

"We'll have breakfast on the sideboard in the morning," Dr. Moretz said, "and you can come down and eat whenever you get ready. We'll leave for church about ten thirty."

"Luke, what's wrong with you?" Ivy asked. "You're not being very sociable tonight."

"I'm sorry, dear. I'm afraid not getting any sleep last night and driving all day is about to catch up with me."

Leah looked at him and thought he looked exhausted. "Maybe we can finish supper and call it an early night," she said.

"That sounds good," Luke replied.

"Oh, Luke," Ivy complained, "I had hoped we could go for a walk. Salisbury beckons, and it's such a lovely night."

"I'm sorry. I'm just not up to it tonight. Perhaps tomorrow night, after I've had some rest."

"Well if an old man's not too poor a substitute, I'd be honored to escort you on a walk, Ivy," Dr. Moretz said.

"Thank you, I'd like that. I need to work the soreness from my joints after today's rough ride." She looked pointedly at Luke. "What about you, Leah? Care to join us?"

"No, thank you, sir. I'm like Luke. I think I need rest more than anything."

"What about you, dear?" He looked at his wife.

"I would like to, but I think I'd better stay here to chaperone Luke and Leah," Frances snapped.

"By the looks of them, they're much too tired to require a chaperone, and we won't be gone long, but as you wish."

Leah felt embarrassed by the insinuation. She looked down at her dessert to keep the blush she felt on her face hidden or from saying something she shouldn't. She would try to act like a lady, even though Frances didn't. The woman shouldn't have been so pointed and direct. She certainly had an abrasive manner.

When Leah finally had herself under control enough to look up, she found Luke watching her. His eyes softened and he smiled slightly in understanding and support. She understood why he couldn't live here. She felt sorry for the doctor, and he was such a nice man.

Leah and Patsy pulled out the trundle bed and got ready for bed. Patsy would get back up to help Ivy undress when she returned from the walk.

"What do you think of this household?" Leah asked Patsy. From experience, she knew servants often picked up on how things stood much quicker than anyone else.

"It would be a fine place it weren't for the missus. There are two servants in the house. You met the one who's the housekeeper and cook, because she served you tonight. There's also a free former slave girl who helps in the kitchen and does much of the cleaning."

"What do they think of Mrs. Moretz?" Leah asked.

"The housekeeper says she's not too bad, whatever that means. The helper has a hard time with her. She says the missus is even hard on little Maggie. She dotes on Teddy, though, and she's fighting mad he won't inherit the bulk of the property. It seems most of that goes to Master Luke."

Leah must have been asleep when Ivy came in, but she woke up when she heard Patsy get up and help Ivy undress. Ivy didn't appear to be in a good mood, so Leah pretended to be sound asleep.

CHAPTER FOUR

Salisbury

Ivy was still asleep when Leah got up the next morning. She checked the time. Already seven o'clock.

She just slipped on the travel dress from yesterday for now. She would change for church when Ivy got up.

"Come down and get some breakfast," Leah whispered to Patsy, when she saw her awake. "I'm sure Ivy won't be up for a while."

The sideboard held apple cinnamon muffins, biscuits, bacon, eggs, and grits. They both filled a small plate, but Leah couldn't convince Patsy to eat with her.

"You're going to get us both in big trouble, Miss Leah."

"I don't think anyone who'd mind will be down for hours, but I'll go into the kitchen and eat with you then."

"You'll do no such thing. Pardon me, miss, but you sit down right there and eat your breakfast like a proper lady."

"Yes, Patsy. You've gotten terribly bossy in your newfound freedom, haven't you?" Leah smiled at the slave.

Patsy saw the reversal of roles and smiled herself. "Yes, Miss Leah. Begging your pardon." As she left with her plate, they both laughed.

"Now, what was that all about?" Luke asked as he came in the room.

"Just a private joke."

"You're up early." He stepped to the sideboard, chose a big plate, and filled it.

"I've never been one to sleep too late." She waited for him before she started eating.

"Neither have I." He sat down across from her. "Frances might have her faults, but she does set a good table."

"Yes, she does."

Luke bowed his head and said grace for them.

"With it being Sunday, are you going to be able to get Patsy's papers today?"

"I plan to set up the appointment today, but take care of it first thing in the morning. I don't like to do business on Sunday, anyway. We probably don't need a lawyer, but I thought it might be wise to have one, in case any questions arise later."

"How far do we need to travel tomorrow?"

"We'll go at least as far as Yadkinville. It's the county seat of Yadkin County, but there's not much there. I'm not even sure if we'll find a decent place to stay the night. If not, we'll camp out at the wagon. If we get an early enough start, however, we might make it to Wilkesboro. It's larger. Are you all right with this traveling? I know it's hard and grueling, and the worst is yet to come, as we go up the mountain."

"Yes, I'm fine with the travel. I'm looking on it as an adventure enabling me to see new places and meet new people."

"That's a good attitude, but I don't think Ivy feels the same way."

Leah looked at Luke. She wasn't sure how much she should confide in him. After all, he'd introduced Ivy as his fiancée, so he must have proposed to her, and Leah had known from the beginning they intended to wed. Well, they were going to be living in the same house, so he'd find out soon enough.

"Ivy's been the most pleasant to me on this trip of any time I remember, so perhaps you're a good influence on her. However, she prefers the comforts of home."

"I'm surprised she agreed to come, then."

"To be honest, I was, too."

He looked at her for a moment. "Thank you for being open and honest with me. I hope you'll always trust me that way."

Leah did, but she wasn't sure why. She'd only known him for a short time, and she didn't know much about him, but she did trust him. Something about him reminded her of Papa, but she wasn't sure what. They certainly didn't look similar or have the same views on issues like slavery. Perhaps it rested more in their honest, caring nature. But Luke cared about Ivy, not her, she reminded herself.

"Well, here are the two people I wanted to eat breakfast with." Dr. Moretz came into the room with a big smile on his face.

"Good morning, Father," Luke said. "You seem happy this morning."

"It's a beautiful Lord's Day, and I have my oldest son home for a change. What's there not to be happy about? How are you this morning, Leah?"

"Very well, Dr. Moretz."

"Good. That's what I like to hear. A doctor doesn't hear those words very often, you know. I see you two are almost finished. Will you sit with me while I eat? Get you another cup of coffee or tea. You may need them to get through the sermon."

"Father, you shouldn't joke about church." But Luke smiled.

"What are your plans for today, Leah?"

"I'm waiting for Ivy to get up, so I can get dressed for church. After that, I haven't made plans."

"Would you like to ride through the town sometime today? Sunday is always a good time for sightseeing. There are some lovely homes around."

"I'd like that."

"Leah's interested in herbs and medicine," Luke said. "I told her she and Granny would have a lot in common."

"My, yes. Mama has treated folks who couldn't get to a doctor for as long as I can remember. She learned it from the Cherokee when she was a teenager. She's one of the reasons I decided to become a doctor."

"I look forward to meeting her. Is she by herself now?"

"I've got some folks looking in on her to make sure she doesn't need anything," Luke said, "but she's pretty independent. I'm sure she'll do fine. She married young and is just in her early sixties."

"Were you her only child?" Leah asked the doctor.

"No, I have an older sister who lives in Salem, north of here. I had two younger brothers, but they were both killed, one by a bear and one in a hunting accident."

"I'm sorry. I just lost my papa not long ago, so I know how hard losing a loved one can be."

"Ivy told me you and she grew up on a plantation, but Luke tells me you agree with us on the slavery issue. How's that?"

"You know, I'm not sure. It was the only issue on which Papa and I disagreed. I'm not sure why I feel as I do, but slavery has always seemed wrong to me. I grew up with slaves as part of my family, and I learned to love many of them."

"But, that's true for many children on plantations, and yet they don't grow up to be against slavery," Luke said.

Leah nodded in agreement. She didn't really know what made her feel the way she did, unless it had been God's leading.

"The more west you go in the state, the more people you'll find who don't understand or support it," Dr. Moretz said.

"I heard some of the men in Anson County discussing the Kansas-Nebraska Act," Luke told his father. "It looks as if more of the power might swing to the free states."

"I read that, too. I think it's needed, but it may cause a wider chasm between the two sides."

"It seems to me the issue of state's rights versus the federal government's rights will also figure in," Leah said. "The slave states are going to say the states should have the first say on things pertaining to that state."

"You're probably right," Dr. Moretz said, "but you amaze me, Leah. How does a young lady like you know so much about politics? I've talked with many a man who couldn't carry on a conversation the way you are."

"I'm afraid you can blame Papa. He encouraged me to learn as much as I could about anything I wanted. He and I used to have discussions like this all the time."

"Don't apologize. I think it's wonderful. I wish you were going to stay for an extended time. I would enjoy being a substitute father. I love such discussions myself. I don't guess you'd consider letting your sister marry Luke here, and you stay with me, while they go on to the mountains? That way, I'd be sure to get to see the wedding, too."

"I don't think Frances would take too kindly to that arrangement," Luke said.

"Also, I've told Ivy I'd go to the mountains with her," Leah told the doctor. He nodded.

"I'm guessing Ivy doesn't agree with your views on slavery," Dr. Moretz said.

"No, she doesn't. First of all, she's always enjoyed the benefits of slavery. Secondly, she hates discussions about politics. She doesn't want to think or hear about what might happen."

"Love doesn't care about politics, either," Luke answered.

"It will sooner or later," the doctor said. "Besides, are you sure you love Ivy or her beautiful face? Wait now. Just think about it, son. You know I want what's best for you, but marriage is an important undertaking. I had a very good marriage with your mother. I missed her so much I married too hastily the second time. I'm determined to make the best of it, but I want better for you. Just make sure it's love, and it's what you really want."

"I shall, sir."

Leah felt she'd intruded on a conversation she shouldn't have heard. "I'll check on Ivy. She should be getting up soon, so she'll have time to eat breakfast and get ready for church."

"It must take her over two hours to get ready, then," Dr. Moretz said.

"She can usually get ready in close to two hours if she hurries," Leah said as she left.

"Was she teasing or serious?" she heard Dr. Moretz ask as she left the room.

"I have no idea," Luke answered.

Ivy had just gotten up when Leah entered the room. Patsy stood ready to help her.

"Has Luke already eaten?" Ivy asked Leah.

"Yes, he and Dr. Moretz just finished."

"Be a dear and go down and bring me up a plate. Oh, never mind. I hear Frances in the hall. I'll just go down and eat with her before I dress for church."

"Shall I help you get ready, Miss Leah?" Patsy asked after Ivy had left.

"I'd appreciate that, Patsy. You do my hair so much more efficiently than I can."

Patsy laid out Leah's emerald gown. "I ironed the wrinkles out of this one after supper last night, when I did Ivy's dress. Will it do?"

"It will. Thank you, Patsy."

Patsy smiled broadly.

Leah hurried, and, with Patsy's help, she finished dressing before Ivy came back. Leah left the room for Ivy to get ready. Her sister didn't seem in a good mood this morning, either.

As Leah went down the stairs, Luke started up. He backed up and waited, since her hoops took up so much room.

"You look especially lovely this morning, Leah," he said, as he watched her descend the last steps. "I agreed with father last night. The dress you wore to supper suited you very well, but this one's even better. It makes your green eyes sparkle."

"Thank you." She looked at him perplexed. She knew he was sincere, but why was he showing her this kind of attention or voicing such thoughts? Ivy would be so jealous if she heard. He shouldn't be noticing how nice Leah looked, when he was engaged to her sister, and he certainly shouldn't say it.

She went to the parlor to wait for the others. Dr. Moretz sat there reading a newspaper. He had already dressed for church, too. "Any good news?" she asked.

"Not that I've seen so far." He looked at her. "Is something wrong, Leah? You look as if something's bothering you."

This kindly man reminded her more and more of Papa. Maybe it was mainly because the doctor also preferred her over her sister. Not many people did. "Oh, it's nothing." She laughed, hoping to ease the situation.

"Did Luke say something to offend you? I heard you two at the stairs, but I couldn't hear what you said."

"He just complimented my dress."

"And you think it was improper for him to give you such attention, when he is planning to marry your sister, right?"

She nodded. She was finding Dr. Moretz to be both perceptive and wise.

"Don't be too hard on Luke, Leah. What social graces he has, he's taught himself when he went to college. If he could have grown up here in Salisbury, things would have been different, but it would have been too hard for him in this household after I remarried. You'll find the culture in the rural mountain areas to be different."

"I understand," she said, and she did. She saw another problem, however. "Ivy is better versed in etiquette and the proper way to do things than anyone I know. She holds great stock in such things."

"I hope I can be honest and confide with you, Leah, and I think I can. I'm worried about Luke marrying Ivy. They don't seem at all suited for each other to me. I'm afraid, even if Luke comes to realize it, he'll still marry Ivy, because he's promised it. I'm hoping she'll realize Luke's not the one for her, and she breaks it off. I think they've both seen the other as the person they want them to be and not who they actually are. That's why I said what I did to Luke last evening."

"I get the same feeling sometimes, but I know Ivy and Luke will need to be the ones to discover it. It won't work for someone else to try to meddle."

"You're a lot like my mother, Leah. You often say what you think and can be honest to a fault."

"Oh, I'm sorry. I didn't mean you were meddling last night."

"It's fine, dear. I'm like that, too, and I like people who're honest."

Frances came in with the children, and their conversation changed. "Is there going to be enough room in the carriage?" she asked her husband.

"I feared there wouldn't be with those awful hoops you ladies wear, so we'll take two carriages. One of you ladies should go in the second carriage, so they'll be enough room."

Luke came in next. He looked dashing, but, unlike him, Leah made no comment. Luke's good looks didn't seem to affect him. Ivy knew she was extraordinarily pretty, and she used her beauty to get what she wanted. If Luke knew how good looking he was, it didn't show.

Ivy came in last, and she made quite an entrance. She was breath taking in a pale-blue gown, with her hair arranged in ringlets at the back of her head.

"The wait was worth every minute," Luke told her. "You're stunning." Ivy beamed.

"Well, shall we begin loading the carriages?" Dr. Moretz said.

The ride to church didn't take long, and the large redbrick building in a Federal style looked impressive. Ivy kept gawking as Luke helped her from the carriage.

Dr. Moretz seemed to be well known, and many people came up to talk with him. Luke stayed with his father, while Frances led the women and children inside.

Toward the end of his sermon, Reverend Thompson used Matthew 7:13-14 to say many of those seated in the churches around the world would be flabbergasted one day to learn they'd not made it into heaven. "It's not so much what you do, although that's important," he told them. "The real criterion is that you've accepted Christ into your life and allowed Him to change you. You've got to change your heart and give total control to God, and most of us refuse to give up control. We want to shape our own future. Well let me tell you, dear folks, God does a much better job of shaping our futures than we do."

"Do you recall when Jesus tried to show the Pharisees their attitudes were warped? They thought they were pious people in God's good graces. They certainly knew the Scriptures, practiced all the rituals, and upheld the laws of Moses, but their attitudes were wrong. They were self-righteous and did nothing from a loving heart. How is your heart this morning? Do you love others as much as yourself? Do you have a servant's heart?

"I truly believe many more of those slaves up there," he pointed to the balcony, "will make it to heaven than you down here in the fancy clothes and fat pockets. They've been taught to be humble, and they know how to serve. They're more like Jesus than many of you."

There was a huge gasp from the congregation, and over half of them got up and angrily walked out. Ivy and Frances looked at Dr. Moretz and Luke to see if they would also leave. The men stayed seated.

"Did he just say the slaves are better than most of us?" Frances whispered in disbelief.

"I guess that cleared out those who are not serious about following Christ and are just sitting on the premises rather than standing on the promises," the pastor said and continued with his sermon. Then, he asked for a commitment.

"Theocentricity is seeing God as the center of everything . . . creation, Scripture, our families, and our lives. God must be Lord of all your life or not Lord of any. We must accept Him completely, because He allows no half-ways. Will all of you who are willing to give God total control of your lives, come forward and kneel in prayer? Think about this now. You don't want to make such a promise to God and not be serious. It's fine to ask for His help, because we are all human, and this will be hard, but if you make this commitment, God is going to expect you to try and live up to it. If you fail, you should ask forgiveness and try again."

About a third of those remaining got up and walked to the front. Luke, Dr. Moretz, and Leah were among them. Frances and Ivy stayed seated.

"You in the balcony may just stand at the railing," Reverend Thompson called out and then joined those who knelt up front.

"Well, that will be the end of Reverend Thompson in this church," Frances said, when they entered the house. "I guess he might be able to find a church up North somewhere."

"I fear you're right," Dr. Moretz said, "but I respect the man more than I can put into words. What a courageous thing for him to do."

"He is right, you know," Luke added. "When we get to heaven, there won't be a slave section. If you can't tolerate all being together here, you'll probably go in the other direction."

"Of all the nerve! Are you saying I'm going to go down *there?*" Frances spit the words at Luke and pointed at the floor.

"Luke wouldn't say something so rude," Ivy told her. "He didn't mean that at all, did you, Luke?"

"It's not for me to judge who goes in which direction," Luke replied.

"I can't believe you also went to the front, Leah," Ivy said.

"Then you really don't know me at all," Leah told her. "I wish God would take total control of my life. Decisions and choices wouldn't be so hard then, but He requires I make the choices all through my life. I want to follow Him completely, however, and I like learning more about how to do that."

"Bravo," Dr. Moretz said, and gave Leah a big smile of support.

Sunday dinner looked delicious, but Frances still raged. She feigned a headache and retired after only a few bites.

If Ivy had been in a testy mood earlier, it'd only become worse. She chose to ignore the other three adults at the table.

"I think Leah and I are going to go for a ride this afternoon," Dr. Moretz said. "It's a beautiful day. Would you and Luke like to come, too, Ivy?"

"No, I am going to rest after dinner. After that ride yesterday, I don't want to be in a conveyance any more than I have to."

"What about you, Luke?" his father asked.

Leah could tell he felt torn. "I should stay here, too," he finally said. "Perhaps Ivy and I can walk in the garden, if she gets to feeling better."

That seemed to please Ivy. She liked for Luke to put her first.

"I hope you'll reconsider," Dr. Moretz said. "You'll have plenty of time to spend with Ivy from here on out, but you and I rarely get to be together. I miss you, son. The post is so slow and not really reliable, and I like to see your handsome face."

Luke didn't reply. He looked at Ivy, as if he hoped she'd tell him to go, but she didn't.

Dr. Moretz and Leah went for a ride directly after the meal. They took the open carriage and moved slowly down the lanes. Downtown, he showed her the large courthouse building, which was nearing completion.

"It's being built by local contractors, Conrad and Williams," Doctor Moretz told her. "It's classic Greek Revival." He seemed proud of the imposing structure. "Doesn't it look like a Greek temple with its two stories and tall Doric columns?"

"Yes, I remember seeing the style in Papa's books, and this one does look like one of the ancient temples. It should be set on a hill, though."

Leah saw a sign that read BOGER & WILSON, WATCHMAKERS. She wondered if they might want to buy and resell some of her jewelry. She would ask Dr. Moretz later.

They passed two attorneys' offices and several more doctors. Besides three stores selling general merchandise, Leah saw a tannery and a cobbler, and she didn't think they drove by all the businesses.

Dr. Moretz proved to be an excellent guide. Not only did he know the families and businesses of Salisbury, but he showed wit and humor. Leah couldn't remember when she'd enjoyed a Sunday afternoon more.

"Salisbury has made its contributions to history, too," he said as they started back. "Daniel Boone's parents moved to the area from Pennsylvania, and he lived out in the country before he opened the way west through the Cumberland Gap. George Washington also visited town, and Andrew Jackson, our seventh president, studied law here for a time. However, Jackson is nothing to brag about, as far as I'm concerned. He forced the Cherokee from their lands and forced them to march all the way to Oklahoma."

Leah appreciated Dr. Moretz's concern for others, even those some people would be prejudiced against. In fact, she admired the man more all the time.

"Salisbury has some very nice homes." She turned to face the doctor. "I like the town."

"We used to be considered the backwoods and the western part of the state, but with expansion and development, that's changing. Salisbury is becoming quite the cultured town. There's even talk of starting a railroad line here, and I think it'll happen soon."

"I can see it's a growing place, but I'm afraid I'm more accustomed to country living and open spaces. I think Salisbury may be getting too populated for my taste."

"Mine, too, sometimes." He studied the scene for a moment before he turned to her again. "By the way, Luke managed to talk to the lawyer I recommended today at church. He made an appointment for eight in the morning. It should only take a few minutes. Only Ivy will need to go with him to sign the papers. I'm sure Luke will tell Ivy about the arrangements."

"That's good. Patsy is very excited. I can't imagine what it'd be like to be bought and sold and have your family members ripped from you. This takes all that away from her."

"Not to mention being beaten or forced to become someone's mistress." The doctor frowned.

Leah must have looked surprised or embarrassed, as he quickly continued: "Oh, I know it's not supposed to be discussed in polite company, but you've demonstrated your intelligence and your broad education. I feel I can talk to you without having to tiptoe around. After all, refraining from talking about it doesn't make it any less true."

"You're right," Leah agreed. "We need to talk about injustices, or they'll never change. In fact, I've shocked people by mentioning such things myself."

"That's the spirit. I'd be a lot more excited about Luke's wedding, if I were getting you for a daughter-in-law. I still feel you'll be part of the family, though. I was serious when I said you can always come to me for anything you need. Consider me your surrogate father. I'd always happily help you in any way I could."

"Thank you. I appreciate that, and I feel we've made a special connection. It's so rare anyone even notices me when Ivy's around."

"You don't seem to be as jealous of that as most women would be."

"I'm not. I decided long ago I wanted to develop my character. There was little I could do about the physical features God gave me, but I felt my moral fiber was more important, anyway."

"I'm amazed at those sentiments coming from one so young, and let me tell you something else. I think you're prettier than Ivy. Oh, I know Ivy is the classic beauty, and there are those who would disagree with me, but I think your beauty is natural. I can tell part of her appearance has been cultivated. Much of what she wears or does is for effect. Her beauty is a casing to cover a petty, spoiled, selfish woman. You're yourself, and the beauty of it is reflected in your countenance. With your rich-brown hair, luminous green eyes, and beige skin, you're an enchantress in your own right. Where Ivy is a traditional beauty, you're an exotic one. Sarah, Luke's mother, was much like that, and I've never seen a more beautiful woman, inside or out."

"I wish half of what you just said were true."

"Oh, it's true. I don't believe in empty flattery. It's a waste of time. I know I can speak my mind with Mama, Luke, and now you, too. Perhaps that's why I end up saying too much with you."

"I would never think you say too much. I love it when you talk with me as an equal."

"Honey," he laughed. "I'm not sure you'll ever find your equal. You are way above most. Luke may be the closest one you'll ever find."

"Is there someplace I might sell some of my jewelry here, and will there be time tomorrow morning?" Leah changed the subject. The conversation was beginning to venture on dangerous grounds. She appreciated the fact Dr. Moretz would like to see her matched with Luke, but it could never be. Ivy had claims on Luke, and Leah would never try to change that. Never.

"Yes, there's a jeweler here with whom I've done business, and he seems to be fair. Why? Do you want to sell some of your jewelry?"

"Yes, I have too much of it for one thing. Some of it I've never worn. I also think it would be wise to have a little money available. I know Luke is spending a lot on this trip, and I'd like to help out."

"I can tell you right now, Luke's not going to accept any of your money. He would see it as an insult. Mama and he actually have more available cash than most of the mountain families."

"Then, I think it would be wise to travel with a little money of my own in case of an emergency. I'd also like to have some money of my own for Christmas presents or whatever later on."

"I'll tell you what. Let me see the pieces you'd like to sell. I'll pick out what I think would make good gifts for Frances, and I can sell the others to the jeweler."

"Thank you, but you'd better not give me more than they're actually worth. I wouldn't take kindly to that."

"You've got a deal."

They were pulling up to the house. "Thank you so much, sir. I've had a delightful time."

"So have I, Leah. I hope you'll allow me to write to you from time to time. I write to Luke, but he's not always prompt in answering. I'm guessing you'll do better."

"I would like that very much."

Ivy and Luke were at one end of the garden, and Frances and the children were at the other end. Frances sat where she could see the couple but couldn't hear what they were saying.

"I see Frances is taking her job as chaperone seriously." The doctor laughed. "Shall we join them?"

Leah wasn't sure whether Dr. Moretz meant to join the couple or Frances and the children, so she followed him. He walked toward Luke and Ivy.

"You two look better," the doctor observed.

"I feel better," Ivy said. "I managed to take a nap before we came out."

Supper turned out to be a simple affair of sliced beef, ham, cheese, bread, and fruit. "We give our help Sunday afternoons off," Dr. Moretz explained.

"How much help do you have?" Ivy asked.

"We have the housekeeper, the maid, and a man, who serves as driver, stable hand, and gardener," Frances said.

"I thought the gardener was part time," Luke said.

"He used to be, but that one found a better paying, full-time job, and we hired Jim to take care of it all."

"I'm surprised you haven't been called out to doctor someone this weekend," Luke told him.

"Frankly, I am, too. Weekends like this are very rare. I think there may have been some divine intervention to give me time to spend with my wonderful guests." He looked directly at Leah.

"Didn't you promise we'd go for a walk?" Ivy asked Luke.

"We can do that if you'd like, but remember, you need to be up and ready by seven thirty in the morning."

"Let's walk some, and I'll be more ready to sleep when we get back."

Leah went upstairs and chose the dress she would wear to-morrow. Patsy said she would iron the simple, everyday dress the first thing in the morning.

"I'm sorry I didn't get to launder your travel dress," Patsy said. "Miss Ivy has a couple, but I see you only brought the one."

"It doesn't matter. I think this one may be more comfortable, anyway."

When Leah came back downstairs, Luke and Ivy were returning. They'd not walked long.

"Where are Maggie and Teddy?" Leah asked. She hadn't seen them since supper.

"I've taught them to stay in their rooms, unless they're invited to stay down," Frances said. "They're not in the way, then."

"You seem to like children, Leah," Dr. Moretz said.

"I do. I like children and animals, and they seem to like me," she smiled.

"I've always heard animals and children sense what a person is really like," the doctor said.

"I don't think so," Frances said. "Dogs and cats seem to take an instant dislike to me."

"And, I don't like animals or little children, either," Ivy added. "They're dirty and messy."

Dr. Moretz looked at Leah with an expression, which said, "See, that's exactly what I meant." Leah had a hard time suppressing her laughter, which threatened to bubble up. She felt Luke's gaze, and, when she looked at him, his eyes crinkled and told her he'd understood the joke, too. She looked away, if he smiled, she knew she wouldn't be able to keep from laughing.

"Well, I'm going to turn in," Ivy said. "I don't want to keep Luke waiting in the morning."

"I think that's a good idea," Frances said. "I need to see the children to bed, too."

"I'll be up shortly," Leah told Ivy.

"Did you have a good ride today?" Luke asked, when the others had left.

"I did," Leah answered. "Your father is an excellent guide."

"I had a good time, too," Dr. Moretz added. "I had a most delightful companion, who is able to carry on the most interesting conversations."

"I'm sorry I missed it then," Luke said, and he sounded as if he really meant it.

"I am, too, son. I certainly am."

"Good night," Leah said as she got up to go upstairs.

"Sleep well, Leah," Dr. Moretz said in a soft voice.

"See you in the morning," Luke added.

CHAPTER FIVE

Yadkinville

Leah heard Patsy get up and slip out of their bedroom before sunup. She got up and realized Patsy had taken her dress down to iron. Ivy began to stir.

"It's too early," she complained.

Leah hurried and quickly slipped on the dress she'd already worn. She would wash and change when Patsy had her dress finished.

"Get me the dress you want to wear today," Leah told her sister, "and I'll take it down for Patsy to iron."

Ivy reluctantly got out of bed. She took a travel dress from the wardrobe and handed it to Leah.

Leah took it downstairs and gave it to Patsy. "Here's the other dress," she told her.

"You're lucky to have your slave traveling with you," Frances said. "It would be much easier if Clifton allowed us to own them. As it is, we can only afford to hire a limited staff."

"She's not my slave. She's been Ivy's, but that's about to change. Luke has convinced Ivy to give Patsy her freedom."

"What a waste," Frances said. "That girl is valuable property. Why, she must be worth at least eight hundred dollars. It's like throwing money away."

Leah didn't reply. Instead, she turned and went back upstairs.

To Leah's surprise, Ivy had also put on one of the dresses she'd already worn.

"I wanted to tell Patsy to be sure not to use too much water on my dress. That material doesn't dry quickly and can remain damp, even when ironed." She left to go downstairs, and Leah followed to collect her dress.

Suddenly, Ivy let out a loud scream. Leah looked and saw a huge black stain on Ivy's dress that Patsy had been ironing. The men must have heard the scream too because they came running.

"You stupid, good-for-nothing . . . ," Ivy yelled and hauled back her hand to hit Patsy.

Leah stood close enough to grab Ivy's wrist. "Stop!" Leah demanded. "What are you doing?"

"You stop!" Ivy demanded. "You're hurting me."

"I didn't do it, Miss Ivy," Patsy said. "It was Missus Moretz, not me."

"I am sorry. I didn't know," Frances said to Ivy. The older woman looked horrified.

"What's going on here?" Dr. Moretz asked.

"I found a bottle of ink in the larder." Frances said, almost fearfully. "I was taking it into your office, when I stumbled and it splashed on the dress."

"It's ruined," Ivy said in dismay. "Ink will never come out."

"What was a bottle of opened ink doing in the larder?" Dr. Moretz asked. "It doesn't make any sense."

"And, what were you about to do, Ivy?" Luke asked. "Were you going to hit Patsy?"

"I thought she'd ruined my dress," Ivy said.

"Even if she had, you should never lay a hand on her. How would you like for someone to slap you because you made a mistake?"

"You just don't understand slavery, Luke," Ivy said. "You have to keep them in line and let them know who's boss. Otherwise, they would all get out of hand."

"Does that include hitting, beating, and torture?" Luke asked, his voice cold and hard.

Ivy lifted her chin defiantly. "If necessary."

"Tell me again, Frances," Dr. Moretz said, "how did you ruin Ivy's dress?"

"I didn't know it was her dress, I thought it was . . ." She stopped.

"You thought it was Leah's?" the doctor finished for her.

"No, no,"—Frances tried to recover—"it was an accident, like I said. I'm so sorry, Ivy."

"We'll buy you another dress," Dr. Moretz said to Ivy. "And, Frances, I hope you did not intend to ruin what you thought was Leah's dress. Surely you wouldn't stoop that low." The look he gave his wife kept her silent.

"I don't think we have time for new purchases," Luke said.

"Then I'll give you the money for one," Dr. Moretz said, as he looked at Ivy. "Frances, you get with Ivy and figure out how much I should give her and let me know."

"That won't be necessary," Leah told the doctor. "We've enjoyed your hospitality for free, and Frances said it was an accident."

"It's what I intend to do, nonetheless. I'll take it out of what Frances spends on dresses. One less dress won't hurt her."

"Go up and choose another dress for Patsy to iron," Leah told Ivy. "You and I can go ahead and eat breakfast, while Patsy finishes with your dress."

Patsy waited in the bedroom when Ivy and Leah went up from breakfast. Patsy was adept at helping Ivy dress, and Leah felt in the way, so she went back downstairs. She'd also tucked the jewelry she wanted to sell in her pocket. Leah could get ready while Ivy and Luke were out.

Luke and his father were talking in the dining room, and Leah could hear them from the parlor. She started to join them, until she realized what they were discussing. She decided to sit down in the parlor, instead, since she didn't want to be put on the spot about what had just happened. She thought of the ugly ink spot. No, she didn't want to be put on that spot at all.

"I can't believe Frances would do such a mean-spirited thing," Dr. Moretz said. "Did you read it like I did? Did Frances deliberately stain the dress, because Leah brought it downstairs, and Frances thought it was Leah's dress?"

"That's exactly what I thought," Luke said.

"I knew she was against you, son. That's why I sent you to live with Mama, but I had no idea she would be mean and conniving against anyone she didn't like."

"Frances didn't surprise me so much as Ivy did. I knew firsthand what Frances could be like, but Ivy was actually going to strike Patsy, even before she found out what had happened."

"She would have hit the girl, too, if Leah hadn't stopped her."

"I know you've tried to warn me about Ivy," Luke said, "but I couldn't see it. I still can't believe it."

"I think you've seen Ivy as you thought she was, instead of what she's actually like."

I'm beginning to see that, Father, but what am I to do? I've taken her from her family and brought her to a strange place. I've proposed to her and promised her a home with me. What kind of man would I be to go back on my word?"

"Maybe a wise one."

"Like you're going to abandon Frances?"

"If Frances and I weren't already married, I would run as fast and far from her as I could. That's what I am trying to make you see. After you marry Ivy, it'll be too late to change your mind. Do something now, before it's too late. Take her back to the plantation where she belongs. Otherwise, you may find yourself married to a younger, prettier Frances, but a Frances, nonetheless. I think it was Ben Franklin who said to keep both your eyes wide open before marriage and half shut afterwards. It's time for you to have your eyes wide open and me to keep mine half shut."

"I can't take Ivy back to the plantation, because she could still be forced into a bad marriage. I can't go back on my word to her, unless she wants that, too." Luke sounded sad but determined.

"What are you going to do, then?" his father asked.

"First, I'm going to see that Ivy signs the papers to free Patsy. If she doesn't, I've already told her she will stay at the plantation, so I'll take her back."

"I never thought I'd be hoping for someone to remain a slave," Dr. Moretz said. "But, I would sacrifice even that for your happiness over your misery. Heaven help me, but I would. I love you that much."

"If Ivy does sign the papers, and I think she will, I'll take her to Granny's, like I promised. But I won't marry hastily. I'll give it more time for Ivy to get to know me better. We'll wait until late fall, and I'll pray for God's guidance and His hand in the matter."

"I'll be praying incessantly myself," his father told him.

"Well, I'd better get upstairs, pack my few things, and check on the wagon and mules so we'll be ready to leave when I get back. I imagine Ivy's going to be ready later than we planned now."

"I love you, Luke."

"I love you, too."

Leah got up and entered the dining room. She didn't want to be caught eavesdropping. She almost wished she hadn't heard their private conversation. Yet, although she found it upsetting and confusing, something told her she had been meant to hear it.

"Ivy should be ready soon," she said. "What time is it?"

Dr. Moretz looked at his pocket watch. "A little after seven. You handled that earlier situation this morning very well."

Leah knew which situation he meant. "I'm just glad I happened to be close enough to stop Ivy. She flew into a rage when she realized the dress had been ruined, and she wasn't thinking."

Dr. Moretz looked as if he started to say something but changed his mind. "I'm going to hate to see you and Luke go," he finally said.

Leah noticed he didn't include Ivy. "I brought this jewelry down for you to see." She held out the five pieces she'd wrapped in a handkerchief.

"I see some of these are a little on the elaborate side. I know Frances will like them. Let's see." He studied them for a minute. "I'll give you four-hundred dollars for the lot."

"Is it a price that's fair to both you and me?" Leah asked. She'd never bought jewelry and had little idea of its worth. She feared Dr. Moretz might try to pad the price in her favor.

"It is, Leah. There are some very nice pieces here with precious stones. If I sell some of them, I'm sure I'll get at least that much."

"Thank you then. You've made this easy for me, and no one else will need to know."

Ivy came down a few minutes later. She looked lovely in her traveling suit of slate gray trimmed with pink piping. Luke came in from outside, and they left to meet with the attorney.

"I'd better go get ready myself," Leah said and went to the bedroom, where she found Patsy waiting for her. It didn't take her long to get ready. Patsy even plaited her hair and wound it into a chignon at her neck.

"This will hold better for you on the journey," Patsy said, "and you won't even have to use your snood."

Luke and Ivy came back about a quarter after nine. Ivy seemed subdued. Leah couldn't determine if her sister pouted over freeing Patsy or if Luke had spoken to her about how she'd acted earlier.

"Here you are, Patsy," Luke handed her an official looking paper. "This proves you're a free woman." The smile Patsy gave Luke could have wrapped halfway around the world.

"Thank you, Master Luke. Thank you ever so much." She clasped the paper to her chest.

"Leah, I want you to keep this copy. Put it in a secure place in case it's ever needed." She nodded and accepted the second document.

"Now let's say our farewells and resume our journey."

They headed west from Salisbury. The terrain had already begun to become hillier and seemed to have more lush growth.

Ivy sat quietly and looked straight ahead most of the time. She inched closer to Leah, as if she didn't want to touch Luke. If Luke noticed, he didn't let on.

Before long, Leah felt stiff and sore again. Luke must have felt the same.

"It won't be long before we get to the Yadkin River," he said. "We'll take a break and give the team a drink. There may not be water for them when we stop to eat."

"Will we have to ford the river?" Leah asked, "Or is there a ferry?"

"Neither. There's a toll bridge where we'll cross."

The Yadkin River ran swifter than Leah expected. She got out of the wagon and walked down to the river behind Luke and the mules. Ivy and Patsy got down and stood beside the wagon.

"Is the Yadkin a major river?" Leah asked Luke, as they stood and watched the rapids.

"It is in this area," Luke said. "It gives water to many of the farms and towns, but it's also prone to flooding. Mountain streams feed into it, and it rains often there. If there's also heavy rain down here, the river will come out of its banks and leave deposits of rich silt. The fields along the Yadkin produce some good crops, especially corn, if a spring rain doesn't cause them to be washed away."

Luke took the mules back to the wagon, and Leah took a private moment. Patsy and Ivy joined her.

"What were you and Luke discussing?" Ivy asked her.

"The river. He shared some information about the Yadkin River."

"How interesting," Ivy said scathingly.

They walked up the slight incline to the wagon. "Here you are," Luke said as he stood waiting to help them into the wagon.

"Well, thank you, Luke," Ivy said in a sarcastic tone. "I was wondering where I was."

Luke gave her a hard look. "We've still got a long trip ahead of us, Ivy. You can either be civil or keep quiet, but I expect you to appear respectful."

Ivy stuck out her bottom lip. "You go first," she told Leah, when Luke started to help her into the wagon. Luke hesitated for only an instant, before he reached out to Leah and helped her up. This would put Leah beside Luke and Ivy at the end.

Leah began to think she liked this arrangement better. It made it easier to carry on a conversation with Luke. She didn't have to talk over Ivy. Time moved by at a much faster rate than the wagon did, and dinnertime came before Leah realized it.

They stopped once again. Frances had told the housekeeper to pack them enough food to see them through breakfast tomorrow.

Luke spread an old quilt from the back of the wagon and Patsy laid out meat, cheese, bread, and fruit for lunch. Luke had filled the water barrel, and the women drank from the tin cups. Luke used his canteen. Ivy picked at her food and said little.

"How much farther today?" Patsy asked.

"We should be almost halfway to Yadkinville."

"I guess the town gets its name from the river," Leah said.

"Yes, and the county, which was just formed from Surry County in 1850. The county seat was formed in 1851, but they planned to name it Wilson, then. When the leaders discovered there was another Wilson, North Carolina, down East, they voted to change the name to Yadkinville. I don't know if I would call it a town yet, though. The last time I was through here, calling it a settlement might even be stretching things."

"You don't seem to be pushing the mules as hard today as you did Friday," Leah told him. "We seem to be taking our time."

"Father and I listened for information when we were in Salisbury. I thought Paul might talk to Lawrence and come to Salisbury, because father lived there, but no one seemed to be asking about us. We got started too late this morning to make it to Wilkesboro before dark, but we have plenty of time to get to Yadkinville."

They finished eating and got back in the wagon. "I want to ride in the back this time," Ivy said. "I'm tired of the wagon seat, and the sun is going to play havoc with my skin." Patsy took Ivy's place on the other side of Leah.

Leah found it interesting that many of the farms along the way were growing tobacco. Papa had always planted most of his fields in cotton, but then, cotton had a long growing season. The farther west they traveled the shorter the growing season would become, and somewhere along the way it would become difficult to grow cotton or tobacco. Also, as the terrain became hillier, the fields became smaller.

"I can't wait to get out of this wagon and into a room," Ivy said from the back. She must have come closer to the front, so she could hear what was being said.

"I don't know if there'll be a place for us to stay the night in Yadkinville or not," Luke told her. "We may be sleeping on the ground."

"What about in the wagon?" Ivy asked.

"There's not going to be room for all of you in the wagon with the supplies I'm hauling," Luke told her, "but I can make room in it for you, if that's what you'd prefer."

Ivy seemed placated by Luke giving her preferential treatment. She even smiled.

True to what Luke said, there wasn't much to Yadkinville. Leah saw a small general store and a few other buildings scattered about. It looked like the smallest county seat she'd ever seen, but it probably looked even smaller to her after coming from Salisbury.

Luke stopped at the general store and asked about where they could find a place for the night. The clerk indicated there wasn't a suitable place for the women.

"If we're going to camp, we might as well move on west a little more," Luke said as they headed for the wagon. "We'll stop when we find a suitable place and at least an hour before the sun starts going down."

"Do you have a pot?" Leah asked. "We could go back to the store and get something to cook a hot meal. We've eaten all the meat Frances sent, anyway."

"That's a good idea. I did get some things in Salisbury in case we needed to camp somewhere along the way."

At the store Leah chose some fresh onions and peas, since those were coming in the gardens now. She also got a few potatoes and a strip of side meat.

"I've got flour in the wagon," Luke told her when he saw her looking at some in the store.

"I don't suppose you have any milk and butter?" she asked the proprietor.

"I can get you some." The man called his son. "How much do you need?"

"About a quart will do."

The boy went out with a bucket and came back with the milk and a half pound of butter. The proprietor poured milk into a smaller tin container with a lid. There seemed to be more than a quart but probably not a half gallon. Luke paid, and they left with their supplies.

"I'm interested in seeing what you'll make with the things you bought," Luke said. "Which one of you will do the cooking?"

"Well, it won't be me," Ivy said wrinkling her nose.

"I learned from the cook at the plantation," Leah told him, "and I actually like to cook. I would've bought beans, but they need to be soaked first, and they still take a longer time to cook. The peas should be tasty, since they're fresh. They'll provide a change, anyway."

CHAPTER SIX

Camping

They rode for about another hour. The sun set low in the sky and straight in front of them, making it hard to see.

Luke pulled the wagon well off the road in a level grassy area. He tied the mules to some trees with long leads, so they could graze but couldn't reach the wagon. Patsy and Luke gathered some wood from under the trees.

Luke made a ring with rocks to contain the fire. After he had it going, he went to the back of the wagon and pulled out the iron pot on legs. He also had tin cups, deep plates, and spoons.

Leah put some water in the bottom of the pot and set it directly on the fire, while Patsy shelled the peas and peeled and diced the potatoes and onions. As the water started to boil, Leah added small hunks of the side meat. When Patsy had finished the vegetables, she added those, too.

"Do you have any pepper?" she asked Luke.

"I do. How much flour will you need, and I'll get it at the same time?"

"About a cup. Just put a pinch of pepper in the flour and a little salt, too, if you have it."

Luke nodded. He came from the back of the wagon and handed it to her in one of the cups.

Leah cooked the mixture until it looked almost dry and set it off to cool some. She poured half the milk into the pot and placed the flour mixture into the container with the milk, beat it with a fork, and shook it until it was smooth. She poured it into the pot and stirred well. Then she set the pot over to one side of the fire so it could continue to cook but hopefully not scorch. She didn't want it to boil too quickly either, because it tended to form lumps when it did.

She stirred the soup until it barely came to a boil, and then she set it off the fire. "It's ready, whenever you want to eat."

"I'm ready," Luke said. "I became hungry just smelling it."

Leah dipped the food, while Patsy got out the bread Frances had sent. Luke said grace and they began to eat.

"This is really good," Luke said. "I had my doubts when you were getting it ready, but it's delicious."

"I could have cooked some dumplings in it, but I knew we had plenty of bread."

"I like it just the way it is," Luke said.

"It is good," Patsy said. "I'm glad you can cook, Miss Leah. I can cook a little, but I've been trained as a lady's maid."

Ivy didn't say anything, but everyone must have liked it, because they cleaned the pot.

"I ate too much," Luke said. "That's the problem. When the food tastes this good, I tend to overindulge."

After supper, Luke laid out three of the bedrolls and rearranged the back of the wagon for Ivy's bedroll. He also put out the things they would need in the morning. When he'd finished, they sat around the fire and talked for a while.

"Tell us about your mother, Luke," Ivy said. She seemed more satisfied since Luke said she could sleep in the wagon. "I don't remember you telling me anything about her. What was her name?"

Leah looked up in surprise. Luke had mentioned his mother to her.

"Her name was Sarah, and she was a very special person. She was beautiful with long, black hair and dark-brown eyes. She did everything she could to make Father's and my lives easier. Father met and married her when he was home with Grandmother after he'd finished college. Then they moved to Salisbury, where she wasn't always accepted into the social circles."

"Why not?" Ivy asked.

"Mama was half Cherokee Indian. Her mother was a full Cherokee, and her father was Irish-American. I never knew them."

Ivy's mouth flew open, but, thankfully, she didn't say anything.

"That must be where you get your dark, good looks," Leah said before she thought, and then felt her face grow warm with embarrassment. She hadn't meant to be so forward. She had considered it inappropriate when Luke complimented her on her looks in Salisbury and here, she'd done the same thing.

Luke smiled at her. "Mother died of a high fever, when I was five, and Father married Frances a little over a year later. Frances never liked me from the very beginning, although she pretended to until they were married. Father eventually saw how difficult Frances made things for me, so he sent me to live with Granny and Grandpa. Grandpa died about three years ago. After her own children were born, I think Frances has resented me even more. "

"I've never seen a Cherokee," Ivy said. "They have dark skin, don't they?"

"All Indians have darker skin," Luke said, "but not as dark as your slaves. What does skin tone have to do with anything?"

"Not a thing," Leah said.

"Well, everyone knows you don't mind dark skin," Ivy said to Leah. "If you did, you wouldn't let yours tan, because it's just not becoming. You wouldn't have been so friendly with the plantation slaves either."

"My skin's darker than Leah's," Luke said.

"It's different for men," Ivy said. "It's acceptable for men to be outside enough to have tanner skins but not women."

"So if my father had been a Cherokee, and my mother had been white, that would have been fine?"

"Certainly not. I think everyone should marry their own kind. That's what birds do."

Leah knew Ivy was parroting things she'd heard before. "What about animals like dogs, cats, cattle, and horses?" she asked her sister. "They mate with different breeds and colors." Ivy looked confused and didn't have an answer.

"What about me?" Luke asked quietly. "I'm one-fourth Cherokee, and my children will be one-eighth Indian."

"I never thought of that," Ivy said.

"Do you still want to marry me? I'll take you back to your home, if you want. I realize I failed to tell you about this before you agreed to marry me, but I didn't think it might be an issue. I assumed you were marrying me because of our love for each other."

Leah knew she and Patsy shouldn't be hearing this conversation, but she sat mesmerized. She couldn't bring herself to get up and walk away to give the couple privacy.

"No, I can't go back now," Ivy said. "How would I face everyone? It would look as if you didn't want me."

"That doesn't sound like a good reason to get married, Ivy. Marriage is forever. You need to be sure I'm the man for you."

"I'm sure," Ivy said, but she didn't sound sure at all.

They all sat in silence for several minutes. Leah couldn't believe Ivy. She always knew her sister to be shallow and vain, but not to this extent. Leah felt nothing but shame over the way Ivy had been acting, and she felt so sorry for Luke. She'd heard him tell his father he planned to live up to his promise to marry Ivy, but would he do so no matter what Ivy said or did?

Leah felt in a precarious place herself. She hesitated to tell Luke he shouldn't marry Ivy, although that's exactly what she thought. Leah also found herself more and more drawn to Luke, but it wouldn't be right for her to try to pull Luke and Ivy apart.

"How long will the trip tomorrow be?" Patsy asked to break the silence.

"A little longer than today, but we'll get an earlier start. We're going to stop in Wilkesboro, because I have some business there.

"Have any of you ever camped out before?" Luke asked.

"Of course not," Ivy said.

"I haven't," Patsy answered, "but, until I was twelve, I lived in a slave cabin, and there's not much difference."

"I've camped out for fishing and hunting with Papa and Paul a couple of times when I was younger," Leah told him, and Luke smiled.

"See what I've been telling you," Ivy said. "Leah has been allowed to run wild."

No one said anything, and Ivy gave a huff. "I'm going to lie down soon," she said. "Come with me, Patsy. I want you to brush my hair. Just because we're out in the wilds doesn't mean we can't be civilized."

"Ivy is rather hard on you, isn't she?" Luke said when Ivy and Patsy were in the wagon. He spoke quietly, so his voice wouldn't carry.

"Ivy's never liked me," she said. "That's why it surprised me so much when she asked me to come with her."

"I told her I wouldn't bring her unless she had a chaperone. She said she could bring her slave, but I knew that wouldn't suffice in most people's eyes. I guess you were the only one she thought she could convince. When she said she would ask her sister, I had no idea she also planned to bring her slave, too."

"Yes, I guess I must have been her most logical choice. Ivy doesn't have many female friends and none who are close. The other girls have always been too jealous of her looks."

Luke remained silent. He looked deep in thought.

"Are you sorry you agreed to bring us?"

"I can see now it may have been a mistake. I'm wondering if Ivy is going to be happy in the mountains. I tried to explain to her how different things would be, but it seems she didn't hear any of it."

"Ivy tends to hear only the things she wants to hear. She makes up her mind and becomes intent on getting her way." Leah looked at Luke. She realized she could depend on him to answer her questions truthfully. She couldn't blame him for wishing he'd left the three of them back at the plantation. They'd become a terrible burden for him. Patsy came back and joined them around the fire, and the more personal conversation ceased.

"Would you mind fetching my medicine chest?" Leah asked Patsy. "I have some lotion I've made to help keep insects away, and we may need it tonight." Patsy quickly returned with the chest, and the three of them applied the lotion to their exposed skin.

"What about Ivy?" Luke asked. "The mosquitoes will certainly fly into the wagon."

"Patsy can ask," Leah told him, "but Ivy won't use it. She says she doesn't like the smell, and she's afraid it might make her skin look less than perfect."

"If the insects don't like the smell, that's all I care about," Luke said.

"Miss Ivy refused the insect lotion," Patsy said when she came back. "Where are we going to sleep? I'll put out the bedrolls."

"I'll take care of mine," Luke said. "I'm going down closer to the mules. You can choose wherever you like close to the wagon. Many people sleep under the wagon."

"I think I'd rather be out in the open tonight," Leah said. "Put our bedrolls between the fire and the wagon," Leah told her. "It doesn't look like rain."

Patsy got up and began clearing the area of twigs and debris, before she put out the bedrolls. When she was through, she came back to Leah. "I'm going to lie down," she said.

"I won't be long," Leah told her.

Luke pulled out his Bible and slipped closer to the fire for the light. "I'm going to sit here and read for a while," he said.

"Would you mind reading some aloud?" Leah asked.

"Not at all." He read several chapters from Psalms. The words came out strong and sure as he read. When he got to Psalm 57, he looked up at Leah. "Be merciful unto me, O God," he read, "be merciful unto me: for my soul trusteth in Thee: yea, in the shadow of Thy wings will I make my refuge, until these calamities be overpast. I will cry to God most high: unto God that performeth all things for me."

Leah realized Luke had tried to tell her not to worry. Everything would be all right, because God was in control. They might not have things figured out, but God did. Luke looked up at her again, and she smiled at him in understanding and appreciation.

Leah slid into her bedroll fully dressed and lay looking up at the stars. It had been a tiring day, and it felt good to stretch out, but she didn't fall asleep. Her mind sifted through the situation with Luke and Ivy.

Leah knew Ivy would not take kindly to the fact Luke had Cherokee blood. Ivy was one of the most prejudiced people Leah knew. She was almost as bad as Archibald. Leah knew for a fact, Ivy had hit Patsy before when the girl did something Ivy didn't like.

Ivy had told the truth, however, when she'd said she wouldn't go home and have it rumored Luke had rejected her. Ivy had always cared a great deal about her image.

Leah decided she needed to pray for God's will to be done. It would take God to straighten out this mess.

Luke lay in his bedroll almost numb from the events of the last few days. How could he have been so blind? Ivy had turned out to be so different than he'd thought. He'd seen her as a vision, a dream come true. To him she'd been everything a woman should be—beautiful, sweet, kind, innocent, loving, and caring. He'd realized she wasn't as knowledgeable as he would have liked, but no one was perfect. The reality of how far off he'd been in his assessment had just begun to set in.

His father had tried to warn him, but it'd been too late then. He'd already asked Ivy to marry him and made her promises. He knew God expected him to live up to his promises. He'd just have to trust the outcome to God. Luke would be like David, when he refused to kill Saul, even though Saul was determined to kill him. Luke would do what was right and honorable and leave the rest to God.

His thoughts turned to Leah. He had never met anyone like her. She *was* smart, knowledgeable, and had a strong faith.

If Ivy had much faith, she'd never shown it. She certainly didn't try to live by the principles in the Bible, as far as Luke could tell. Would marrying her make him unequally yoked? Would that be grounds to call off the wedding? He should have thought about all this before he asked her to marry him, but the forced marriages had made it necessary to rush things. Surely God would eventually give him the answers and work everything out for the best. He always had.

It had been cooler sleeping out on the ground than Leah had expected. After all, this was June. Her bedroll felt damp from the heavy dew, which had fallen during the night. Maybe she should have slept under the wagon, Leah thought to herself. The ground had also become hard and uncomfortable by morning, but she stayed where she was until she saw the sky begin to lighten.

When she heard Luke moving around to collect wood for the fire, she got up. She went through the things Luke had brought out for breakfast. She saw coffee, but no tea. At least someone had ground some of the beans, so she took a small cloth and tied enough coffee to make a pot-full. That way she wouldn't have to wait for the grounds to settle in the bottom before they could drink it. She added the water and set it aside to wait until Luke got the fire going.

They still had enough bread left, and the housekeeper had sent a small crock of fresh strawberry jam. They also had butter left.

Luke came up carrying a big armload of branches and twigs. "Good morning," he said. "Did you sleep well?"

"I slept okay once I got to sleep. What about you?"

"I lay awake for a long time, but I feel fine this morning." He smiled at her, as if to prove his point. He didn't appear as worried as Leah would have been in his place. Luke had the fire going in no time, and Leah set the coffee on.

Patsy roused. "Is it already morning?"

"Yes, sleepyhead," Leah laughed, and Patsy laughed with her. They sat around the fire.

"Patsy, has Ivy hit you before?" Luke asked.

"Yes, sir. Whenever I did something she didn't like."

"How often?"

"Oh, about once a week, I guess. It's common practice with slaves. The missus would do the same, maybe even worse. The Master, Paul, and Miss Leah never struck anybody, as far as I know."

"I can believe that," Luke said, as he looked at Leah. "You know you don't have to be Ivy's slave any more. You don't even have to be her maid."

"Yes, sir, I know, but I think it's best that I do be her maid for now."

"As long as you don't feel forced. Don't let Ivy mistreat you, either. If she does you let me know, you hear?"

"Yes, sir, I surely will. I won't take it no more. I promise."

"Why don't you speak like most slaves, Patsy? Your English is pretty good."

"When I first come to be Miss Ivy's maid, my talk bothered her. She said it grated on her nerves, and, if I wanted to stay in the big house, I needed to learn to speak proper. Miss Leah, she said she would teach me, and she did."

Luke gave Leah a look of admiration. "Did Leah also teach you to read?"

"No, sir. Miss Ivy didn't allow us much time, and I didn't want to know how to read and get Miss Leah into a heap of trouble. It's against the law to teach a slave to read, you know."

"Would you like to learn to read, Patsy?" Leah asked. "I could teach you now that you're free."

"Yes, miss, I'd like that very much."

"We may not have much time during the summer," Luke said, "but the winters on the mountain can be brutal. There'll be plenty of time inside for reading lessons then."

"Why is it illegal to teach slaves to read?" Luke asked. "I've heard plenty of slave owners argue slaves are inferior and incapable of learning. If they're incapable, why would you need a law to prevent them from being taught?"

"It doesn't make much sense, does it?" Leah said. "Nothing about slavery really makes much sense to me. Most of the harsher laws designed to keep the slaves subservient came about because of the Nat Turner rebellion. The law preventing the education of slaves was one of those. The slaveholders became obsessed with fear their slaves would revolt and kill them in their sleep. The slaves outnumber the whites on many of the big plantations."

Luke nodded.

"Do you think slavery will ever end?" Patsy asked.

"I'm sure it will one day," Leah said.

"The coffee smells good. Is it about ready?" Luke asked.

"It should be. I'll pour the coffee. Patsy, would you get us the plates, bread, and jam? How do you drink your coffee?"

"Just black for me," Luke said.

"I'll put some sugar in mine, if that's all right." Patsy said.

"Help yourself," Luke told her. He asked the blessing on the food, and they began to eat.

"Do I smell coffee?" Ivy asked, coming from the wagon.

"Yes, come have some breakfast with us," Luke said.

"I don't drink coffee without cream," Ivy said.

"I just put some sugar in mine," Patsy said, "and it's good."

"The coffee helps wash down the bread and jam," Leah told her. Leah thought it all tasted pretty good. The bread was a little dry now, but the strawberry jam must have just been made, and it was very good.

Leah looked at Ivy. "I see the mosquitoes found you last night." She had red welts scattered over her neck and what was exposed of her hands and arms. There were even some on her face.

"Oh, my," she looked at her arms in disgust.

"Leah's repellent worked great," Luke said. "I heard a few mosquitoes buzzing around last night, but they didn't land on me."

"I didn't have any problem, either," Patsy smiled.

"What are you smiling about?" Ivy snapped. "Stay away from me. I don't want to smell that awful concoction."

"That's going to be hard when we all have it on," Luke told her. "I don't think it smells much at all, certainly not bad."

"I'll ride in the back, then. You three can have the seat." She stomped off to the back of the wagon. Leah could hear her rambling for her hand mirror.

When they all got into the wagon to resume the trip, Patsy took the end, which left Leah beside Luke again. Leah began noticing how often they touched, especially on some of the bumps. If the ruts were molded in certain positions, one of them would almost fall into the other, and, when the wagon leaned left, Leah would slide his way. Her face reddened at her thoughts. She almost wished Ivy would come back up and sit between her and Luke again. This was uncomfortable in more ways than one.

As the road became rougher, Patsy clutched the edge of the seat to keep from bouncing off, even though the wagon wasn't going fast at all. Ivy must've been really bouncing around in the back.

"Take hold of my arm, if that would help you brace," Luke told Leah.

"And, whose arm do I take hold of?" Ivy asked crossly from the back.

"Mine if you want to switch places with Leah."

"Never mind," she replied. "I can hold to the side of the wagon."

Leah held onto Luke's arm and tried to ignore the way her heart picked up and the odd tingle that ran through her. *Lord, help me. Don't let me feel attraction for my sister's fiancé.*

They came around the bend to find a freight wagon in the middle of the road with a broken wheel. The driver had a spare wheel, but he was having a hard time jacking up the wagon and changing the wheel by himself. He'd already unpacked most of his crates to make the wagon lighter.

"Looks like you need some help there," Luke called out.

"I sure do," the driver replied with a grin. "I'm tickled pink to see somebidy come along." The burly man looked like a lumberjack with wide shoulders and thick arms.

"Ladies, you might as well get down and stretch a bit." Luke helped them down from the wagon. Then, he went to the broken wagon. "I'm Luke Moretz," he said to the driver and held out his hand.

"Jack Soots here." The driver shook Luke's hand. "If you'll help me raise the wagon up some, I can hold it while you slip the new wheel on."

He had a log laid across a thick tree section as a lever under the wagon. Luke helped him raise the wagon. As he'd said, Jack held it there, while Luke took the broken wheel off and slipped the new one on.

Jack eased the wagon down and came around to secure the wheel. "That should hold until I get to the next wheelwright."

"Do you need some help to reload the wagon?"

"I guess I do." He sounded reluctant. He put the log and tree trunk in the wagon, and started loading.

"It looks like you came prepared, anyway. Where are you headed?"

"I've had this happen a few times, so I carry the stump and beam with me. I'll stop briefly in Yadkinville, but I'm going to Salisbury."

"We just came from there. What are you hauling?"

"Just some farm products."

"Produce?"

"It ain't exactly produce. It's more like corn products . . . corn juice."

Luke helped him load the crates. "Does the road get worse as we go west?"

"I reckon it does. You be careful. Breaking a wheel's bad enough, but you break an axle, and you're in big trouble."

"You take care, too," Luke told him. "You don't want to break your cargo."

"That's a fact. I'm hopin' I got it packed and padded enough. I appreciate the help, Luke."

Luke helped the women back into the wagon, and they moved forward again. They had lost about an hour.

"What did he mean about his cargo?" Leah asked.

"He must be hauling corn liquor. There are stills all through the region, especially Wilkes County and up the mountain."

"Oh, my!"

"I don't drink any strong drink," he added. "I don't like the idea of not knowing what's going on or not being responsible for what I do. I guess I don't like losing control to anything or anyone but God."

"Does that mean you are authoritative and bossy?" Leah teased.

"What do you think, Leah?" he answered with a question, but he sounded serious.

"I think you're fair and reasonable," she said, matching his tone.

He was actually too fair sometimes, like in dealing with Ivy. It might be better if he could be a little more authoritarian there.

They rode without talking for a while. Leah could tell Luke tried to be careful how he hit the ruts and holes in the road. He didn't want to damage the wagon and be stranded. They met a few other wagons, but they managed to get over and let the other wagon pass.

"Do we have enough food left to have a little to eat?" Luke asked. "Since we lost some time back there, I'm getting hungry."

"There's some since we bought food, and I cooked for supper yesterday. I think there's some bread, cheese, and apples left."

"That'll do. I'll pull off, when I can."

"Do you have anything for this incessant itching, Leah?" Ivy asked when they'd stopped.

"Not with me," Leah told her. "Luke, do you have any oats for porridge or apple cider vinegar?"

"I have some oats. Granny is partial to them in the winter."

"I can make a paste by crushing them more and adding a little water. It will curb the itching and help the welts heal."

"What will it look like?" Ivy asked.

"It'll show some, but so do the red bumps. If you apply it carefully, it'll help disguise the redness and look more skin toned."

Ivy nodded. Leah prepared the paste after they ate, while Luke took the mules to a small stream. Ivy applied the paste very lightly and rubbed the edges, so the affected skin did look better.

"Apply it thicker tonight before you go to bed," Leah told her. "It will make them heal faster."

When they resumed the trip, Ivy took the end seat, and Patsy got in the back. Leah still ended up beside Luke, but Ivy must have decided she didn't like the bumpy ride in the back.

Leah realized her attraction to Luke continued to grow, but she didn't know how to stop it. She wondered if he felt it, too. Because of the way Ivy was acting, they seemed to be thrown together more and more.

If Luke minded Ivy's pouts, he gave no indication. He allowed her to withdraw from him and didn't appear bothered. If Ivy sought to punish Luke, it might just prove to punish Ivy more.

"Look," Luke told Leah. He pointed to a dark-green, tree-covered mountain in the distance.

"Oh, that's pretty," Leah said. She'd never seen a mountain before. She'd seen pictures, of course, and Papa had told her about them. He and Paul had been in the Uwharries, but Papa said they weren't good examples, since they were old and worn down to almost hills.

"That's the start of the Brushies," Luke told her. "Wait until you see the Blue Ridge and the Appalachians."

CHAPTER SEVEN

Wilkesboro

They arrived in Wilkesboro about five o'clock. It looked smaller than Salisbury but much larger than Yadkinville. They crossed Cub Creek and headed straight down Main Street. Luke stopped at the first inn and secured two rooms for them. The larger one had a bed and a trundle, and the women would take it. Luke left them to freshen up, while he went to stable the mules and wagon.

"I feel so wilted and as wrinkled as dried fruit," Ivy said. "I can't wait to get into a fresh dress." Leah agreed. Camping had left her feeling grimier than usual.

"Here, Patsy. Take this dress downstairs and see if someone will let you use an iron," Ivy said. "Be quick about it before you're in the way of supper preparations."

"Yes, Miss Ivy." She took Ivy's dress and picked up Leah's, too.

"Wilkesboro seems a little more civilized than I expected," Ivy said. "Since we left Salisbury, I feared we would see nothing but wilderness. This town gives me hope."

"I'm glad you're pleased." It was about time Ivy found something likable.

Patsy came back with their ironed dresses. "The lady was going to charge me for this, but when I helped her move some heavy pots of water, she said never mind about the fee."

"Thank you," Leah said. Patsy smiled and Ivy frowned.

Ivy poured water from the pitcher into the bowl and washed up first. Leah went downstairs, emptied the bowl, got fresh water, and washed up next. Patsy had offered to fetch the water, but Leah didn't want to continue treating her like a slave.

"I don't like you washing right in front of me, Patsy," Ivy said. "You should go somewhere else or wait until I go down to supper."

"She's not a slave anymore, Ivy," Leah said.

"She's still a darky, though. No papers are going to change that."

"Yes, when the Europeans immigrated to America, many of them were discriminated against, too, but they were eventually disseminated, and today it is hard to tell one from the other. The Irish seem to be the European group on the bottom right now, but eventually they'll fit in, too. The Africans are never going to be able to do that in the same way. Prejudiced people are always going to be able to pick them out."

"Save your highfalutin lectures for Luke. He seems to appreciate them. I don't."

When Luke knocked on their door and came in, he had cleaned up, too. Leah's breath caught, and she quickly looked away. This growing attraction just wouldn't do.

"Are you ladies ready to eat?" he asked. "We didn't have much for dinner, and I'm ready for supper."

"Whatever you think is best," Ivy said, and smiled sweetly at Luke. He seemed as surprised as Leah. Leah looked at her sister. What was she up to now? She must have decided to change tactics, since her pouting hadn't worked.

"I'll just go on down to the kitchen, get a plate, and bring it back to the room to eat," Patsy said. "They'll probably think I'm getting it for one of you, anyway."

The proprietor came to take their order. "We have some nice beef stew, but the Missus is in the process of frying up some fresh catfish, and I'd recommend it. It's just coming out of the pan."

Leah and Luke ordered the catfish, and Ivy wanted the stew. The catfish came with boiled potatoes in an herb butter sauce, coleslaw, and cornbread. Ivy had the stew and wheat bread.

"Where did you get this catfish?" Luke asked, when the owner came by. "This is really good."

"It is, isn't it? I just had me a sample piece. A passel of brothers must've gone fishing today. They came by with a slew they'd just caught. I bought them for a good price, and they even cleaned them for us. Agnes is going to serve them up until they're gone, then it'll just be the beef stew. It's a good thing you folks came a little early. He looked at Ivy. Would you like me to bring you some catfish, Miss?"

"No, thank you," Ivy said. "I'm happy with my stew. I don't care for fish."

"I heard Father say he thought fish is good for the skin and hair," Luke told her.

"Do you think my skin and hair need help, Luke?" She said it as if she knew the answer, but her tone was honeyed, and she seemed to be flirting.

"No, I certainly don't. I don't think you could improve on anything, as far as your appearance goes." He gave her a melting smile, and she beamed.

"The mules are getting privileged treatment. They're being housed in the courthouse," Luke told them with a twinkle in his eye.

"Is that true?" Leah asked him.

"I know you haven't known me long, but have you ever known me to lie?" His eyes still held that teasing look.

"No, I don't, but there's more to the story than you've told us."

"Yes, there is," he laughed. "The first courthouse was a log structure. The court ordered it moved from the square in 1830 and a new courthouse built. They moved the log building from the site and turned it into a stable. So, you see, the mules are staying in a courthouse." He laughed again.

"Or what used to be a courthouse." Leah laughed, too.

"That was a good one, Luke," Ivy cooed, but her eyes showed no merriment.

"Would you ladies like to go for a walk before it gets dark?" Luke asked.

When they agreed, he asked Leah to go up and get Patsy.

"Do we have to take her?" Ivy asked sweetly. "Wouldn't it be better to leave her in the room?"

"I think Patsy would enjoy seeing the town, too," Luke told her. "She's probably never been off the plantation, and it'll be good for her to see new things."

"You're always thinking about others, aren't you, dear?"

"According to the Bible, it's what we're supposed to do."

"Of course it is." Leah could tell Ivy wanted to appear agreeable, but she didn't really agree.

Leah left to get Patsy. She didn't know if she preferred the pouting Ivy or this honeyed, sweet one. She'd been getting more nauseated by the minute, almost like when she'd overindulged in rich desserts as a child. She wished she could get a sister somewhere between the two extremes.

First, they walked east, the way they'd come into town. Not far down Main Street they saw the Presbyterian Church.

"I like the simplicity of the building," Leah said. "Isn't it Greek Revival style?"

"I think you're right," Luke said. "Don't tell me you know architecture, too."

"Not really. Papa had a few books on it. The church is made of red brick I see, and look at those massive white stucco columns."

"They almost look too big for the tiny church," Ivy said.

"The style is similar to the courthouse they're building in Salisbury," Leah observed, "but this is a much smaller version."

"You're being quiet back there, Patsy," Luke said.

"I don't have nothing to say, Master Luke. I'm just taking all this in."

"Why don't we dispense with the master and switch it to mister or, better yet, just Luke? 'Master Luke' makes me uncomfortable. I'm no one's master."

"That's not exactly true, Luke," Ivy said. "You're my master." She gave him a theatrical smile, one she had practiced many times for its allure. Luke appeared to stifle what he started to say. As they admired the church, they heard, "Well, hello. Are you folks interested in coming to church? I'm Reverend Pharr, the pastor here."

Luke introduced them and said, "We'd like to come, but I'm afraid we'll be leaving before Sunday. We're on our way to the mountains."

"It's a pretty church," Leah said.

"Thank you. We're rather proud of it. If you're seeing the sights, you'll also want to see St. Paul's Episcopal Church up on the hill past the courthouse headed west. It was built by Dameron, the same builder who built this church. You'd never know it by its looks, though. The Episcopal is Gothic in style."

"I've heard of it," Luke said. "The faculty and students from the seminary at Valle Crucis in Watauga County walked all the way down here for the opening ceremonies."

"How far was that?" Leah asked.

"About fifty miles, I'd guess," Luke told her.

"The Episcopal church was built in 1848, about a year before this one," the minister told them.

"Thank you for the information," Luke said and shook his hand.

"You're welcome, and come to church anytime you can. We'd love to have you."

They seemed to be getting out of the main part of town, so they turned around and headed west. The town seemed to contain many private homes. There were businesses, too, including three general stores, three doctors, and three attorneys.

The new courthouse had been made of brick but had a rock foundation, which Leah found odd. It still looked impressive, however.

"It looks almost majestic, doesn't it?" Ivy said.

"I think I heard someone say this is one of the best courthouses in the state now," Luke said.

Luke pointed out a large oak tree standing nearby. "They call it the 'Tory Oak,'" he said. "In 1779, during the War for Independence, Colonel Benjamin Cleveland's scouts caught about five Tories, who'd stolen some horses. They hanged them on this oak. The British sent a captain with two men to capture Cleveland. They were also taken prisoner and hanged on the Tory Oak."

"How do you know all this?" Ivy asked.

"I guess living in the area helps, and I pay attention to what people tell me. Plus, I've always been interested in history and learning. Besides, Cleveland is considered a hero in these parts."

Much of the town seemed to be clustered around the courthouse. Past it to the right, as the pastor had said, the Episcopal Church sat on a hill.

"It indeed does look different, doesn't it?" Luke said. "And, to think, this builder also built the Presbyterian Church."

"He must have been talented," Leah said. "Although, about the only things the two churches have in common are their bell towers and their brick."

"Look, there's the post office," Luke said. "I think I'll write Father before we leave and post it from here. If any of you would like to include a note or letter, you can."

"I'd like to do so," Leah said. "I'd like to at least send him a letter of thanks for his kind hospitality."

They walked a little farther, but soon turned and went back to the inn. As dusk began to settle, Leah sensed the streets might be getting more dangerous. She saw a man, who'd been behind them, stop and stare. When he realized Leah had noticed him, he quickly turned his eyes elsewhere. Maybe he had just been looking at Ivy, because her sister often got stares.

The women slept well. They'd been so tired from the jolting wagon ride and camping out, the bed felt particularly comfortable. They went to bed early and were asleep almost immediately.

Leah awoke earlier than the other two. She quietly washed from the basin and put on her same dress. When she went downstairs, Luke sat at a table drinking a cup of coffee.

"I'm glad to finally have someone to talk with," he said, as he held out the chair for her.

"Have you been up for a while then?"

"I have. I think this is my third mug of coffee, but I haven't eaten yet. Shall we order?"

"We might as well. Ivy will sleep until much later, and Patsy won't eat with us anyway."

"Are they both still asleep then?"

"They are."

"Let them sleep as long as they can. I plan to stay here today, and we'll leave early in the morning, weather permitting. I don't want to deal with a heavy rain."

"Do we have a long distance to go?"

"It's only about as far from here to Boone as it was from Yadkinville here, but the steep grade will slow us down. The farm is on the other side of Boone, toward Grandfather Mountain, too."

"Will we make it in a day?"

"We should if we get an early start, and we don't have any mishaps or hold-ups along the way. I'm planning on driving all the way to the farm."

They were served boiled eggs, butter, and a basket of muffins and breads warm from the oven. Luke continued to drink coffee, and Leah had tea.

"Ivy seemed more pleasant yesterday, didn't she?" If she could, Leah wanted to see what Luke had been thinking about Ivy's behavior.

"Yes, she was. What do you think of her change of attitude?"

"I don't know. She doesn't confide in me. Do you think she's decided to look forward to the wedding again?"

"That is the important question, isn't it? However, most people don't change their minds on basic beliefs and values that quickly, unless God is involved."

"I've seen no signs of her turning to God."

"I know you told me you've been baptized. Has Ivy?"

"No, she hasn't. She said she didn't want to get all wet and mess up her hair."

Luke shook his head. "I don't think I understand her."

"I'm not sure I do either, but I do love her. I don't want anything bad to befall her, but I think I care more for her than she does for me. We're just so different that it's been better for us to stay away from each other as much as possible. It's sad when you think we're sisters and only two years apart in age."

"So you're seventeen, then? I knew Ivy was nineteen, but I'd never heard your age."

"Yes, I'll turn eighteen in September. What do you think of the way Ivy's been acting?" There. She'd been blunt enough for sure. Luke had a knack of turning the conversation to Leah every time they talked.

"I'm just going to wait and see how she feels when we get to the farm. Perhaps the uncomfortable trip has made her irritable. But, I promised to marry her, and that's what I still plan to do, if she still wants to marry me. I began to wonder after the way she reacted about my Cherokee heritage. I'm not going to rush things, however. I see now we both need to take the time to really get to know the other. I'm glad she's out of her bad mood, though. It'll make things easier for everyone."

"I admire your patience, Luke. It's a virtue I sometimes find I lack."

"It's easier when you give your life to God and know everything's in his hands."

"I know that, too, but thank you for reminding me. I need to remember it more."

"Well, I have some business to take care of this morning. What are your plans?"

"Do you think it would be okay if we walk around town and maybe go to the store?"

"Normally, it would be fine, especially if you stayed in the central area, but I'm a little cautious, since we left secretly. If someone had trailed us, they could easily grab you and Ivy. I'd prefer you'd stay inside unless I'm with you."

"Do you think they're still searching for us?"

"I don't know, but I sensed someone might be following us yesterday when we walked around town."

"I thought I saw someone, too."

"I don't know how long I'll be," Luke said, "but I'm certain I'll be back for dinner."

Leah went back to the room. Patsy had already gotten up and gone down to the kitchen, but Ivy still slept. Leah got out her Bible she'd moved from her trunk to her travel bag, sat down in the chair near the window, and began to read.

Patsy came back shortly and smiled at Leah, but they didn't speak, so they wouldn't disturb Ivy. Both preferred the peace as long as possible. Patsy quietly moved a chair closer to the window and began to mend some clothes.

Leah read several chapters then remembered she wanted to write Dr. Moretz. Luke had already written his letter and had let Leah borrow his pen and ink and have some paper. They would mail them after dinner. She wrote a brief letter and read back over it.

Dear Dr. Moretz,

I wanted to thank you again for your warm hospitality. I enjoyed our visit ever so much.

We didn't find a suitable place to stay in Yadkinville, so we camped beside the wagon Monday night. It turned out to be a lovely night, and everything went well. We bought enough produce at a store in Yadkinville to cook a warm supper.

Thank Frances and your housekeeper for the food they sent. It was appreciated by all and lasted as long as we needed it. We finished the last of it for the noon meal Tuesday.

We arrived in Wilkesboro about five o'clock Tuesday afternoon. We would have been here earlier, but the road grew very rough, and we were delayed by a freight wagon with a broken wheel. I think he was hauling libations, but Luke helped him with his wagon, and we were able to continue west.

Wilkesboro is a quaint town, but it has some impressive buildings, especially the courthouse and churches. The inn, where we're staying, is clean and sufficient, and the food is quite good. How long has it been since you were here?

We plan to start out early in the morning. I'm eager to see the mountains, and to meet your mother. I pray we encounter no problems on this, our last part of the journey.

I hope this letter finds you well. Please reply soon and let me know how things are there and all the latest news. I shall be eagerly waiting to hear from you.

Yours truly,

Leah Morgan

Much later, Ivy woke up. "My, I needed that." She stretched. "I was tired."

"You've missed breakfast," Leah told her, "and you probably need to start getting dressed for dinner." Leah knew Ivy never got ready quickly.

"Where's Luke?"

"He said he had some business to take care of this morning, and he would meet us back here for dinner."

"So, you saw him, then?"

"Yes, we had breakfast together this morning."

"How cozy. Look, Leah, a fool could see you are becoming besotted with Luke. Don't go getting any ideas. He's mine, and he's not going to look at another woman."

"I would never try to take Luke from you."

"That's good to hear. See that you don't." It appeared Ivy's sweetness only extended as far as Luke.

Ivy got ready, and Luke still hadn't returned. They could've heard him moving about next door if he had.

"I'm getting tired of this room," Ivy said. "I'm going to the store. At least it will be something to do. Do you think Luke might have an account set up there?"

"I don't know, but I don't think you should charge anything without his permission."

"Never mind, I have the money from the ruined dress."

"Luke said he wanted us to stay inside in case someone was following us."

"Nonsense—if someone were following us, we'd know it by now. I'll go alone, if you don't want to go."

Leah would never forgive herself if Ivy went alone and something happened, so the three left the inn. Leah and Ivy walked together, and Patsy followed closely behind. They hadn't gone far when Leah looked back and noticed the same man she had seen last night, and this time he didn't seem to be hanging back. In fact, he walked fast enough to be gaining on them.

"We're being followed," Leah whispered to Ivy.

Ivy looked back. "It's your imagination, you ninny." Leah looked back again and saw no one. She knew she'd seen the man, but had she just imagined he'd been following them?

Luke came out of the store just as they started in. They almost collided. "What are you doing here?"

"Ivy insisted on coming, and I didn't want her to come alone," Leah said.

"Didn't Leah tell you I wanted you to stay in the inn?"

"No, she didn't. I'm sorry, Luke. I wouldn't have come if I'd known."

"I heard Miss Leah tell you," Patsy said as she backed up out of Ivy's reach, "but you said you'd come by yourself if she didn't want to come."

"Well now," Luke said with a frown, "standing in the street arguing isn't going to solve anything. Let's go get something to eat. Maybe some food will make us all feel better."

"Leah's as jumpy as a marionette on a string." Ivy said as they ate. "She said someone had followed us, but when I looked, I couldn't see a soul."

"That's why I didn't want you to go out. It would be easy for someone to grab two unescorted ladies."

"Well, I don't know about that. I think Leah and I together might put up enough resistance for it to take more than one somebody."

"There could be more than one man."

"It sounds like a lot of crying 'wolf' to me. There could be a lot of things."

Luke didn't say anything else, but he looked troubled. Leah's worry ratcheted up a notch, too.

"I've got one more thing to do today," Luke said as they finished their meal. "If you have your letter written, Leah, I'll go by the post office, while I'm out."

"I finished it this morning."

"Since we can't go out without you, won't you let us go, too?" Ivy asked.

"Not this time, but I won't be gone as long as before. I just have two stops to make."

Ivy stuck out her lip, but said nothing. She didn't like not getting her way.

"Come," Luke said, "I'll escort you ladies to your room and get Leah's letter."

True to his word, Luke came back within an hour. When he returned, he wanted them to walk to the courthouse with him.

"I just saw the most fascinating thing," he told them as they left. "Two strange-looking men, joined at the waist, just went into the courthouse. I think I remember Father once mentioning something about conjoint twins touring the county as a side show, but I've never seen anything like it."

As they started up the steps to the courthouse, Luke saw someone he knew. "Rayhue, what are you doing in Wilkesboro?"

"Well, hello, Luke. I had some business here. I bought some land just across the county line. I thought one or more of the boys might need it someday."

Luke made the introductions. Rayhue looked to be close to Dr. Moretz's age and seemed friendly and talkative.

"What are you doing at the courthouse?" Rayhue asked.

"I just saw a strange pair of twins go into here. I wanted the ladies to see them."

"Yes, I've met Eng and Chang Bunker. They were born in Siam, but when they were sixteen, they were put on show around the world. They traveled for ten years, but became tired of it. One of their shows had been in Wilkesboro, and they loved the town and people, so they decided to settle here. They ran a store in town for a while, but ended up buying a farm north of town. They married sisters and have two households and children, I hear."

About that time, the twins came out. Sure enough, they were joined at the mid-section.

"Hello there," Rayhue said to them. "I'm Rayhue Wilcox. Do you remember meeting me at the doctor's house? I live near Stony Fork."

"Yes, yes, we remember."

"I'd like you to meet my friend, Luke Moretz, who owns a farm in Watauga County. These ladies are his fiancée, Ivy Morgan; her sister, Leah; and their maid, Patsy. This is Eng and Chang Bunker."

"Beautiful young women," Chang said.

"Must go quickly," Eng added. "Need to buy supplies and get home."

"Nice to meet you," Chang said as they left.

Ivy continued to stare at them as they walked away.

They were fascinating, but Leah tried not to stare. The twins must get too many of those.

"What did you ladies think of Eng and Chang?" Luke asked as they walked back.

"I could hardly believe what I was seeing," Ivy said. "I've never seen anything so bizarre. And to think they are each married and have children. I just can't fathom it."

"It must be hard for them, always being stared at and treated as oddities," Leah said. Luke smiled an agreement.

"Well, they are oddities," Ivy said. "Their oriental looks make them stand out, and then to be joined like that."

"What a handsome little boy." Ivy now stared at a family getting out of a farm wagon in front of a store. "That could be your son in a few years, Luke."

Leah looked. The boy seemed to be about ten, and he was already handsome enough to turn heads.

"Come on, Tom, don't dawdle," the woman said. Tom had been staring at Ivy.

"What can I do for you today, Miz Dooley?" Leah heard the store clerk ask, as they walked by the door.

CHAPTER EIGHT

Up the Mountain

Luke knocked on the women's door at five thirty Thursday morning. They could have slept later, except Ivy needed extra time to get ready. Even then, it was a little after seven when he got them down for breakfast. They ate quickly and left about seven thirty.

"This is later than I planned to start," Luke said.

"Is it that far?" Ivy asked.

"Not in distance, but it is in time. You'll understand when you see the two mountains we have to climb."

"I like this," Leah said as she took in the landscape. "I can see it has already started to get hillier, but it's a pretty area. I like the streams that wind through the fertile farmland."

Luke watched Leah when the silhouette of the mountains rose majestically in the distance to touch the sky. She looked elated.

"This is breathtaking," she said. "I could live here."

"You can have it," Ivy said. "Don't tell me we have to go up one of those." She pointed at the high peaks ahead. Luke chose not to answer.

The farther they traveled, the larger the mountains ahead loomed. "'I will lift up mine eyes unto the hills,'" Leah quoted from Psalm 121, "'from whence cometh my help. My help cometh from the Lord, which made heaven and earth.' He made a beautiful earth, didn't He?"

"Yes, He did." Luke looked at the largest peak. "I love these mountains. I'm free here. My spirit soars."

Luke looked over at Leah. Ivy partially blocked his view, but Leah seemed to alternate between watching the landscape beside them and looking upward toward the summits. When she stared at the mountains ahead, her face turned radiant, as if she beheld the presence of God.

He looked back at Ivy and the grimace on her face. Ivy's sweet disposition had only lasted about a day. Even though he knew she'd been making a concerted effort to appear agreeable, he'd hoped it would last longer.

Although Ivy wasn't as pleasant as she'd been for the one day, she wasn't angry and pouting, either. Her remarks often showed a petty and selfish nature, but she didn't seem mad at the world, now. That attitude had worried him more than he wanted to admit. Still, he realized the chance of her being happy on the mountain farm seemed to dissipate with each mile they traveled west.

He glanced at Leah again. He must try to hold her at arm's length. It wouldn't do for him to become too interested in her while being engaged to Ivy.

Why couldn't Ivy be more like her younger sister? Being her mother's favorite, Ivy had been spoiled and pampered all her life, but Leah had grown up in the same household and been her father's favorite. Yet, Leah had depths Luke dared not explore, and she cared about others. What made the difference?

God. God must be the difference. Leah's faith seemed strong and vibrant. He thought Ivy believed in God, but she didn't show much faith. The three of them, God, Ivy, and Luke, needed to work on that.

Soon the incline became steep. "We'd better get off and walk until we clear the steepest part," Luke said.

"You mean we have to walk," Ivy complained. "I'll ruin my shoes."

Luke remained silent.

"It's fine with me," Leah said. That wagon seat gets hard, and I could use a stretch. Besides, the road has narrowed, and when the wagon hits a rut and tilts toward the cliff, it almost looks as if the wagon might fall over the ledge."

"Are you disparaging my driving?" Luke teased.

"Not at all," Leah countered. "If not for your driving, I'm sure we would have already rolled down to the valley below."

"How do those freight wagons get up the mountain with a heavy load?" Patsy asked.

"They usually have a large team of strong mules," Luke said. "Even then, it's not easy. That's why anything brought over the mountain is more expensive."

Luke walked along beside the wagon, as he held the reins. Leah and Patsy came along not far behind. Ivy tended to lag back, and Luke could tell her breathing had become labored. Patsy saw him looking back at Ivy.

"You want me to go back and walk with her, Mister Luke?"

"That might be a good idea, Patsy. I don't want to stop the mules on the mountain. It would be harder for them to get the wagon going again."

When Patsy stopped to wait for Ivy to catch up, Luke realized he and Leah would be together again. He hadn't thought of that.

"I can tell the air is getting thinner, the farther we go," she said. "It may take us flatlanders some time to get used to this."

"You don't seem to be having much trouble with it."

"I'm used to roaming over the plantation and often putting in a day's work. I guess that's helped my stamina."

"How do you like the mountains, so far?"

"They're lovely and welcoming."

"Welcoming? How so?"

"I don't know. It's hard to explain. It's almost as if they're wrapping their arms around me. I feel as if I'm coming home."

"I know the feeling, Leah, but I *am* coming home. I'm surprised to hear you feel it, too."

"I'm rather surprised myself. I've never even seen a mountain before."

"I wish Ivy felt the same way." The words came out before he could stop them.

"Don't be too hard on her," Leah said. "She's never liked drastic change. Give her time, and she'll probably come around."

"I'm surprised she wanted to come at all, then."

"I was, too, but she really didn't want to marry Lawrence. Mother had always helped Ivy get what she wanted, but Mother continued to push her to marry Lawrence and wouldn't consider you. It's ironic, but if Papa had been alive, I think chances are good he'd have allowed you and Ivy to wed at Gold Leaf."

"What about Paul? He seemed reasonable to me."

"He usually is, but he and Ivy have never gotten along well, and he's wrapped up in his own affairs."

Luke wondered, if he had married Ivy at the plantation and brought her up the mountain as his wife, would things have been better? Would Ivy have acted differently? He doubted it. Something told him things might have been worse.

Luke realized he had a strong aversion to a contrary, unhappy wife. The very thought frightened him. Frances came to mind, and he mentally shook himself.

"How did your business go in Wilkesboro?" Leah asked.

"It actually went as I'd hoped. This year, I decided to grow a large crop of cabbage to sell for extra cash. Cabbage grows quite well in our cool, wet climate. I decided to take advanced orders in

Wilkesboro, and I'll do the same thing in Boone and deliver them in the fall."

"That sounds like a good idea. I take it you got some orders."

"I did. I'll be able to take a large wagon load down the mountain. I haven't asked in Boone, yet, but I'm hoping for orders there, too."

The wagon topped the ridge, and Luke stopped the wagon to wait for Ivy and Patsy. "We'll be able to ride the wagon from here into Boone," he said.

Luke helped the women into the wagon. "I'm glad that's over," Ivy said. "I don't think I could have made many more steps."

Luke started the mules up, and they had just rounded a curve, when they had to stop for a huge tree across the road. "Now, what?" He got down to take a look, and three men on horseback rode out with guns pointed on Luke.

"Hands up, Moretz," one of them commanded.

Luke raised his hands. "How do you know my name?"

"We've been trailing you for days. I planned to do the snatch in Wilkesboro, and we almost got the chance, but then it fell through."

"We got a beauty," another of the men said. "Have you looked at her, Burt?"

Burt looked at Ivy. "Whoo-ey! I like that. It may be worth it to keep her and forget the bounty."

"Who's paying you to do this?" Luke asked.

"Some Biles fellow down in Anson County, but he said he had the brother's permission."

"I'll take the sister. She's a looker, too. Can we keep 'em, Burt?"

"Shoot, that just leaves me the colored, Hank." Patsy had stuck her head out of the wagon to see what was happening. "Oh, well, she ain't half-bad either. We ain't goin' to marry them, no how."

"Let's git them down and git out of here. We can decide on what to do later."

"I don't like those plans," Leah said. "We'd rather stay with Luke." Somehow she held Luke's rifle aimed at the one called Burt. Luke had no idea how she'd managed to pull it from the bottom of the wagon without anyone seeing her.

"Go on, boys," Burt said. "She ain't goin' to be able to shoot."

"I'd think again, if I were you," Leah said. "I've been hunting with my father and older brother, and I could outshoot both of them."

"Now, you ain't goin' to kill us, little miss." Burt didn't sound as sure anymore.

"I won't have to kill you," Leah told him. "Just some strategically placed shots should take away your threat of harming women."

Luke's mouth dropped open. He couldn't believe she'd said that. Was this gentle, caring Leah, and was she bluffing, or did she mean what she'd just said? Even he didn't know. She sure appeared calm and in control. The barrel of that rifle didn't move at all, so she wasn't shaky.

Luke started for the wagon. Leah did remind him of his grandmother sometimes. Luke could see Granny standing down bounty hunters, if the need arose.

"I'll take over now, little lady," a new voice said. Luke hadn't even seen the sheriff ride up. He'd been too taken back by Leah. "Good job. I could use you as a deputy." He nodded at Leah and laughed.

The sheriff had his gun on the three abductors, so Luke moved to the wagon and took his gun from Leah. She sat down in the seat, as if her legs suddenly gave way.

With the two guns on them, the sheriff made the men pull the tree to the side of the road and then tied them to their horses. Luke kept his rifle on them the whole time.

"I don't think these three will bother you anymore," the sheriff said. "I saw them follow you out of Wilkesboro, so I trailed along. I had some business up this way, anyways. I'm glad you filled me in, before you left, Moretz."

"I am, too. Thanks, Sheriff." Luke shook his hand.

"Well, I might have been too late, if that little gal hadn't taken things in hand. You be careful, Luke. I'd hate to get on the wrong side of her." He laughed again.

"Will we have to appear in court?" Luke asked.

"Since I witnessed what was going on, and they ain't denying it, I think I can handle it. If that changes, we'll let you know. I'll get with Sheriff Horton in Boone. We'll make sure justice is done."

Luke walked over to Leah's side of the wagon, and the sheriff left with his prisoners. "Thank you, Leah. I don't know how you did it, but you saved us. Even if the sheriff hadn't come along, I could have taken over, and we'd have been all right."

"I was scared to death, Luke. I knew I had to try to do something. I couldn't let them take us, but I have never been so frightened."

"You didn't show it. You were great." He had the strongest urge to take her in his arms and comfort her, but he knew he couldn't. "Could you indeed shoot, if you'd had to?"

"Yes, what I said was true. I can hit what I aim at. I had no intention of letting them take us, but I was hoping I wouldn't have to pull the trigger." She gave Luke a weak smile.

He picked up one of her hands, squeezed it gently, and quickly let it go. He'd felt a shock at the touch of her hand, and, by her reaction, she'd felt it, too. He walked around the mules and got into the driver's side of the wagon. Now, he felt shaken. He wasn't sure what had just taken place, but he knew he'd better not touch Leah again.

"What Mister Luke said is true. You saved us from a fate worse than death," Patsy told Leah. Leah reached back and hugged Patsy. Patsy wrapped her arms around Leah and squeezed. Good. Leah needed a hug.

"Yes, thank you, Leah," Ivy said. She sounded subdued.

"Burt was the man I saw following us in Wilkesboro," Leah told them.

"I saw him, too," Luke said. "That's why I went by the sheriff's office before we left. He said he'd keep an eye out."

"Do you think it's over," Leah asked, "or will there be others?"

"Most likely that's it." Luke wasn't nearly as sure as he sounded, but he knew the women didn't need another scare right now. "Let's get to Boone."

———

"What a pretty place," Leah said. "It must be atop a mountain or ridge, it looks much more level."

"This is Deep Gap," he told them. "The longest climb is over. There'll be little change in grade to get to Boone. Between Boone and the farm will be more mountainous."

Luke had planned to stop in Boone and try to contract to sell some more cabbage, but he felt it would be better to get the women on to the farm. After their escapade, he didn't feel like stopping now, either. He could come back to Boone on another day.

He turned left, while they were still in the east side of town. They would go south and then turn right to head southwest.

Leah looked exhausted. The Deep Gap incident must have left her emotionally drained.

"Look at Grandfather," Luke said. He pointed to the mountain in the distance.

"The mountain?" Ivy asked.

"Yes, the Cherokee called it 'Tanawha,' which means great hawk or eagle in their language. The settlers named it 'Grandfather Mountain.' Look at it. See it looks like the profile of an old man with a beard. He's reclining horizontally. Can you see?"

"I don't see an old man," Ivy said. "All I see is a mountain."

"It's the head of a man with a beard," Leah told her. See the first rise is his forehead. The sharp, thin peak is his nose, then comes his chin and beard. Can you see it?"

"I can see it now," Patsy said excitedly.

"We're getting close to where we turn again," Luke told them.

They passed a few plowed areas, where the soil gleamed as black as cow manure. These were small plots, not big enough to be called fields.

Luke turned the wagon onto a lane barely wide enough for the wheels in some places, and they started climbing again. Luke didn't mind the narrow, winding mountain path, but he knew the women would.

Ivy gasped and clutched the edge of her seat. Leah didn't seem to notice it, and that worried Luke. He didn't know if she was distracted by the scenery or remembering the incident.

"Sometimes it looks as if we're driving off the side of the mountain," Ivy said.

"Close your eyes and don't look," Luke told her. "When you get used to it, you won't even notice."

Leah looked over at them. "You can trust Luke's driving," she told Ivy. "He'll get us there safely."

Luke gave her a grateful glance. "I've done this many times," he assured them.

"Look at all the beautiful pink flowering bushes!" Leah exclaimed. "They're gorgeous."

"Those are rhododendron," Luke told her. "You'll see them all over the mountains during the month of June." At least the scenery seemed to distract Leah from thoughts of what'd happened.

"Everything is so lush and green," Leah remarked, "and there are little streams of water trickling over rocks and down the mountain all along. The forests look almost enchanted, and the soil's black and fertile. What a remarkable place!"

A wave of pleasure washed over Luke. He loved Leah's descriptions.

"It's cold here, even in June," Ivy said.

"It's cool and refreshing," Leah said. "It smells fresh and clean. I feel close to the earth and on top of the world, all at the same time."

"You've gone giddy on us. What's wrong with you?" Ivy asked.

"Nothing's wrong, Ivy. At this moment, in this place, everything's right."

There weren't many homes along the way, but the ones Leah saw were primitive, rustic log cabins. None of them looked big enough for a family. However, some of them had a number of barefooted children running about them.

They must have climbed the steepest grade again, because the land leveled out. Leah looked up to see a larger log house come into view. It nestled back on a small rise, as if it had been waiting patiently for their arrival. Mountains seemed to loom in the distance all around them.

A slender, spry woman with graying hair pulled straight back into a bun came to the porch, paused to look, and then quickly came down the steps to meet them.

"Land alive, is that you, Luke? I was hoping you'd make it in soon."

She stopped in her tracks, when her eyes settled on the three women. Luke jumped down from the wagon.

"I brought you some company, Granny," he said. "In fact, I brought my fiancée."

His grandmother already had Luke locked in her arms, but she stepped back to look at Leah and Ivy. Luke moved to help them all down from the wagon.

He lifted Leah down first, since she sat on that side of the wagon. She turned to find herself locked in a bear hug. The woman was stronger than she looked.

"I'm so pleased to meet you, honey. I've been thinking Luke was going to bring himself home a bride one of these days."

"No, no, Granny. This is my fiancée, Ivy Morgan. Ivy, this is my grandmother Emmaline Moretz."

"Pleased to meet you, Mrs. Moretz," Ivy said, but she didn't sound too pleased. Leah guessed she was peeved Luke's grandmother had mistaken Leah for Luke's fiancée.

"Well, I'll be," Luke's grandmother said. She looked from Leah to Ivy and back to Leah again. The twinkle in her eyes made Leah wonder if the spry lady wasn't glad she'd made the mistake.

"And, this is Ivy's sister, Leah."

"Well, we already greeted each other, now, didn't we?" she laughed. "Y'all just call me 'Granny Em' like everyone else around these parts, except Luke. I'm just plain ole Granny to him."

Luke helped Patsy from the wagon. "Granny, this is Patsy. She's a freed slave, who used to be Ivy's maid."

"Now, Luke, she may be free, but you know she's still my maid."

"I'm sure y'all are weary of traveling, so come on in the house, now."

"I didn't expect a log cabin," Ivy said to Luke.

"I told you, Ivy."

"Well, I didn't hear you."

"I love it," Leah said. "It's suited to the mountains."

"You love everything here, don't you?" Ivy said. "The next thing, you'll be telling me you love Luke."

"Ivy!" Leah exclaimed. "What are you talking about? Now who's letting her imagination run wild?"

"You need to quit sharpening your tongue at your sister's expense," Granny Em said to Ivy. "It seems way too sharp already."

Ivy gasped in dismay. No one had ever talked like that to her before.

CHAPTER NINE

The Farm

"Come on, girls. You have a seat in the sitting room. I'll get you a good cool drink of water. You've never tasted good water, until you taste it straight from a mountain spring."

"I'll just go back to the kitchen," Patsy said as they entered the house.

"Whatever for?" Granny Em asked. "You'll be spending enough time in there to help get all our work done. No, you go on in the sitting room for now."

Leah found the house attractive. The layout looked much as Luke had described it, but the furnishings weren't as primitive as Leah had expected. She sat down on the end of the sofa and looked around.

Patsy gingerly sat on the other end from Leah. Leah knew Patsy had never sat in a parlor before. Ivy walked by the empty seat between them and took a chair. Luke then sat down between Patsy and Leah.

Logs formed the interior walls of the house, too. Wide boards, held in place by flush pegs, made up the flooring, but a braided rug spread out across the center of the sitting room. A large rock fireplace, capped by a thick wooden mantle stood centered on the end wall.

"I like your house," Leah said when Granny Em came back with the water. "It seems solid and substantial."

"It is that. Edgar's father built it. Of course, then, it was just this downstairs part. Edgar and I added the upstairs, when our third child came along. This house has seen many a storm, and it's still standing strong."

"Just like you, Granny," Luke smiled.

"That's right, son."

"This is wonderful water," Leah said. "I've never tasted as good."

Granny smiled and gathered the glasses.

Leah continued, "I see you have a spinning wheel and loom. You'll have to teach me some of your patterns. The slaves just made the simplest, solid homespun for their clothes."

"I'll be glad to," Granny seemed pleased. "We'll probably wait until winter, because that's when I usually do the spinning and weaving. I'll show you some of the plants around here we use for dyes, too."

"Only the slaves would wear homespuns at home," Ivy said as she looked at granny's dress and apron.

"Well, I'll go out and unload the wagon," Luke said.

"I'll help," Leah said. "I've sat enough lately, so I could use some exercise."

"I'll help, too," Patsy agreed.

"Luke, you know the upstairs. Just put them in the rooms, as you see fit."

Patsy took her bundle and Ivy's travel bag, so Leah grabbed her bag and medicine chest. Luke took two of his pieces. Ivy still sat in the chair.

"Follow us upstairs," Luke told her, "and we'll get you settled."

The stairway led to a hallway with a small window at each end. "There are two bedrooms on this side," Luke said, pointing to the side of the hall with two doors. The front one has a trundle bed, so two of you will need to take it, or all three of you can sleep there, if you'd prefer. There's also another bedroom beside it. You can decide who will be where. My bedroom is the large one across the hall. There is another smaller bedroom, but we've been using it for storage."

"I'll take the back bedroom," Ivy said.

"That's fine," Leah told her. It didn't surprise her that Ivy didn't want to room with Patsy. "Come on, Patsy."

Leah went into the front bedroom and set her things on the floor. The walls here were log, just like the ones downstairs, and a woven rug in shades of green covered much of the floor. The curtains and bed coverings coordinated.

Leah found herself pleasantly surprised by the beauty of the room. She'd not expected anything this nice. She heard Luke struggling on the stairs, and she went to help. He wobbled under the weight of one of Ivy's large trunks as he tried to maneuver the narrow stairway.

"Here, let me take one end," Leah said. Somehow she managed to get her heavy end up the steps and into Ivy's room. When they set the trunk down, Leah looked at Ivy's room. It appeared just a little smaller than hers but very similar, except it had been decorated in blues. She followed Luke back down to help with the other trunks.

"How's your room?" Luke asked.

"Very nice," Leah replied. "I'm actually pleasantly surprised how pretty the house is. When you said it was a log home, I expected things to be more primitive."

"It was very primitive in the beginning, but things have been added over the years. You'll find this is one of the nicest places outside of Boone, but Granny doesn't like to make a show of it. She doesn't want to appear any different than the neighbors."

"I think I like the logs. They look thick and protective, as if they make the house a fortification and haven, all in one."

"I hope you're keeping a journal, Leah. You have a wonderful way with words."

"I've never taken the time to keep a diary, but it might be something I'd like to try here."

"I see you and Patsy are in the same bedroom. I hope that's agreeable to you. I actually thought Ivy and Patsy might room together, since Patsy is still acting as Ivy's maid."

"Ivy said she wanted the other room, and that's fine with me. I'll actually like rooming with Patsy better than I would have Ivy. Patsy's much more amicable, and I can begin her reading lessons, whenever we have time."

"Do you have any books to use?"

"Only my Bible. I didn't bring any from Papa's library."

"I'll see what I have that might help."

When they got the trunks upstairs, Leah offered to help Luke unload the supplies he'd brought, but he declined. She returned to her room and began unpacking. Patsy had gone to Ivy's room to help her.

Leah took her dresses from the trunk and shook them out. All of them would probably need to be ironed again. She lay two soiled dresses she had worn to the side for the wash. She would hang the others outside to air out before they were brushed and ironed. She put all of her worn undergarments into the wash pile.

With that done, she went downstairs. Granny Em flittered around the kitchen cooking.

"What can I do to help?" Leah asked.

"I've got the meat in the pot cooking," the older lady said. "I'm making a stew, and I'll add the vegetables a little later. Do you want to peel and dice the potatoes, carrots, and onions and shell a handful of peas or make cornbread or biscuits?"

"I'll either make cornbread or peel the vegetables," Leah said. "My cornbread is fine, but my biscuits are usually either on the dry or hard side."

"You make some cornbread, then, if you don't mind, and I'll sit at the table and fix the vegetables." Granny Em handed her a bowl and large spoon. "You'll find cornmeal, flour, and such in the larder through that door. I just sent Luke down to the springhouse to fetch some milk and butter."

Leah took the bowl into the larder. The room now also held the supplies Luke had unloaded from the wagon. She found what she needed and went back to the kitchen.

Luke had just come in from the springhouse. "I brought some buttermilk, too," he said. "I didn't know if you'd need it or not."

"I can use either," Leah said.

"I see you've enlisted some help, Granny."

"Not enlisted," Granny Em said. "I accepted a volunteer."

"Well, I can testify, Leah can cook. She cooked some delicious concoction for supper the night we camped beside the wagon. I don't know what it was, but I ate until I almost popped."

"That's good to know. You'll have to tell me what concoction Luke's talking about."

"It wasn't anything fancy. I just made a cream of pea and potato soup. I added some onions and side meat. It probably tasted better to Luke because we were camping."

"It sounds good to me," Granny Em said. "The garden peas are just coming in now, so we should have enough for a soup soon. The onions are growing good, too. Luke got the potatoes in the ground just before he left, but we still have a few left from last year."

"Clouds are rolling in, so it might be getting ready to rain," Luke said. "We often have an afternoon shower in the summertime.

Sometimes it gets into a pattern, and it'll rain the same time for days in a row. At least it waited until we got the wagon unloaded."

"It sounds good for the crops," Leah said. "We had to worry about having enough rain on the plantation."

Leah cut the lard and a little butter into her meal mixture. She added the eggs, stirred them in, and slowly added a little buttermilk and regular milk.

"I see you cook like me by just throwing the ingredients together until it looks right," Granny Em said. "That means you've had some experience."

"I've cooked quite a bit, but not so much whole meals as dishes here and there." Leah then turned to Luke. "I guess it stays cold here longer than it does in Anson County."

"It does," Luke confirmed. "We don't plant much before the first of May. I've seen it come a big snow in April, and it's snowed in May, although that's rarer."

"Since I've lived up here," Granny Em said, "I've seen a lot of snow, and I've heard tell of it snowing in every month, except July."

"Really? Which pan do you want me to use?" Leah asked Granny Em.

"Just grab the spider from the hearth there behind you."

Leah picked up the iron skillet with legs and greased it well. Then, she poured in her cornmeal batter and placed the lid over it. She set it in the edge of the fire but not in the flames. The pan would need to be turned along. She added some hot coals to the top of the lid to make the bread bake more evenly. She noticed the baking oven built in one side of the fireplace, but it would only be used once or twice a week to bake yeast bread and such.

Patsy came down. "When do you usually do wash, Missus Moretz?"

"I just do the laundry whenever there's a need," Granny Em told her, "but I don't want to hear any of this 'Missus Moretz.' You just call me 'Granny Em' like the rest. We can do some wash on

Monday. Luke probably has some things he needs washing now, too. Do you need it before then?"

Patsy responded, "No, it can wait until Monday. Miss Ivy is resting now. She said to call her when supper is ready."

"She did, did she? My mama always said, 'He who doesn't work, doesn't eat,'" Granny Em responded.

"I think John Smith said something like that to the first settlers at Jamestown, when they wanted to go off looking for gold, instead of getting food for the winter," Leah said.

"Ooh, she not only works, but she's smart, too." Granny laughed.

"Granny, you don't know the half of it," Luke told her. "You should have seen her sneak my gun and stand down three rough men who planned to kidnap the ladies."

"You're joshing!"

"Not in the least."

"That's right, Granny Em," Patsy said. "Leah's something. She used to read, study, and work so much the slaves wondered where she found the time for it all. She's the one who taught me to speak proper, and she's going to teach me to read now, too."

"Enough," Leah said. "I don't like you talking around me, like I'm not even here."

"It's better than talking behind your back," Granny Em retorted. Leah smiled.

"You want to walk outside, Leah? I'll show you around the farm before the rain starts." Luke said it before he thought, but something told him Ivy wouldn't be interested in seeing the farm. He shouldn't be alone with Leah, however. It would be proper, since they'd stay close to the house, but his emotions might be in jeopardy.

OWN IN DARK SOIL

o you need me to help here?" Leah asked Granny.

"No, Patsy and I can handle it from here. We'll rotate your pan of cornbread. Supper should be ready in about forty minutes."

Leah followed Luke through the larder and out its exterior door to the barn. He pointed out the barn, pigpen, and chicken houses.

"Some of the people up here let their pigs and chickens run free, but I find the wild animals take most of them when I do. Besides, the ones who range the hogs usually have more and drive them to market. I don't try to sell that many. I just raise them mostly for us."

"I'm assuming you let the chickens out during the day and shut them up when they come in to roost in the evening."

"Yes, that's right. The sow already has a litter of spring pigs, too." Luke showed her the piglets, and she laughed.

"It's amazing how cute they are when they're young, and how ugly they grow up to be. Will you keep them all?"

"Probably not. There's eight there. I'd like to sell four soon, since they're old enough to wean, and another two in the fall to be butchered. With the two grown hogs, that'll give us plenty to butcher and still have a pair to keep over."

Luke pointed out the large garden, granary, woodshed, smoke-house, and spring house, as they walked away from the barn. Behind these were three small fields. He showed her the cabbage he'd set out in two.

"I know these probably don't look much like fields to you when you think of your huge ones back on the plantation. With the steep inclines in the mountains, there's just not that much suit-able land for vast fields, and it's also hard to get them cleared. I guess what we do could be called 'patch farming.' I have a field of potatoes farther away. You can't see them from here. We can use them to feed the animals through the winter if we run out of hay or grain."

"You need some sons to help you." Leah said and then looked away in embarrassment.

"It's okay," he told her. He guessed the proper ladies had been taught to watch what they said to a man. "You can feel free to say anything you want to me. After all, we're going to be family."

Luke felt glad he wasn't the only one who sometimes said things before he thought. Yet, Leah seemed an odd mixture of speaking her mind and trying to adhere to societal rules.

"Besides, we are a little more independent and freer in the western end of the state. Look at Granny. She's pretty outspoken."

"I like her, though. She seems honest and down-to-earth."

"She is that. I kind of like her myself."

"I can't believe how rich this soil looks." Leah bent over, scooped up a handful of plowed dirt, and felt it as she pushed it through her fingers.

"It is rich. Most things grow well in it."

She walked back to the garden for a closer look, and Luke followed her. The potato plants were up and looked healthy. The onions had a good stand, and pods were forming on the pea vines.

"I'll start planting some other things tomorrow," Luke told her. "The threat of frost is gone now. I have some wooden boxes of dirt with seeds I planted before I left, because I knew I was going to be gone. I put them in the smokehouse. Granny has been setting them in and out as needed, so they'd get sun. We have cucumber, tomato, pepper, and squash seedlings. I'll need to plant the rest of the vegetable seeds, too."

"I'll be glad to help you. I like to work outside."

"I may take you up on your offer. I'm a little behind this year, since I've been gone longer than I'd planned. It may take all of us tomorrow to get it done."

"How much land do you own here?"

"Over five hundred acres, but most of it's in forest, and much of it's mountainous. My grandfather built this place for my grandmother and him. His older brothers were getting his father's place at Meat Camp."

"It's a beautiful place."

"Thank you. I like it. There's apple, pear, persimmon, walnut, and chestnut trees, too. In addition, the summer offers wild strawberries, cherries, blackberries, gooseberries, and huckleberries to pick."

"I'll look forward to all those."

"You really mean that, don't you?" Luke looked at her carefully. He'd never met anyone so eager to work and learn. She accepted changes as an adventure and challenges as an opportunity.

"Yes, of course." She said it as if it was common and ordinary. Luke knew better. Even most of the women on the mountain, who worked arduously and long, did so because the work needed doing, not from wanting to do it.

There was nothing common and ordinary about Leah. He found it hard to believe she and Ivy were related, much less sisters. Ivy might have the advantage in the beauty category, but Leah seemed to excel in everything else.

Luke cautioned himself not to form opinions too quickly. He had seen what he'd wanted to see in Ivy at first. He should have taken more time to get to know her before proposing, but he didn't have the time. He needed to get back to the mountains, and Ivy felt her mother pressuring her into marrying right away.

Would Lawrence and Ivy have gotten along better than she and Luke? At least Lawrence could offer her the plantation lifestyle and wealth she seemed to crave. Luke would never be able to do that, and he had no desire to do so.

"Come," Luke told Leah. "I want to show you the pasture." They walked side by side past the barn. Luke watched Leah's face as she took it all in. He and Grandfather had enclosed the small grassy pasture with a split rail fence. Large, gray rocks cropped up here and there. Spring flowers added splashes of color to the green, grassy carpet. Toward the back of the pasture, three cows and a bull grazed peacefully. One of the cows already had a calf by her side. The mules were standing to the other side in a pose of contentment. When a pretty chestnut horse saw Luke, he came galloping up. Luke reached out to pet him.

"How did you get to Anson County?" Leah asked as she watched Luke pet the chestnut.

"I rode a mare. This fellow had been favoring a leg at the time, but I see that has cleared up. I sold the mare when I bought the team of mules."

Leah looked back over the pasture. "It looks like a marvelous painting by a master artist."

"It is."

"God," Leah finished for him.

Luke would love to show her every inch of his land and the mountains. The temptation to do so seemed almost too great to resist. *Nonsense.* God didn't allow anyone to be tempted beyond what they could withstand, and He would also provide a means to escape it. The Bible said so.

He looked at Leah, who still gazed across the pasture. He wanted to take her in his arms and hold her tightly against him. He wanted to taste her lips and explore these new feelings within him.

He mentally shook himself. What was he doing? Exactly the thing he told himself he wouldn't do. This was not like him at all. He had more self-control than this. He now understood better what Paul meant when he wrote, "the evil which I would not, that I do."

"It must be time for supper," Luke said. "We'd better go in."

"You're just in time," Granny said. "I just sent Patsy up to get Ivy. Leah, what did you think of the farm?"

"I like it very much, but it looks like a lot for you and Luke to handle alone."

"It can be," Granny said, "but Luke and I are both hard workers. Besides, I think I've got me some good help now."

"I do, too," Luke said. "Leah just volunteered to help with the planting tomorrow."

"Well, now, that's good, because there's a heap of things we need to get in the ground right away."

"I set your cornbread on the hearth, Leah. It looked done, if you want to take it up. Just grab one of the plates to put it on. The rest of you go ahead and seat yourself."

Luke watched Leah turn the cornbread out on a plate. It slid out easily without sticking at all, and it smelled wonderful. She sliced it into eight good-sized hunks. Granny set a bowl of stew in front of everyone.

Luke held out Ivy's chair for her. Patsy remained standing beside the table. She looked uncertain and confused.

"Well, take a seat, Patsy," Granny Em said. She put Patsy's dish on the table across from her place and to the right of Leah.

"I'll just take mine to the back steps to eat," Patsy said.

"You'll do no such thing. You sit down right here and eat your food like somebody, now."

"She's used to eating apart from white folk," Ivy said.

"Well, she can just get unused to it. She's part of this family now, and she's going to eat with us. That's all there is to it."

"Well, just don't put her beside or across from me." Ivy picked up her spoon and started to eat, but she saw everyone else was waiting. "Oh, I forgot," she said and lay her spoon back down on the table.

"You'd better not be forgetting to thank the Lord," Granny said. Luke hoped Granny wasn't going to be too hard on Ivy. If she did, there'd be a war for sure.

Luke said grace, and they began to eat. The cornbread tasted as good as it smelled.

"You did an excellent job with the cornbread, Leah," Granny said. "I don't ever think I've tasted better."

"Thank you. The stew is good, too."

"I've had better," Ivy said.

"Well, the next time, you're welcome to do the cooking," Granny snapped, "and if you don't want to help, don't complain."

Luke sat between Granny and Ivy, and he felt he might be in a precarious position. He looked at Leah, who sat across the table from him. She looked concerned, too, as her eyes moved from Ivy to Granny. When they came to rest on him, they softened, and she quickly looked down at her plate.

Was Leah having similar thoughts about him? That disconcerted and thrilled him, all at the same time. If Leah felt halfway as drawn to him as he was to her, he'd have to be doubly cautious.

"We always have our family devotion each night before we go to bed," Luke told them after they'd eaten. Let's go ahead and do that, and then everyone can go to bed when they're ready."

"Would anyone like to play a game of chess or checkers?" Luke asked after the devotion. He hoped this would be something he and Ivy could enjoy together.

"I don't like such things," Ivy said. "I brought some embroidery to work on, but the light's getting too dim now."

"I'll play either game you want," Leah said.

"I don't know," Luke teased, "with the way things have been going, you might beat me too badly."

"Luke Moretz," Leah laughed, "I believe you can hold your own in about anything you try."

"Let's play checkers, since it's usually a shorter game. We're tired from all the traveling, and we need to put in a full day's work tomorrow."

As soon as they started, Luke realized he would have to be on his guard. Leah took a double jump and got two of his checkers after only a couple of moves. He buckled down and concentrated. The game ended in a draw with him sliding a checker in a corner and Leah moving after him, but never being able to take it.

"We'll have to have a rematch soon," Luke told her. "I think I'm going up to bed now."

"Do we have to go to bed this early?" Ivy whined. "It's only a little after eight."

"We're all tired," Leah said. "It's been a long, eventful day."

"I'm not tired," Ivy said.

"That's because you napped while we were cooking supper," Granny said. "Go up and read until you get sleepy."

"I don't like to read," Ivy said.

"Just what do you like to do?" Granny asked.

"Order new clothes, dance, go to parties, and such."

"Pshaw! You've come to the wrong place for such goings on. If you want new clothes, you'll have to make them. There're no dances or parties and such."

"You've got to be kidding."

"Look around you Ivy," Granny said. "We don't even have a church to attend, unless we travel some distance. We get the circuit rider by now and then, except in the hard of winter. If you need dances and parties, you shouldn't have come."

"I guess I shouldn't have," Ivy flung back. "I sure don't feel welcomed here."

"Now that's not true. I was as glad as I could be to see you girls. I haven't had any female company for some time, and I still miss Edgar something awful. But, you can't just sit around and be waited on hand and foot, Ivy. This is a working farm, and that means everyone has to work. We don't need anyone who can't pull their own weight—someone who is always taking and never giving. Luke doesn't need someone like that in his life, either."

Ivy turned and stomped up the stairs, and Patsy followed her slowly. "I'm sorry, Granny Em," Leah said. "I know Ivy can act like a spoiled brat. Mama's always pampered her too much. I'll try to make up for her for her inability to help out."

"You'll do no such thing. Luke didn't bring you here to be a servant. Ivy needs to learn to do work, if she plans to marry Luke. Far from burning her candle at both ends, she won't even light the wick. You don't need to go apologizing for her bad behavior, either. We're all responsible for our own choices and no one else's."

"Thank you, Granny Em." Leah walked over and kissed her on the cheek, and Granny looked pleased. "Good night, you two."

"Good night, Leah. Sleep well." Luke would've liked a good-night kiss, too, but he chided himself for thinking such a thing.

"Granny, could I talk to you a minute?" Luke said as she started toward her bedroom.

She turned, came back, and sat down across from Luke at the table. He thought for a few seconds before he began.

"Granny, I think you're being too hard on Ivy. I know what you said is true, but we can't expect Ivy to be able to do everything at once. When it comes to work, she won't know where to begin. I think it would be better to give her one task at a time and show her what to do. Begin with easy things, like washing dishes and gathering eggs."

"Okay. I can do that, but what if she refuses? What then?"

"I don't know. I hope she won't." He realized Ivy might very well refuse, especially if it came from Granny. Those two had already butted heads, and it was just the first day. "Maybe I can coax her into helping."

"You do that, and you'll be a miracle worker. I'll tell you one thing right now, though, Luke. You picked the wrong sister. Leah fits in here, as if God made her just for us. You're probably too blinded by Ivy's pretty face, but Leah would be a perfect fit for you. She's smart, enjoys doing tasks well, has many of our values, and I'm guessing holds a strong faith in God. She's also very pretty. If it wasn't for her always being compared with Ivy, she'd be considered a beauty, too."

"And, you can see all this in just a few hours?" Granny had hit much too close to the truth for Luke. He had been trying to keep himself from thinking those same things.

"I can. Ivy and Leah are so different it doesn't take long to see. Why in the world did you choose Ivy over Leah?"

"I met Ivy before I ever met Leah," Luke immediately realized he'd said too much.

"You had already committed to Ivy by the time you met Leah?"

"Yes. Ivy seemed much different on the plantation, too. All the work there is done by the slaves, so I didn't realize how inept Ivy really was. Ivy seemed sweet and agreeable until we started to travel."

"You rushed into this, Luke," she told him. "You were at Lawrence's, what, two weeks or so? That's not enough time to get to know someone. You shouldn't have proposed so quickly."

"There were some other things happening. Ivy's father died, and her mother and brother wanted her pledged to marry. They planned for Leah to marry Archibald Biles, and I understand he's a horrible, cruel man, who tortures his slaves, and anyone else he can, if they displease him."

"Well, you should've married Leah and left Ivy to marry someone more suitable. Who had they planned for her?"

"Actually, as I found out much later, it was Lawrence."

"Well, he's a good man, right?"

"Yes, he is, but Ivy didn't want to marry him. She said she wanted to marry me."

"So you pretty much stole your best friend's girl, and she turns out to be a spoiled handful. You've got yourself in a real fix this time, Luke, and it's not like you to be so impulsive. What are you going to do?"

"I didn't know Lawrence was the man her family wanted her to marry at the time, and I don't have much choice. I promised Ivy I'd marry her, and that's what I'm going to do, if she still wants me."

"When is this wedding supposed to be?"

"We haven't set a date, but I'm thinking it should be before winter sets in."

Granny looked almost as if she were about to cry. He'd never seen Granny cry, except at his grandfather's funeral. She reached out and put her worn hand over his.

"I'll be praying for you, son. Please do your own praying. Don't marry Ivy if you don't feel it's what God wants."

"I'm trying to leave it up to God, Granny. I want to be patient and wait on God, but things seem to be moving too fast. I do find myself liking Leah more and more. I'm almost drawn to her, like steel to a magnet, and I know it's not right, not when I've promised to marry Ivy. You go ahead and say your prayers for me. I surely can use them right now."

She patted his hand, got up with her eyes watering, and went into her bedroom. Luke knew she didn't want him to see her tears, and she didn't trust herself to hold them back if she spoke.

He went upstairs to get ready for bed himself. As he went to his room, he became conscious of Leah's bedroom directly across the hall from his. Why did he think of her first now? It should be Ivy.

CHAPTER TEN

Boone

Friday all five of them worked in the garden and fields. Leah didn't know how Luke managed to get Ivy to help. It could have been a combination of what Granny Em had said to her and Luke's persuasiveness. Maybe Ivy really did care for Luke.

Luke saw that Granny Em began to tire with all the stooping and bending, and he sent her to the left field to plant the corn. He asked Ivy to go help her, since the seeds were easier to plant than setting out the seedlings. Ivy had already destroyed a few plants by being too rough with them. The corn seeds would be tougher.

Mid-morning Granny Em went in the house to prepare dinner. Ivy feigned a headache and went in also. Leah, Patsy, and Luke finished the planting.

As Leah sowed the corn seeds, she imagined she sprinkled her hopes, dreams, and desires into the rich, black soil. Maybe the fertile soil would grow them along with the crop. Maybe someday, she'd be sown into the mountain and producing a crop of hearty mountain children. She shook her head before her thoughts drifted to places they shouldn't go.

When they stopped for lunch, Leah's back and legs had started to ache. No wonder Granny Em had grown tired. Patsy must have felt much the same.

"I'm not used to this field work," the former slave said.

"I don't usually try to get all this done in one day," Luke said, "but I'm a little behind this year. If we don't get it in the ground, the frost will be here before everything makes."

"Couldn't we finish up tomorrow?" Patsy asked.

"We could, but you can never trust the weather here. It could very well be raining tomorrow."

They took a long dinner break, and Leah felt some better when they went back outside. Granny Em stayed behind to clean up the kitchen, and Ivy went to her room to rest. They'd put out all the seedlings already, so the remaining work wouldn't be so back-breaking or take as much time. Granny soon joined them again.

"I'm glad that's done," Patsy said later, as they went into the house.

"Let's all go lie down for a spell, before time to start supper," Granny said. "I figure we've got about an hour to spare."

"That's a good idea, Granny," Luke said. "I couldn't get to sleep for a long time last night, and I'm worn out."

Leah and Patsy went to their room, washed up, and lay down. It felt good to stretch out.

"Do you think Miss Ivy is going to make it here?" Patsy asked. "She appears to hate it."

"I don't know. Luke tried to tell her how it would be, but she didn't seem to hear him. The only skill she has involves being the mistress of a plantation, and telling others what to do. She's totally out of her element here."

"I am, too," Patsy said, "and so are you. We've never done work like we did today. I've always been a house slave, and, although you've learned many things on the plantation, I never saw you in the fields."

"Are you unhappy here, too?"

"No, Miss Leah, I'm all right. I realize we all have to work to eat. It's not like I have to do anything the rest of you don't do, except for Miss Ivy, that is. I probably need to learn to cook and do more things myself. If I have a family of my own someday, I'll need to know how to do more than just be a lady's maid."

"Do you like it here, Patsy?"

"Yes'm. I like it just fine. It's a good place for me to be right now. I'm also glad I'm rooming with you, instead of Miss Ivy."

Leah laughed. "I'm glad I'm with you and not Ivy, too." Leah felt sorry for her sister, though. No one had ever gotten along well with Ivy for any length of time, except for Mama. Leah found this to be very sad.

"We'll probably need to sleep together in the big bed when winter gets here. I suspect it's going to be hard to keep warm," Leah told Patsy and heard her make a soft, contented sigh.

Leah must have napped. She woke up to the sound of Granny Em in the kitchen starting supper. Leah eased out of bed trying not to wake Patsy, hurried to dress, and went down to help.

"I'm just starting," Granny Em said. "I'm going to fix sauerkraut, sausages, potatoes, and cornbread. What had you rather cook? I'm hoping cornbread for one. I think your cornbread is better than mine."

"I'll bake the cornbread, and what do you think about cooking potatoes with a thick white sauce?"

"It sounds good."

"I'll make the cornbread and potatoes, then."

"You get the cornbread made, and I'll be peeling the potatoes for you. I've got the sausages browning now, and I've already rinsed the kraut. All I'll have to do is pour it over the sausages, add a little sugar, and let it cook some. I guess Patsy must be sleeping. She looked pretty tuckered out, but she's a hard worker."

"We all were tired. Is Luke still resting?"

"No, I think he was the first one up. He's got a lot on his mind, poor boy. He's out in the barn sharpening some tools or something."

"What's bothering him? Is it Ivy?"

"That's a big part of it. I know Luke's trying to leave everything in God's hands, but that's often easier said than done."

"He told me the same thing the night we camped out. He seems to really try to live his faith. Why is his faith so strong?"

"Luke's not had an easy life. His mother was the kindest, gentlest person you'd ever meet. She would've done anything for Luke or his father. Luke accepted Christ and was baptized when he was only eight, right before he came here to live, but he'd grown up in a Christian home, and he was smart for his age, too."

"It devastated Luke when his mother died. We all felt it. Clifton was beside himself and so upset and grief stricken. Only their faith in God helped them survive."

"When Clifton met Frances, he knew Luke needed a mother and saw in her what he wanted to see. He married her before he got over his first wife, because he just wasn't thinking straight. That second marriage turned out to be a big mistake, and he knows it now."

"Frances treated poor Luke like dirt and made him even more miserable. When she started physically abusing the boy, Clifton brought him to live with Edgar and me. We were as pleased as we could be to have him. Since that time, Luke has always worked hard to help out. We never had to fuss at him to get him to do his chores. He did them eagerly and then some."

"We talked Luke into going to college in Chapel Hill. Clifton especially wanted him to go and paid his way. Luke didn't like it there and wanted to come back to the farm. I sure was glad to have him back, because Edgar's health had begun to fail, and I needed Luke's help. When Edgar died, I don't think I would've made it without Luke."

"How old is Luke now?"

"Let's see now. Luke must be twenty-four, but back to your first question. Through all this, Luke's relied on God. Even when he went off to college, he didn't go carousing around like a lot of boys. He stuck to his studying and learned all he could. Through all the hard times, Luke's faith has multiplied. That's my one hope in all this mess with Ivy—that Luke'll rely on God, and let Him take charge. I'm trusting God won't want Luke unequally yoked. I know in my heart Ivy would only hold Luke back in his walk with the Lord."

"I'm sorry Ivy's causing so much trouble. She and I have never gotten along well, but even I've discovered more of her bad side on this trip."

"None of this is your fault, Leah, and it's not all Ivy's fault, either. As much as I hate to say it, Luke brought some of this on himself. Like his father, he saw only what he wanted to see and didn't give the courtship the time it needed."

"Do you think Luke regrets asking Ivy to marry him?"

"He hasn't said it, but yes, I do. Any man would under the circumstances. I wonder if Ivy's not feeling the same way. They're just not suited to each other."

"If she is, she hasn't said anything to me, but, then, she probably wouldn't. We've never been close."

Luke came in from the barn, and their conversation ceased. Leah needed to be like Luke and try to leave it all with God. She would trust Him to have everything under control.

"Supper's ready to put on the table. You want to go fetch the other girls, Leah?"

"I'm sorry I stayed in bed so long and didn't help with the cooking," Patsy said.

"That's okay," Leah told her. "Granny Em and I managed just fine, and we had a long conversation about Luke."

"You think a lot of Luke, don't you?"

Leah looked at Patsy. She knew the former slave would say nothing to Ivy about anything she told her. "I'm afraid I'm beginning to think too much of him, but I'm trying hard not to."

"I don't know how you're going to do that, Miss Leah. It's a difficult thing to try to control what you think."

"With God anything is possible."

"Amen to that."

When Leah got back to the kitchen, Granny Em had already put the food on the table, and Luke set out the last of the dishes. Leah tried to hide her surprise, but she'd never seen a man set the table before.

Granny must have read her thoughts. "Luke's been helping me with everything he could, ever since he came to live here. We really do well together."

They all sat down. Luke said grace, and they began to eat. "These are really good potatoes," Luke said. "I've never had any quite like them."

"Leah fixed them, and they are good. What'd you put in them?" Granny Em asked.

"Oh, they're easy," Leah said. "I just boiled hunks of potatoes and added butter, salt, and pepper. I made a white sauce with milk and flour. I think the French call it 'béchamel.' You pour that over the buttered potatoes and bring it to a boil while gently stirring. That's all there is to it. It's similar to the white sauce I put in cream soups, but I make this one thicker."

Ivy ate her potatoes, cornbread, and the insides of her sausage, but she didn't get out any kraut. "I don't really like sauerkraut," she said. Granny Em let it pass without comment.

"Since we've worked so hard today and got everything planted, I propose we take the day off tomorrow and go into Boone, if the nice weather holds," Luke announced. "I'll put four of the pigs in crates and take them along. It'll be easier to sell them on a Saturday, because there'll be more people in town."

"Let me think on it," Granny Em said. "I'm not sure I'll be up to a long wagon ride tomorrow."

"I've been thinking on whether or not to sell two of the mules or not. What do you think, Granny?"

"Now, that's your department, Luke. You know more about those things than I do."

"Will you need them to haul the cabbage?" Leah asked.

"Not so much down the mountain, but that is something to consider. If I want to bring anything much up the mountain, I'd need all four."

"Well, there you are, then," Granny said with a gleam in her eye. "Two heads are better than one, especially when both of them are about as smart as they come."

Saturday morning Granny decided she didn't want to ride into Boone. The way she moved, Leah got the feeling she might still be sore and stiff from the garden work.

"I made biscuits, ham, and fried eggs for breakfast," Granny Em said. "I made enough so they'd be leftovers to pack for your noon meal. If you'll each fix what you want, I'll put them in a pail for you to take. Biscuits will keep better in a pail than a basket or a sack. They won't dry out as much." Leah fixed a ham biscuit and an egg biscuit to take with them.

"I think I'll stay with Granny Em." Patsy told them. "A day of rest sounds better to me than another trip in the wagon."

Ivy looked lovely in her cornflower blue silk dress, which flared out to the hem from the hoops and crinolines. She seemed excited to be going anywhere, but she wasn't excited about hauling the four pigs.

"I didn't intend to end up with a hog farmer," Ivy mumbled, as Luke went around the wagon to get on. Leah didn't think Luke heard. She hoped not.

Leah chose not to wear her hoops and crinolines. The billowing skirts made it too cumbersome to get in and out the wagon, and they took up too much room around the seat.

"I'm glad both of you aren't wearing hoop skirts," Luke said. "There wouldn't be any room for me."

"I declare, you and your daddy sound just alike," Ivy said. "You seem to resent it if a woman is well dressed."

"You won't find many well-dressed women in these parts. In fact, I don't know of a one who wears hoops. They're just too impractical."

Winding down the mountain seemed more treacherous than going up had. Ivy shut her eyes and clenched the seat tightly. The pigs squealed in the back every time the wagon hit a bump, and their cries seemed to warn of danger. Leah hoped the wagon brakes would hold.

She looked at Luke. He seemed to have everything under control. No, God was in control. That's what she needed to remember.

They made it down just fine. When they got to the valley and rolled toward Boone, Ivy opened her eyes and breathed a sigh of relief. "I don't think I'll ever get use to those steep drop-offs," she said.

"Sure you will," Luke said. "It won't be long before you won't even notice them."

"I doubt that."

Leah looked as they approached Boone. She couldn't remember much about it from before.

"What's that single mountain looming over us?" Ivy asked, looking up to the right. She sounded as if she fancied it might hurl itself down and crush them.

"That's Howard's Knob," Luke told her.

"That log house is about the same size as yours, Luke," Ivy pointed out.

"John Greene lives there. He and his brother, Jerry, originally owned all this land. They've been selling it off to people who want to open businesses or build houses."

"I think Boone will be growing," Leah said. "It's in a pretty setting between the mountains."

"I agree," Luke said. "One of the main industries here is the saw mills. They supply wood for building in the area. Boone was first called Councill's Store, because of the store run by the Councill family. I hear the post office operated here as early as 1835."

"Speaking of post offices, will we check to see if there's mail for us while we're here?" Leah asked.

"Are you expecting a letter?" Ivy asked in a sarcastic tone.

"I thought Dr. Moretz might have written, but, even if he has, it probably hasn't had time to get here."

Luke smiled at her. "I always check the post office when I come into town. Let's see if we can sell these pigs first, so we can leave the wagon."

The businesses ran mainly along King Street. Leah saw a courthouse, a rather large store, and a few other buildings. It looked as if a number of people had decided to come to town today.

Luke pulled the wagon into a large area between two buildings. Leah saw other farm wagons had been left there, and a few seemed to have something to sell or trade. Luke set the pig crates on the ground by the wagon.

"Why don't we go walk around," Ivy said to Leah.

"I'd rather you wouldn't," Luke said. "There could be more men hunting for you, and you two are much too pretty to be walking around without an escort."

Ivy frowned, but she seemed placated by Luke's flattery.

"How much ye askin' fer the peegs?" an older man asked Luke. They bargained for a few minutes, finally settled on a price, and the man took two.

"Ya'll heared 'bout the meetin' goin' on at one?"

"No, what's happening?" Luke asked.

"A new preacher man come to town and done got this here idee to hold a preachin' fer folks who only git to town but once in a blue moon."

"That sounds like a good idea. Where's it going to be held?"

"In that thar log buildin' on the east end of King Street."

"I'll take them other two pigs for a dollar each," said a younger man, who looked cleaner and neater. He must have taken some pains to clean up before he came into town. He kept glancing at Ivy but tried to do it without anyone noticing.

"Grover, you about ready?" a woman called from a wagon on the other end of the lot. Leah couldn't tell if it was a mother, wife, or some other relative.

Luke carried one of the pigs, and the young man took the other. "Well, that's done," Luke said when he came back. "I'd like to go to the preaching service at one. If we hurry and get our business done, we can go and leave from there for home."

They went to the post office located in the back corner of the store, but they had no mail. Luke checked with the store owner about taking some of his cabbage.

"I don't know they'd sell," the man said. "Too many people grow their own around here. Maybe some of the sawmills would take some, since they usually feed their men at least one meal a day and some more'n that. The boarding house might also take some."

"Instead of me having to make little stops like those, why don't you just take some, and let the others buy them from you. That way you can mark them up and make a profit."

"Hmmm. That's not a bad idea. I bet the missus would like to have some, too. She could even make some kraut."

"Maybe there'd be some others here in town, who'd feel the same way?"

"Okay, you talked me into it. Bring some by, and I'll see how they do. If they sell well, I'll take more next year."

Ivy had been looking around the store, while Luke talked. "Do either of you need anything?" Luke asked them before they left.

"I don't see anything to my taste," Ivy said. "Everything is so backwoods."

"No, thank you," Leah said. "I may come shopping when you bring the cabbage in the fall."

They got back in the wagon and rode to the east end of town. They sat in the wagon and ate their biscuits and drank some apple cider. Although they'd arrived early, this section of town seemed to be filling fast. Leah noticed none of the ladies she saw wore hoops and crinolines like Ivy.

The preacher, a Reverend Whitley, must have done a good job of spreading the word about the meeting, because the small building looked packed. Luke found Ivy a seat near the back and Leah one nearer the front. Luke sat on the other side with a group of men. Luke and Leah could see each other from where they sat, but they couldn't see Ivy.

Reverend Whitley must have been in his late forties or early fifties, and he had a booming voice, which he used to rattle the room. No one would fall asleep here.

The service only lasted about an hour. They sang a couple of well-known hymns from memory, and Reverend Whitley delivered a rousing sermon. He preached on hell so convincingly, someone would almost think he'd been there himself.

When they got up to leave, Ivy stood beside the door waiting for them. She looked excited.

"What did you think of the sermon?" Luke asked.

"I couldn't hear it that well from where I sat," Ivy said. Luke and Leah looked at her in disbelief. As loud as the preacher had been, she should have heard it clearly. Ivy had probably just tuned out everything, like she often did in church.

"Well, let's head home," Luke said. "We should make it by suppertime."

Leah watched Grandfather Mountain grow larger and larger as they traveled toward it. They couldn't see it from the farm, so it must be either too close, or something blocked the view. Leah hoped she would get a chance to explore some of the land around the farm. She'd like to see it all.

The steep section didn't seem as scary this time. They went up it at a slower pace than when they'd descended. In addition, the pigs were no longer in the back squealing in fright. Maybe Luke had been right. Maybe Leah would get used to this soon.

She looked over at Ivy. Her sister had her eyes open now, but she still clutched the seat in a death grip.

Halfway up the steepest section, the mules became skittish. Luke managed to control them, but he had to work at it. The drop off the side looked more ominous to Leah then. She held her breath, but Luke kept the mules from pulling toward the cliff.

A black bear with two cubs started down the incline on the forest side of the road, then stopped, and smelled in the air. Luke picked up his rifle and got it ready. The mother then turned and climbed the slope back into the woods, and her cubs followed.

"Are bears common here?" Leah asked.

"Very common," Luke said. "I never go out of sight of the house without a gun. When you start picking wild fruits or berries, always let me know."

"This indeed is the wilds, isn't it?" Ivy said.

"I think that's one of the things I like about it," Luke told her. "I like the untamed, natural spirit of the mountains. I like living close to nature, and I don't think I'd enjoy town living half as much. I know I didn't like Salisbury or Chapel Hill as well as I do here."

"But, it seems so dangerous," Ivy said.

"Everywhere has its own dangers," Luke said. "Different places just have different ones."

Leah might need to reconsider exploring the area. At least she could shoot. She wondered if Luke had an extra rifle.

"Is there another gun I could use if I go out?" Leah asked him.

"I still have grandpa's rifle," Luke said, "but it's a muzzle loader. I think I'd prefer to go with you when I can."

Leah nodded. That might be better, because Leah found Luke to be a good guide who shared a wealth of information. She could learn a lot about the place by talking with him.

She'd take Patsy or Granny Em with them. She knew Ivy would never go.

"Strawberries might be ripe now. We'll go look for them Tuesday. You'll need to get your washing done on Monday."

"What about tomorrow?" Ivy asked.

"Tomorrow is the Lord's day. When there's no circuit rider, we have our own worship."

"We just went to preaching today," Ivy said. "Won't that suffice?"

"No. It won't be preaching, but we will study the Bible."

They pulled up to the farm, and Luke helped them down from the wagon. Ivy's hoops and crinolines almost engulfed Luke as he handed her down.

Granny Em came out to meet them. "Supper's almost ready," she said. "Patsy's stirring the gravy now."

"I'll just go put the wagon up and the mules out to pasture. Then, I'll be in."

"Supper smells delicious," Leah said as they went in. She saw the chicken had been roasted on the spit. Granny had made gravy from the drippings she'd caught in the drip pan.

"There's also biscuits, roasted potatoes, leather breeches, and chow-chow," Granny Em said.

"What's chow-chow?" Ivy asked.

"It's like a pickle relish with cabbage," Leah said.

"What's leather breeches, then?" Ivy wrinkled her nose.

"That's dried green beans," Granny Em told her. "We call them leather breeches because they can be tough if you don't soak them first and cook them a long time."

Supper tasted good, and Leah found herself eating too much. She wondered if this fresh, mountain air had given her a bigger appetite. On the plantation, it would be getting too hot to eat anything but breakfast right now. The others would eat, but she and Ivy often just picked at their food.

In the summers on the plantation, the humid air would hang heavy and thick, like a damp, bulky blanket ready to suffocate. The slaves in the fields would roast in the sun, basted in their own perspiration, and baked to a crisp. It could be a miserable time. Leah appreciated the difference here.

Ivy didn't eat any of the leather breeches or chow-chow. When supper was over, she went up to her room. Patsy followed to help her.

Leah heard the rain start again. It came a little later today than yesterday. She was glad it hadn't come when they were going up or down the mountain. A muddy mountain road might prove treacherous.

Leah got up from the table and began to clean the dishes. Patsy came back down and helped. Luke sat at the table and stared at nothing, deep in thought.

"Why don't you get out your fiddle, Luke," Granny Em said. "I got a hankering for some music."

"Do you play, Luke?" Leah asked.

"I try."

"He's right good, if you ask me."

He surprised her by how good he played. He played some melancholic tunes to start with but then switched to some toe-tapping songs.

"Help me sing, girls," Granny Em said.

"Ivy's the one with the pretty voice," Leah said. "I love music, but singing isn't one of my talents. Our music teacher once told me the only way I would stay on key is if I sat on one used for the door."

Luke and Granny Em both smiled.

"I'm not asking for a performance, Leah. My voice's not pretty, either. Just join in." Granny Em began singing "Pop Goes the Weasel" in an exuberant voice.

Leah joined in and so did Patsy. Luke also played many hymns and one or two popular songs. Leah liked to just sit back and listen to him. The music soothed her.

They spent the evening in music and song and had their devotion. Everyone seemed to be in a better mood when they decided to retire. Leah could especially tell a difference in Luke, who joked and laughed as they climbed the stairs.

"I'm surprised Ivy didn't come down and join us," Luke said. "I know she heard the music."

"You never know about Ivy," Leah remarked.

"That girl has a disposition that would sour milk," Granny Em mumbled as she moved to her bedroom.

"She would just have complained and put a damper on everything," Patsy said, and then clamped her hand over her mouth. "I'm sorry. I shouldn't have said that."

"Why not?" Luke said. "It's the truth." He sounded too serious again.

CHAPTER ELEVEN

Missing

Sunday morning, Leah went down to the smell of coffee and hot grease. Granny Em and Patsy were frying pancakes.

"I'm going to have Patsy cooking anything she wants before you know it," Granny Em said. "She sure is a fast learner."

"I've just got a good teacher," Patsy said with a big grin.

Luke came in from milking the cows. "Here comes one of the sleepy heads," he teased.

"Am I late for something?" She smiled to soften the statement.

"No, I just wanted you to get a hot breakfast. Have you ever had buckwheat pancakes?"

"I don't think so, but they smell delicious. How do you make them?"

"They have a little heavier taste than the wheat ones, but Luke likes them better. I use equal amounts of buckwheat flour and regular flour, eggs, buttermilk, soda, and a pinch of sugar."

"I brought some molasses back, so you can have that, honey, or preserves on them," Luke said.

"I think there's some blackberry preserves left." Granny Em added. "The strawberry and cherry's all gone until we make some more."

"Should I go get Miss Ivy or let her sleep?" Patsy asked.

"Aw, just let her sleep," Granny Em said. "Maybe she won't be as grumpy. She doesn't seem to like my cooking all that well, anyway."

"Well, the rest of us do," Leah said.

They sat down, and Luke said grace. The stacks of buckwheat pancakes were warm and dripping with butter. They were a little heavier and grainier than what Leah had been used to, but they were good. Leah liked the honey even better. Patsy had blackberry preserves on hers, and Granny Em and Luke ate molasses.

"Let's go ahead and study the Word," Granny Em suggested, when they'd washed the dishes and cleaned the kitchen. "Ivy doesn't seem to listen to such things anyway."

They read the Bible, discussed it, had prayer, and sang a couple of hymns, but Ivy still hadn't come down. Perhaps she was pouting or upset over something again.

"How late can Ivy sleep?" Granny Em asked about ten o'clock. "It's about time to start dinner."

"If she's not up by the time we get ready to eat, Patsy or I'll go wake her," Leah said. "At the plantation, she sometimes slept until one or two o'clock, but that's when she stayed out late at a ball."

"Did you usually go to the balls, too?" Luke asked.

"I went to some, but sometimes I would become tired of them, especially if there were too many in a row. Is that where you met Ivy?"

"Yes, we met at the cotillion given by Archibald's mother. Then Lawrence's family gave a ball, and Ivy and I got better acquainted. I don't think I'd met you until the dinner at your house."

"I'd tried to avoid Archie, as much as possible, so I chose not to go to the cotillion at his house. I'd planned to go to Lawrence's, but Ivy said Archie was planning to spend the evening with me, since her time was spoken for, so I decided to stay home."

"Sounds to me as if Ivy just didn't want you going where you could meet Luke," Granny Em said. Leah hadn't thought of that, but she doubted Ivy would ever consider her as competition.

"What're we having for dinner, Granny?" Luke asked.

"I haven't decided. Patsy and I cleaned two chickens yester-day, so it will be something with chicken. The two hens got their heads hung in the wire and killed themselves trying to get loose. We put the second one in a bucket in the springhouse to keep it cold, and I've got the other one boiling."

"Would you like me to fix chicken and dumplings?" Leah asked.

"Well, now that sounds good."

"Do you want me to cook any vegetables to go with them?"

"No, the chicken and dumplings will be enough. I baked some pies out of the dried apples yesterday to have for today, so I think that'll be enough. We won't even need bread with the dumplings."

Leah got busy. She had everything ready, and Ivy still hadn't come down.

"These look like mountain-style dumplings, light and fluffy," Granny Em said as she peered into the pot. "Where'd you learn to cook like this?"

"I can make the flatter kind that's more like noodles, too. I just prefer these."

When they had everything on the table, Patsy went to get Ivy. She came back without her.

"Miss Ivy wasn't in her room," Patsy said with a worried frown.

"Well, what in the world!" Granny Em said.

"Are you sure?" Luke asked.

"Maybe she just went outside for a moment," Granny Em said. "Let's go ahead and eat. It'd be a shame to waste this food after Leah cooked it for us. If Ivy's not turned up by the time we're through, we'll start searching."

Luke blessed the food and prayed Ivy would turn up soon. "These are really good," Luke said. He ate fast, and Leah guessed he was hurrying to see about Ivy.

"They sure are good," Granny Em said.

They ate in silence. It turned out to be the fastest meal they'd had.

"I'll save my pie until later," Luke said. "Leah you go look around Ivy's room and see if you find any clue. I'll go outside and look around."

Patsy helped Granny Em clean up, while Leah went upstairs. She opened the wardrobe. Ivy's travel bag and some of her clothes were gone. Leah's heart fell to her stomach. This didn't look good. Leah surveyed the room. She saw a note on the desk. It read: "Don't come after me. I can't stand it here anymore. I have an opportunity to leave tonight, and it may be my only chance. Don't worry. I'm doing what's best for me." She'd signed it, "Ivy."

"Dear God, no!" Leah pleaded aloud. Surely even Ivy wouldn't do something this foolish. A lone female, especially one who drew every man's attention, would be easy prey, and Ivy, of all people, knew this. Leah hurried down to tell the others. Luke hadn't come back in yet.

"That girl!" Granny Em declared. "I feared she would be bad news. Poison. Poison ivy. That's what she is, and she's going to blister Luke." She sat down and put her head in her hands.

Luke took one look at them when he came in. "What's wrong?"

Leah handed him the note. He read it, and his face turned white.

"Her travel bag and some clothes are gone," she said.

"Do you or Patsy have any idea what she's up to?"

"None. I didn't have the slightest inkling," Leah told him.

"Miss Ivy asked me yesterday if she left the farm, would I go with her." Patsy looked at Luke. "I thought you and she might be thinking about going somewhere else after you married. I told her I'd rather stay with Miss Leah, and she just nodded."

"She can't have gone far, if she doesn't have someone helping her," Luke said. All the animals are out there, so she must be on foot. I'll saddle the horse and try to find her. You three stay here and pray."

Luke felt upset and confused. He'd never expected Ivy to do something like this. She'd always seemed too proper. If Ivy wanted to go home, why hadn't she asked him to take her? He just didn't understand. He now knew Ivy would never be happy on this mountain farm. He'd been trying to change her into the person he wanted her to be, but that wouldn't work, and it wasn't fair to Ivy. She'd have to make her own decisions. Luke just wanted her to be safe. Traipsing around the mountain was way too dangerous, and, if by some miracle, she made it down the mountain, she could be even more danger. A lone woman wouldn't be safe, and something bad would likely happen to someone as pretty as Ivy.

Luke stayed out until dusk, but then he knew he needed to head back. He would never be able to find her in the dark, and he could become lost himself. It appeared that it would be an overcast, black night.

He clutched the reins in his hands and prayed with every breath that Ivy would be at the house when he got there. Chances were good she'd get so tired or scared that she'd retrace her steps and come back to the house. Ivy wouldn't cope well in the outdoors, not like Leah.

Leah. His heart filled. Would this mean Luke could begin to court Leah? No! He shook his head and detested himself for even thinking it. Until he resolved all this, he wouldn't be free.

One step at a time. He mustn't be running ahead. He needed to find Ivy, and then he could worry about something else. He started praying again.

Ivy hadn't returned. He felt like holding his head for support. Did that mean she would be alone in the mountains all night?

"I picked up her footprints leading away from the farm, and down the road a piece, but then I lost them," Luke told the others when he was back in the house. "Leah, do you have any idea what Ivy might be thinking, or where she might be headed?"

"No, but I know Ivy well enough to know she would never venture out on foot by herself in a place she didn't know well. She also told us she'd never go back to the plantation in defeat. Remember?"

"Yes, she said if she returned, it would look like I no longer wanted her."

"Do you want her, Luke?" Granny asked.

"Now's not the time for that kind of question. I want her to be safe and well, and I've got to find her before we can sort through our problems."

"Did she meet anyone when y'all went to Boone? Was there someone who might be helping her?"

"Not that I know of. We were with her the whole time. Did you see her talk to anyone, Leah?"

"No, I didn't. The younger man, who bought two pigs, seemed interested in Ivy, but they didn't talk. She might have had a chance to talk with someone at the preaching service, but I couldn't see her. Maybe that's why she didn't hear the message. Maybe she didn't stay inside."

"It's a long shot, but it's all we have right now," Luke said.

"That girl's much too good looking for her own good," Granny Em said. "She's used to getting what she wants with those looks, but, one of these days, it's all going to turn around on her."

"I'll ride into Boone early tomorrow morning, and see if I can find out anything," he told them.

They had a devotion and went to bed, but Luke knew he wouldn't sleep. He heard beds rustle and creak all night from across the hall, too.

He got up before sunrise and planned to leave quietly before anyone got up, but it didn't work out that way. Granny heard him and came out of her room.

"I'll fix you some breakfast," she said.

"I don't feel like eating."

"Well, you need to put something in your stomach, so you won't get sick. How about a piece of apple pie and a cup of coffee? At least, that's something."

"I'll try. Make it a little piece."

Leah came down next. "May I come with you?" she asked. Her eyes were red, and he knew she'd been crying.

"I need you to stay here with Granny. She can load the muzzle loader, if you don't know how, but you'd probably be the better shot. Granny's never had to use a gun much. I'm going to take my horse, so the trip will be faster. If I don't find anything in Boone, I might ride on to Wilkesboro, so don't worry if I'm not back for a while. I may have to try to follow her, too, and who knows how long that may take."

Leah knew she needed to stay at the farm and let Luke find Ivy, but she didn't like it. She wanted to go. She wanted to know what was happening.

At breakfast, they said grace and asked God's blessings on Luke's quest and on Ivy, wherever she might be. Luke also asked protection for the women at home.

"You go on," Granny Em said to Luke. "I'll rustle you up some food to take along, and I'll do the milking this morning."

Leah helped Granny Em pack Luke's knapsack and took the bag to Luke. He had saddled his horse and was tying a bedroll on the back.

"I'm sorry, Leah. I should never have brought Ivy here. A mountain farm just isn't the place for her. She'd never be happy here, and I know that now."

"This is not your fault, Luke. Ivy told you she wanted to come, even when you explained to her what it'd be like. She made her own decision. If you hadn't brought her, I'm sure she would have found some other way to leave the plantation and run away. She had made up her mind, and Ivy's quite determined when she decides on something. At least with you, she stayed safe."

"How safe is she now?" Luke voice cracked with emotion.

She put her hand on his arm. "That's in God's hands, Luke. You're better than anyone I know at giving troubles to the Lord. Do what you can to help, but give it all to God. Let Him guide you."

Luke pulled her into his arms, and gave her a quick hug. "Thank you, Leah," he whispered. "I needed to hear that."

Luke said his good-byes and left. Leah still wobbled from being in Luke's arms. She knew it had been a friendly, thank-you hug on his part, but it left her weak-kneed and unable to think straight all the same.

She shouldn't be thinking like this. Here her sister could be in all kinds of trouble, and Leah stood feeling much more than she should for Ivy's fiancé. What kind of person was she? One who was falling in love. She tried to push that thought far away.

Patsy had started washing the dishes when Leah went into the kitchen. Leah followed Granny to the barn to milk.

"Can you milk, Leah?"

"I can. One of the slaves showed me how, but I've never milked much."

"Well, we milk two of the cows. If you'll milk one, I'll take the other, and we'll be finished in no time."

They milked, carried the buckets into the kitchen, and strained it into clean crocks. They tied a clean white cloth over the tops, and Leah carried them to the springhouse.

"Luke had been planning to sell one of the milk cows when he got home," Granny Em told her, "but when you girls came, he decided we might need both."

"We've upset everything, haven't we?"

"No, we're glad to have you here. Ivy has certainly upset the applecart now, but God promises He will bring good things even from the bad for His children. You and Luke are surely His children, and I'm holding on to that promise, Leah. You should, too."

With that done, they started on the laundry. They heated the water in an iron pot over an open fire outside and also used big wooden tubs with a washboard and homemade lye soap. Some of the clothes would need to soak for a while. During the soak, they used hand-hewed sassafras paddles to swish and agitate the clothes from time to time.

"Well, those may be the cleanest clothes ever," Granny Em said. "I think we all took out some of our frustrations on the laundry."

Their days fell into a regular routine. They rose early, cooked and ate breakfast, and worked through the morning. Often, one of them would quit in time to cook dinner, and they usually made enough to eat leftovers for supper.

Granny complained the days were getting too hot to keep using the fireplace three times a day, but it felt comfortable to Leah and Patsy. They'd been used to melting heat on the plantation.

After lunch, they worked until suppertime, had devotions, and went to bed at dusk. The hard day's work left everyone exhausted.

The days weren't as hard, because Leah stayed so busy, but the nights were agony. She had so many questions with no answers, and they constantly followed her around and nipped at her heels like a pesky puppy.

Where was Ivy? Was she alone, or had she run off with someone, most likely a man? Why was it taking Luke so long? Had he found Ivy, and they'd married to keep her reputation intact? If he didn't, would there ever be a chance for him and Leah? The last question almost seemed the most frightening. She felt wrong for thinking such a thing, but it remained, lurking in the background, no matter how hard she tried to squelch it.

Leah and Patsy picked strawberries and made jam. They took care of the garden and farm chores. In addition, they churned and made butter, made cheese, dipped candles, made soap, and gathered plants and herbs.

Granny Em hung many of the plants in the rafters of the smokehouse or granary to dry. When she made the medicines, she stored them in the larder.

Occasionally, someone from the area would come by for doctoring. Often they'd waited until the condition became severe, and the patients seemed humbled. Granny Em would take care of them the best she could. Sometimes they would bring something to give her, but sometimes they wouldn't have anything to bring. Leah assisted, and she and Granny Em learned from each other.

Leah and Granny Em had long conversations about the plants and their uses. All three of them roamed the meadows and woods to collect ones they could use. Leah carried the old rifle with them whenever they went away from the house.

"I learned most of this from the Cherokee," Granny Em told her. "I was captured and taken to a village. Luke's great-grandmother taught me about herbal medicines and doctoring."

"Really?" Her eyes locked on the little lady. "How fascinating! Luke never said anything about this."

"He never met his Cherokee relatives that he remembers, since his mother died when he was five. His parents had always lived in Salisbury, you see."

"When were you captured?"

"I was about fifteen at the time. It was right before Edgar and I married."

"Were you hurt?"

"No, thanks to the leader of the group who captured me, I wasn't harmed. He protected me and kept me safe. As things turned out, he's Luke's great-uncle. I'll tell you the whole story one of these cold winter days coming up."

"I'll look forward to it."

Almost two weeks passed with no word from Luke or Ivy. Granny Em and Patsy seemed about as worried as Leah.

Sunday afternoon, two weeks to the day, Luke rode up alone. He looked haggard and disheveled. When he came into the house, the three of them gathered around to listen to his story.

"I got to Boone Sunday afternoon and heard talk about Samuel Whitley. He's the son of the minister we heard preach the Saturday we went to Boone. His son left that evening and never returned. Reverend Whitley seems terribly upset. His wife died several years back, and Sam has always stayed with his father. According to rumor, Sam had fallen in with a wild crowd, and the reverend's been concerned even before he left.

"Some of the people at the church service we attended thought they remembered Ivy and Sam talking and leaving the building together. I'm wondering if the two didn't make arrangements to go off together sometime Saturday night, but I have no proof.

"I went on to Wilkesboro to see if I could catch up with them, but no one remembered seeing them there. The sheriff said he'd keep an eye out for them and send me word, if he saw or heard anything.

"I realized there was a good chance they could have left Boone and headed south instead of east, so I hired Zeb Brewer, a tracker, in Wilkesboro. I gave him some money now and promised him more if he found Ivy and I got to see her. He could bring her back, if she wanted to come, or tell me where to find her.

"I decided to go on to Salisbury. I still hoped to find Ivy on the way, but I also wanted to see father. A doctor hears news other people might not, and I wanted his advice.

"He seemed almost as stunned as we were at Ivy's disappearance. He hadn't seen or heard anything that would help. I went around town asking for information, but nothing helpful turned up. After a few days, I turned around and headed back.

"Father sent you and Granny letters." He handed them the envelopes. "When I came back through Wilkesboro and Boone, there'd been no other news about Ivy or Sam."

"You look like you're plumb tuckered out," Granny Em said. "Let's get you fed, cleaned up, and put to bed."

"I wish it were that easy," Luke said. "Father tried to take care of me, too, but I can't eat or sleep. I'm so afraid of what might be happening to Ivy, I can't relax at all."

"Maybe a good family devotion will help," Leah said.

"I wish, but God seems to have deserted me now."

"Luke Moretz!" Granny Em exclaimed. "I'll hear none of that kind of talk from you. You of all people! Your faith has been as strong as anyone's I've ever known, and God would never desert you. You're just worn to a frazzle. Things will get better. You'll see. You can't get a bad attitude now. When you start plowing your rows crooked, it's awfully hard to get them straight again."

"Well, supper's ready," Patsy said.

"Let's eat," Granny Em said. "Then we can read our letters, Leah."

Leah looked at Luke across the table, as they ate. He seemed different. She knew God hadn't deserted him, but something had.

Was it just Ivy? Had he loved her that much? Did it take her running away for him to realize how much she meant to him? Granny Em watched Luke, too. Leah knew the older women well enough by now to know she had many questions she wanted to ask, but she was wise enough to know this wouldn't be the time. Luke seemed defeated. Much of the confidence and sense of security he'd always demonstrated had fled. His shoulders slumped, his eyes had lost their sparkle, and he ate very little. Luke then looked up and his eyes met Leah's.

"It's good to have you home, Luke," she told him.

"It's good to be home." He gave her a weak smile. "And it's good to hear you call it home."

His statement gave Leah hope. It wasn't much, but she grasped at it anyway.

After supper, Granny Em and she read their letters from Dr. Moretz. Leah's read:

My Dearest Leah,

I was so glad to get your letter from Wilkesboro and know you made it that far with no problems. Reading your letter makes me wish I were there with you. I hope you're enjoying the mountains and the farm. It's getting so warm here that I'd like to be there.

Although I haven't been to Wilkesboro recently, I remember the town well and have always liked it. I remember when Luke's mother and I went back to the farm the summer Luke was two. We stayed overnight in Wilkesboro. The courthouse was brand new then. It was the last time we got back to the mountains together. I miss Sarah so much, even now. Forgive my memories.

I've been praying for all of you often. I still don't have peace about Ivy and Luke. I guess a father can't help but worry.

I plan to send this letter to Wilkesboro with a friend who's traveling there soon. I'm hoping this will speed its journey to Boone, and you'll get it quicker. Of course, I know it will depend on when Luke is able to get to the post office in Boone to pick it up.

Again, I want to express how delighted I was in your visit. It's rare I meet a young lady as congenial and intelligent as you. In fact, I don't think I ever have, except for Luke's mother.

Please write soon with all the details about what you see and do. I want to be able to see it all from your perspective. Tell me how you feel about the situation there, and what you think about Luke and Ivy. I eagerly await your reply.

Yours truly,

Clifton Moretz

P.S.

I'd already written the above letter in reply to your most welcomed one, when Luke came and gave me the startling news. I decided just to add to what I'd already written.

I am so sorry for what's happened. I know you must be riddled with worry, the same as Luke. I've never seen the poor boy so anxious. I tried to talk with him and have him tell me what he's thinking, but it seems difficult for him to organize or express his thoughts right now.

From what little I've been able to gather, Luke's afraid that Ivy has put herself in a precarious situation. If he finds her, and she's married, that would be the best set of circumstances. Luke would then be free to pursue other interests, and, although he'd never say so, I feel his main one would be you. I can tell he holds you in high regard.

If that's not the case, and Ivy assures Luke no harm has come to her, but she no longer wants to marry him, he'll take her back to your plantation or anywhere else she wants to go that's safe. This would also make things relatively easy.

If, however, Ivy has been ruined and abandoned, Luke is resigned to marrying her, if she wants that. Please be assured, this is not what Luke wants, but he feels responsible for taking Ivy to a place where she felt the need to run away. I've tried my best to dissuade Luke from such a course, but he will not listen. He says it's what's right. He certainly has a strong sense of honor and responsibility.

Well, enough for now. Know that Luke, you, and Ivy are always in my prayers. I shall write if I hear anything at all, and you do the same.

Yours,

Clifton

Leah sat for several minutes looking back over the letter and trying to digest it all. Dr. Moretz had answered some of her questions.

They had the family devotion. Luke read the scripture, but he asked Granny Em to pray.

"Leah's been doing our devotions and asking grace at meals while you've been gone," Granny Em told Luke after she finished the prayer. "She's done a good job."

"That's good," Luke said. "I'm going to lie down now. I may not get to sleep, but my body's tired. I'm sorry. I know I haven't been good company."

"Could I make you some tea that'll help you sleep?" Leah asked tentatively.

"Good idea," Granny Em said. "I'm glad you're still thinking. It's just what he needs."

"I'll take any help I can get," Luke said. "I can't go on like this much longer. Father offered me some drug, but I didn't want the aftereffects."

Leah steeped the tea. She poured Luke a generous cup and added a little honey. She made sure it was hot enough but not too hot, said a quick prayer that the tea would help, and handed it to him. He drank it all.

"Thank you, Leah. I'll see you in the morning."

"We've all been praying for you and for Ivy, and I'll continue to do so."

"Bless you," he said and went upstairs.

"I'm sure worried about that boy," Granny Em said. "I've never seen him like this, not even when he had to come here and leave his father, but, of course, he was just eight then. I wish I knew exactly what he's thinking, but I didn't think this was the time to ask."

"I think he's too exhausted right now to even think," Leah said. "We'll just pray he gets a good night's sleep. I think that would help more than anything."

Leah lay in bed and prayed for a long time. She prayed Ivy would be found safe and unharmed. She prayed Luke would get a good night's sleep, wake up feeling refreshed, and pull close to God again. She wanted him to find peace.

CHAPTER TWELVE

Summer

When Leah awoke the next morning, she quietly got ready and tiptoed out, so she wouldn't disturb Patsy. She had built the fire and put on the coffee before Granny Em appeared.

"Any sign of Luke?" Granny Em asked.

"I haven't seen him, but I guess he could be milking."

"Well, I'm going to see, and, if he isn't, I'll milk."

"Anything you want me to start for breakfast?"

"There's a slab of bacon and eggs in the larder. Go ahead and fry out the bacon. I'll make the biscuits when I get back, or you can give it a try, and we'll scramble the eggs at the last minute, so they'll be warm."

Leah decided to make drop biscuits, since she found it easier to get light, moist biscuits that way. She had the biscuits baking in the covered spider when Luke came downstairs. He looked better.

"I slept all night through for the first time since I left here. Thank you, Leah."

"I'm glad the tea helped."

"Leah." He took her arm and gently pulled her around to face him. His touch sent tingles up her arm, and her heart pumped double time. He may have felt something, too, for he quickly pulled his hand back. His gaze locked her eyes to his with a penetrating look she couldn't pull away from. "Right now my burden is heavy, and I can't express what's in my heart. I hope and pray it won't be like this much longer." With those words, he turned and walked outside.

Leah sat down. She'd suddenly grown too weak to stand. What had Luke just said to her? Was Ivy his heavy burden? Was Leah in his heart, but he couldn't tell her, until the burden was taken from him? Once she had been good with riddles, but this one confused her, or did she just fear the answer?

Patsy came downstairs and began to set the table. Leah had already fried the bacon and broken ten eggs into a bowl when Granny and Luke returned. She added a tiny amount of milk to make the eggs fluffier, and beat them until smooth. She put some butter into the skillet, poured in the eggs, and scrambled them slowly as they cooked.

"That smells good enough to eat," Luke said with a grin. He almost looked like he did before all this happened.

"You'd better wait until you taste the biscuits," Leah teased. "Biscuits have always been my nemesis when it comes to cooking."

"Well, I'm glad to know you're not always perfect," Luke told her with a twinkle in his eye.

"Far from it."

"If you two will quit picking at each other, let's bless the food and eat, before it gets cold." Granny Em said, and Luke complied.

"These biscuits are just fine," Granny Em said.

"They're delicious," Luke agreed. "Everything is. How did you get the eggs so light and fluffy?"

"I mixed in a little milk."

"I'll have to remember that," Granny Em said.

Luke ate his bacon and eggs with a couple of biscuits. Then, he had some biscuits and fresh strawberry preserves. "I feel better than I have in a good while," he said. "I've had a good night's sleep and eaten a big breakfast. Now I'm ready to face the world."

"You just needed to get home," Granny Em said.

"I think you're right," Luke replied, but he looked at Leah.

———

Luke looked across the table at Leah. Did she understand what he had tried to let her know when he'd first come downstairs this morning? He couldn't tell by looking at her. He'd thought about being clearer about his feelings and asking her to wait until these problems with Ivy were resolved, but, that wouldn't be fair to Leah. What if Ivy had been through so much, she now wanted to marry Luke? He hoped not. He hoped he would find her well and happy, wherever she was.

Just seeing Leah after two weeks had been a tonic that lifted his spirit. He realized part of his melancholy had come from missing Leah. He'd grown to care about her more than he'd realized. Despite his efforts to the contrary, he might as well admit it—he loved her.

He loved her in a way he'd never loved Ivy. If he'd ever been in love with Ivy at all, it'd been infatuation. He'd loved the woman he thought he saw, but Leah came so much closer to being that woman. Although she had grown up on a plantation, she had the strong, independent spirit of the mountain people.

"Well, since I've been gone, I guess I need to get to work. I think I'll begin with hoeing the garden and fields."

"I would like to pick the last of the strawberries to make a dessert for supper," Leah said, "but we've already picked a few times. I can carry the older rifle, like I've been doing."

"We've hoed once since you've been gone," Granny Em said. "It shouldn't take you too long to get through it again."

"We'll plan to go pick strawberries right after lunch, then."

"I'll help you hoe, and that way, you'll finish even sooner," Leah told him.

"Patsy and I'll wash some clothes, then," Granny Em said. "There's not as much as the last time we washed, but Luke has some things. We need to get them out early, in case it rains this afternoon."

Leah ran upstairs to gather up her dirty clothes and give them to Patsy. Luke went outside to get the hoes.

"I see there are still a few peas," he said when she came out. "What's the chance I can get some more of that soup?"

"The peas have almost stopped bearing, but I think I can get enough for soup. Perhaps I can fix some for supper."

In each plot, Leah started chopping down the weeds in one corner, and Luke began in the opposite one. They met in the middle. Luke hoped it would prove an allegory for what would be. As long as he and Leah eventually got together, he could patiently work through the problems, just like they were cutting down these weeds.

Luke stopped and let the rush of feelings wash over him. Now that he'd quit trying to lie to himself and pretend he felt nothing for Leah, what he felt seemed overwhelming. He would stay at arm's length, however, until they found Ivy. What if she never turned up? What if something awful had happened? He feared he'd find her used and abandoned, and he'd have to marry her. He'd just have to wait and see, and he couldn't court Leah until that had been settled.

They finished all the hoeing and ate dinner. Then, all except Granny went to pick strawberries.

"I see most of the strawberries are gone," Luke said, "but there are some still in the shady areas. It looks like the cherries and blackberries are beginning to ripen. We can pick them soon."

They'd picked berries for a while, when Luke heard a strange, rattling noise. He knew that sound. "Don't move, Leah," he commanded. He could tell Leah wasn't sure what was happening, but she did what he told her and froze in place. Luke finally spotted the culprit and fired his rifle. Leah nearly jumped out of her skin. Luke moved forward and saw the timber rattlesnake with his head shot off.

Leah cocked her head to one side and held a hand over her ear. The close shot had likely sent her ears to ringing. "What kind of snake?" she asked.

"A timber rattler, and he's a big one." Luke looked at the dull, black snake with rust splotches edged in gold. The snake had been headed right toward Leah.

"I never saw it, even after you told me to stop."

"They blend into the terrain."

"You about scared me to death," Patsy said.

"Me, too." Leah took a deep breath. "I think we have enough strawberries for supper. Let's go back."

Leah cooked supper for them. She made the cream of pea and potato soup Luke liked. Instead of using hunks of side meat, this time Leah added diced ham, and it was even better. She also fixed biscuits and cake with strawberries and sweetened cream for the top.

"I feel like I've just had a feast to welcome me home," Luke said, when they'd finished eating.

"I'm just glad to see you feeling so much better," Granny said. "You had me worried last night."

Leah and Luke played another game of checkers. This time Luke won by the skin of his teeth.

They had their devotion and went to bed. Luke lay in bed thinking. He didn't feel as anxious as he had before. Being here with Leah and Granny had calmed him, and he knew God had been with him all the time. Luke felt His presence now comforting him. Whatever happened, God would be with him.

Luke's return made the farm work go much faster. He could do more than all the three women put together. When he caught up with other work, he chopped and hauled wood for the fireplace. Obviously, they would need a lot to keep them through the winter here.

Leah and Patsy often went with him and helped carry the wood. When they got the logs back to the farm, Luke would saw them into fireplace lengths, split the larger ones, and Leah and Patsy stacked the wood he cut.

Granny had taught Leah what new herbs to look for, and she often gathered some of them while they were getting wood. Ginseng seemed to the most important of the new ones.

They picked blackberries and made pies and preserves. Leah didn't like picking blackberries, but she'd picked them on the plantation. The briars made her arms and hands look as though she'd been in a cat fight.

At odd times, Luke looked at her tenderly, almost as if he wanted to take her in his arms, so she tried to look away. She understood they needed to wait and be patient. She didn't like it, but she understood.

Luke and Leah were together more now than before. If they were out of sight of the house, Patsy always went with them. If Patsy or Granny Em couldn't accompany them, Leah didn't go either, but that rarely happened.

After supper, Luke and Leah often played a game before the devotions and bedtime. They played checkers, chess, or backgammon.

Leah liked to beat Luke in chess the best, and she always tried harder there. Since both of them often took a long time to move in chess, they sometimes played another game on the side. One player could be studying on a chess move, while the other moved in checkers or backgammon. Often they'd leave the chess board set up, because they wouldn't finish a game before bedtime.

"We'll have more time to play this winter," Luke told her.

"It sounds like we're going to be confined all winter," Patsy said.

"That's somewhat true," Granny Em said. "Sometimes, I feel like I'm taking after the bears and hibernating in the winter. Luke usually gets out and does the chores when it gets so cold."

These days turned out to be almost happy times, and Leah marveled in them. It seemed as if they had all pushed Ivy into a corner of their minds, since they could do little but wait. Yet, there were times when Luke would grow pensive, and Leah knew Ivy held his thoughts. Both of them were in a state of uncertainty, waiting to find out about her, so they could get on with their lives in one direction or the other.

Cherries ripened and they picked all they could. Leah liked the black ones better to eat, because they seemed sweeter, but the red ones were great in pies or preserves. They even crushed some and made cider.

Luke would climb the trees and push the limbs down so the women could pick more. He'd also pick from up in the tree. Leah would have liked to don pants and climb into the trees, and she might have, if Luke hadn't been there. She didn't want to do anything that might draw his attention to her in a physical way right now. The attraction between them seemed too strong anyway.

The days grew warmer, but Leah found them comfortable. Here they thought eighty extremely hot while on the plantation eighties in the summer would have been a respite.

The garden produced its bounty, and they enjoyed the fresh vegetables. They made crocks of pickles from the cucumbers and also pickled some beets. They ate fresh green beans and strung them to dry as leather britches to cook in the winter. Some of the fruits, especially apples, would also be dried. They would make hominy later out of some of the corn by soaking hard kernels in the alkali solution from the ash hopper and cooking them. They had leaf lettuce, squash, and radishes, and there'd also be carrots, okra, potatoes, pumpkins, and field peas. Where the early garden peas had been, they planted a fall crop of turnips and mustard greens.

All the root crops, as well as the some of the cabbage, apples, and pears, could be harvested and stored in the root cellar, a small, cave-like room dug into a hillside. It had a thick wooden door and deep earthen walls to keep it from getting below freezing. Just to be on the safe side, Granny Em wrapped the containers in old, worn-out quilts.

Leah liked gathering food and preparing it for the winter. It gave her a sense of survival and made her feel capable of caring for a family. It also connected her with ancestors, who had struggled just like this to settle a new land. It gave her the feeling she belonged.

One Saturday, at the supper table, Luke said, "We've been working hard. Why don't we pack a dinner after breakfast tomorrow and spend the day exploring the mountain? We can take a quilt and have our Sunday Bible study out among nature."

"That's a good idea, Luke," Granny Em said. "These girls have worked their hearts out, and they haven't gotten to get out at all. Leah just got to go to Boone once, and Patsy didn't even do that."

They woke up Sunday to bright sunshine, a rarity on the mountain. Normally, they rose to low clouds and mountains wrapped in fog. It would usually burn off by mid-morning, however.

They packed things for the day and loaded them into the wagon. Granny Em seemed as excited as anyone.

Luke headed up toward higher elevations first. He pointed out important plants and scenes along the way.

Leah felt the impact of the beauty of this land. The valleys and glens were like perfect landscapes. They called to Leah and wanted her to run their hills and sing atop their summits.

The forests were dark and mysterious, but not foreboding. Hardwoods dominated the lower elevations, but, as they went up, the evergreens took over. Ferns abounded, and Leah felt as if she'd stepped back in time to an enchanted European forest.

Luke pointed out blue spruce and Fraser firs, two majestic evergreens unfamiliar to her. Granny told of herbs and plants they could use for home remedies.

They came to a more level section, and Luke pulled the wagon over and stopped. They pulled out the quilt and their Bibles, and they sat to read the creation story from Genesis. It took on special meaning for Leah now, because she sat surrounded by God's marvelous creation. She said as much when they had their discussion.

"Why do you think I feel closer to God in the mountains?" she asked.

"I'm not sure," Luke said, "but I feel the same way. It's almost as if my spirit soars to the mountain peaks, and I'm more aware of God's hand."

They sang some hymns, and Leah felt their voices ring out, as clear as the mountain air. She wished Luke had thought to bring his fiddle, too.

They sat silently for a while to meditate and say their individual prayers. Then, Luke prayed aloud to close their worship time.

They got back into the wagon and rode some more. At the top of the mountain, they got out and walked around. Leah saw many lovely flowers and plants she'd never seen before. One eye-catching lily had small, deep-red flowers. Luke said a botanist had discovered it and named it after himself, Gray's lily. How odd the delicate red bloom would be called "Gray."

"Those Blue Ridge goldenrods are found only in a few locations at the highest elevations," Luke added.

They ate dinner at the top of the mountain, and, even near noon, the air held a chill. A steady breeze blew, and the women pulled their shawls around them. Thankfully, Granny Em had said to bring them along.

Luke put an arm around Granny Em to help keep her warm as they went back to the wagon. Leah looked longingly, wishing that arm was around her shoulders. She shook herself. She knew better but couldn't seem to tie down her wayward thoughts.

"Let's drop by and visit Oralee," Granny Em said. "I haven't seen her in a long time, and I'd like for the girls to meet her. She's about as mountain as they come."

"I thought you were mountain, Granny Em," Patsy said.

"No, no." Granny laughed. "My mother and father moved to Watauga County when I was fourteen. Of course, it was Wilkes County then. I've never talked like the old mountain people. I'm a newcomer by their standards."

"What does that make us?" Patsy asked.

"A foreigner, or 'furriner,' as Oralee would say." Granny Em laughed.

"The families who came in the early seventeen hundreds kept some of their old English language patterns," Luke added. "The way they talk is almost reminiscent of Elizabethan English and Shakespeare's time."

"Do they use 'thees' and 'thous?'" Leah asked.

"No, it's different. Just wait and you'll see."

"The slaves speak their own way," Patsy said. "I used to talk like that, until Miss Leah taught me differently."

"Yes, it's the same idea, except they're different dialects."

"Oralee's husband is dead, too," Granny Em said. "Her grandson and his family live with her. She's some older than me."

They rode up to a log cabin nestled in the shadow of the mountain. It looked smaller, older, and more in need of repair than their log house at the farm.

"Lawsy me, is that thar Emmaline? Hit's been quite a spell, hain't hit?" a weak, but excited voice said when they were ushered into the cabin.

The cabin consisted of one big room, but sacks had been sewn together and tacked up to create a bedroom in the corner. Oralee lay in bed in another corner. Supper cooked in a big pot in the one fireplace. The rest of the sparse furniture looked homemade.

Introductions were made. Polly, Oralee's granddaughter-in-law, had let them in. Three young heads peeked down from a sleeping loft, but they pulled back quickly when Leah looked up.

"Y'all have a cheer," Polly said. "Raymond's in the barn with the two eldest boys. He'll be in to reckley."

"You got a looker thar," Oralee said, looking at Leah. "Come riecheer, girl. Let me have a looksee. You a-courting' her, Luke?"

"No, ma'm," Luke said.

"Bein' a bit choicy, haint yuh? Well, yuh best keep yer eyes peeled, Emmaline. Them bucks'll be swarmin' 'round yer place like bees to honey. How old are yuh, gal? My eldest great grandson's goin' on sixteen."

"I'll be eighteen before long," Leah said, "but I'm not interested in seeing anyone now."

"Now that thar's a right smart thang. Seems yuh got more sense'n most."

The children in the loft kept peering down when they thought no one was looking. They seemed to be staring at Patsy.

"Y'all youngins a-fightin' agin?" Oralee asked when noise came from the rafters. "Thar's no call fer that. Y'all best cut it out 'fore

I git ahold o' yuh with a keen hickory switch. You ort to have a good whuppin'. Y'all've jist 'about wore me plumb out today. How many times have I done axed yuh to quit yer ruckus?"

Leah looked around at the primitive cabin with just the bare necessities. From what she'd seen from riding by, this place must have been typical of most mountain cabins. She realized Luke and Granny Em were well-off compared to most of the other families here.

"How have you been, Oralee?" Granny Em asked.

"Oh, I reckon I'm right pert fer a woman a-gettin' up in years."

"Don't let 'er lead yuh on," Polly said. "She's been right puny lately."

"I never heared tell of sech. Jist 'cause I hain't up kickin' to the ceilin', don't mean I got one foot in th' grave."

"How you do go on, Granny," Polly said.

"Luke, I heared you went off and brung this purty little blonde thang up the mountain, but she went and flew the coop, leavin' you all done in."

"You know you can't believe everything you hear," Granny Em said.

"That's shore 'nuff the Gospel. Luke, wouldja reech over thar and throw another log on the far. I've got a chill and it'll soon be time to start supper."

Luke put a piece of wood in the fireplace. "Well, I guess we'd better be getting back home," he said.

"Can't ye stay a spell longer. Stay and eat a bite with us. You're more'n welcome."

"Thank you," Granny Em said, "but it'll be milking time soon, and we need to be going."

"Well, ya'll come back soon, now, ye hear."

"Patsy, you sure were quiet back there," Granny Em said, as they boarded the wagon.

"I didn't know what to say, and I was having a hard time following some of the conversation."

"What did you think, Leah?" Luke asked as he pulled the wagon back onto the trail.

"Quite interesting," Leah said. "I like to hear Oralee talk. It has an almost melodic rhythm to it, and only some of it was hard to follow."

"You stay in the mountains long enough, and you might get to talking just like Oralee," Luke teased.

"Are you trying to run me out of the mountains, Luke?"

"No, not at all." He looked worried, and Leah wondered if he thought she might leave like Ivy.

"Well, that's good," she told him, "because, as much as I like it here, I think you'd have a hard time running me off." He relaxed and smiled at her.

The days followed one by one in a regular pattern. They worked together like clockwork to get all the work done and be prepared for winter. Even in the summer, winter lurked right around the corner and threatened mountain life. By the end of August, the nights had already started to turn cooler.

Granny decided to kill a chicken to cook. Several of the hens had hatched biddies over the spring and summer, and, if something didn't raid the hen house, they'd have plenty of chickens.

"Luke, if you'll cut its head off, I'll clean it. It's a messy job, and I don't want to ask Patsy or Leah," Granny said.

"I don't mind messy jobs," Leah said. "Someone has to do them."

Luke caught a chicken and took it to the chopping block, a thick stump he used to split wood on. Patsy also came running when she heard the chicken squawking.

"You ladies might want to go out of sight of this," Luke said. "It looks pretty grotesque."

Leah had never seen anyone chop off a chicken's head before, so she stayed. At the plantation, a slave had wrung the chicken's neck. She saw Patsy decided to remain, too.

"Don't say I didn't warn you," Luke placed the chicken's neck across the chopping block and severed its head with a one-handed swing of the axe. He flung the chicken out from him. The headless bird danced around, flapping its wings, while all the time blood spurted from its neck. The bizarre dance took several minutes, and the headless fowl frantically covered a lot of ground, as if it were hysterically searching for its head.

Patsy gave out a scream and ran for the house. Leah stood as if glued in place. Though sickening, the scene appeared so strange, she couldn't turn away. She stared at the weird performance, as if she were watching a stage show. It took several minutes for the poor chicken to finally drop dead.

Luke came to stand beside Leah. "Are you all right?"

She nodded. Her stomach did feel a little queasy, but she didn't want to show it. A farm woman needed to be strong. "That just gave a whole new meaning to 'running around like a chicken with his head cut off.'"

Luke chuckled in appreciation. He put his arm around the back of her shoulders and gave her a quick squeeze.

"I'm going to cut a load of cabbage now," Luke said to Leah and Granny Em. "I plan to take them to Boone tomorrow."

"Well, if you don't mind the company," Granny Em said, "I'd like to do some shopping. I don't guess I'll get a better chance before Christmas, and I don't want to wait until the weather gets cold. I'm sure the girls will want to come, too."

"I'd like the company very much," Luke said. He looked at Leah.

Leah helped Luke cut the cabbage heads. They'd grown so big and hearty it proved difficult to cut through them with a butcher knife. "I think an axe would work better," she told Luke, and he laughed. They loaded them into the wagon, so it would be ready to go in the morning.

CHAPTER THIRTEEN

News

They got up at five, ate a quick breakfast, and gathered a sack of food for dinner. By the time the sun had begun to peep over the mountain, Luke headed the mules and wagon toward the road.

"Well, at least it's not cold, damp, and foggy," Granny Em said.

Leah noticed Granny Em paid no attention to the steep precipices as they went down the mountain. It didn't seem as scary to Leah as it had been the first time, either. Luke looked over and smiled, as if he'd read her thoughts.

They sat squeezed together on the wagon seat. Luke, Leah, Patsy, and Granny Em came in that order. Granny Em had seemed to orchestrate the arrangement. Although none of them were big, the seat had not been designed for four adults. With the load of cabbage, however, Patsy didn't have room in the back, but she would on the way home.

Leah became keenly aware of Luke's side against hers. It caused her heart to race, her legs to turn weak, and her stomach to flutter. Neither did it help that he'd stretched one arm along the back of the seat to give more room, and it almost felt as if he had his arm around her. She tried to put her thoughts on other things.

Patsy hadn't wanted to come, but she didn't want to stay at the farm by herself, either. In the end, she'd joined them. Leah noticed Patsy still brought her papers showing she'd been freed.

181

The store owner seemed pleased with Luke's cabbage. He gave him the price they'd agreed upon without trying to haggle.

"You ladies do your shopping, and I'll walk around town and see if I hear any news of Sam Whitley or Ivy."

"Do you need any money, Leah?" he asked quietly before he left.

"No, thank you. I have some of my own, but you might ask Patsy. She wouldn't take any from me, but you and Granny Em might have better luck." Leah had brought some of the money from selling her jewelry, but she appreciated Luke's thoughtfulness.

"I want you to take this for all the work you've done on the farm," she heard Luke tell Patsy.

"No, sir. You've given me a home, and I haven't worked any harder than anyone else."

"But we all have some money," Granny Em said, "and you should, too."

Leah saw Patsy take the money and hand some of it back. "This will be enough," she said.

Patsy and Leah walked out to the wagon while Granny Em bought her things. Then, Granny Em and Patsy sat in the wagon, while Leah shopped. Patsy gave her a little money and told her what to buy for Granny Em. She must have done the same with the others.

All three of them were at the wagon when Luke came back. "I went back by and picked up the mail," he said. "We have a thick envelope from Father. Shall we open it now or wait until we get home?"

"Let's wait until we get home, where we can take our time and enjoy it," Granny Em said. "I'm getting hungry, too. When can we eat?"

"Let's head out of town. We'll stop in the meadow on the way out. That should be a good place to spread the quilt."

"Did you hear any news?" Leah asked as they began to eat.

"Not much. Rumor has it Sam Whitley has been seen in Wilkes County without Ivy. I don't know how true it is. No one has heard anything about Ivy. The sheriff sounded concerned some counterfeit banknotes might come into the area. Apparently there's been some down the mountain to the south. I'll check on the tracker I sent to find Ivy and try to find more information when I go to Wilkesboro."

"When are you planning to go there?" Leah asked.

"Probably next week."

They finished eating and headed home. Everyone seemed more preoccupied than before. Leah knew their minds, like hers, had settled on Ivy again.

They got home rather late, so they fixed a quick supper. Leah fried some cornbread fritters and eggs. She served the fried egg on top the fritter. Luke ate four.

"That hit the spot," he said.

Granny Em opened the fat envelope addressed to her from Dr. Moretz. She handed Luke a letter and Leah two. Granny Em went into her bedroom to read hers. Patsy went upstairs, and Luke remained at the kitchen table.

Leah sat down in the sitting room and opened the one from Dr. Moretz first. The other came in another envelope and looked to be from Paul. She wanted to postpone seeing what it might say. The doctor had written:

My dearest Leah,

I assume you have not heard from Ivy, since I haven't heard anything from you or Luke. There is nothing to report on this end, either. My prayers are still with all of you every day.

Your brother sent me a letter. He said he wants you to come home and begged me to forward his letter to you, which I have done, although I don't know exactly what it says. I hope it doesn't prove distressful to you. From what he wrote to me, he doesn't seem to know Ivy is not with you.

I hope his letter does not put an additional burden on you. I know you have enough to bear now. Remember, you don't have to answer him. Don't let him pressure you into doing something you don't believe is right or best.

If I can be of any service, don't hesitate to ask. I would love to have you here with me for a while. If you feel you can't stand the mountain winters, please come. Those winters can be fierce, especially to a flatlander. The climate zone of Watauga is more akin to Canada, so don't underestimate winter there. I'll look forward to hearing from you soon.

All my best wishes,

Your surrogate father

With a deep sigh, Leah opened Paul's letter. She read:

Dear Leah and Ivy,

Please come home. Your mother is suffering without you. She's not been the same since you left. I fear for both her health and her mental state. It's getting harder and harder for me to deal with her.

Hester Sue thinks our first child will arrive in May. Although there's little physical indication yet, she is very nervous and anxious. She's afraid something bad is going to happen to her or the baby. Leah, you are good with medicines and herbs. You would know just what to do. Please come home. Just your being here would help relieve Hester Sue's fears. She's far too high-strung of late.

Do not fear we will force you into an unwanted marriage. I promise you both I shall not. I don't know what I was thinking, Leah, when I considered allowing you to marry Archibald. He's a cruel man, and I think too much of you to want such a match. Although Lawrence is a good man, I'll not make you marry him, Ivy, if you're still opposed to the idea. You are pretty enough to get any man you want. I'll approve any match that would be suitable to your station. I'll leave that selection to you and your mother. The only stipulation I have is that you live in this area, so your mother can see you regularly. Perhaps she could even live with you, if that would be agreeable?

Ivy, your mother needs you in the worst way. If you don't come home, I fear for her well-being. Come quickly, before it's too late. Even if you're already married, come for a visit. I could meet you in Salisbury, or I could send someone up the mountain to get you. I eagerly await both your replies. If one of you cannot possibly come, I'm hoping the other will.

Your half-brother,

Paul

Leah leaned her head back on the settee and closed her eyes. Dr. Moretz had been right. She didn't need this right now.

Luke moved to sit down beside her. "Leah, what's wrong?" His gentle concern tugged at her.

She didn't look at him. She just handed over both her letters. When he'd focused on the mail, she watched him, as he read.

"Oh, Leah, I'm so sorry that Paul's put all this on you. What are you going to do?" He almost sounded fearful of her answer.

"I don't know."

"I'll ask you the question Father would ask, if he were here. What do you want to do?"

"I want to stay here." She answered quickly, because she didn't need to think about that one. She saw Luke relax, but she continued. "We don't always get to do what we want, though, do we? Are you doing what you want now?"

Luke grimaced.

"What do you want, Luke?" She whispered it, unsure if she should ask it at all.

He paused. "I want to be through with all this mess with Ivy. I want her to be in a good situation, and I want to be free to follow my heart."

Leah wanted to ask Luke what following his heart meant, but Granny Em came in. She must've heard Luke's last remark.

"Then, what are you going to do about it, Luke? Sometimes it doesn't work to just sit around and let things happen. When you do that, you may be letting others chart your course. Sometimes you need to take control. Only God should control your actions. Seems to me, you've been letting Ivy do that," Granny Em told him.

"Granny Em, Luke's been trying hard to do what's right." Leah said. She felt sorry for Luke. How dare Granny Em be so harsh! "You're being way too hard on him. He's still engaged to my sister."

"You see there, Luke." Granny Em pointed her finger. "Who takes up for you no matter what? Who would support you through thick and thin? Who would never leave you, if you made her your wife? Open your eyes, son. God has sent you a treasure above all others. Don't let your life waste away just waiting to see what happens."

Luke sat as if frozen in place. He seemed to be stunned by Granny Em's words.

"And, Leah Morgan, don't you go telling me Luke's still engaged to Ivy. We know she ran away from Luke of her own free will. She told us as much in her note. If that doesn't break any engagement, I don't know what would. I've watched all summer and held my peace. Well, I just can't hold it anymore."

No one said a word. Leah guessed Granny Em had said more than enough for them all. Luke leaned forward on the seat beside Leah. His hands were clasped in front of him, and he stared at the floor.

"I'm going to bed," Luke finally said. He turned back to Leah, and his countenance softened. He looked like he wanted to touch her, but he didn't. "We'll talk in the morning and decide what's best to do."

She nodded.

Granny Em looked at Leah. "I just couldn't keep a lid on it anymore. You know, sometimes you have to lift the lid and stir things around to ensure it's all right."

Luke lay in bed and knew sleep wouldn't come easily tonight. Why did Granny have to say so much—as if Leah and he hadn't already been anxious enough? He sighed and thought a minute. Maybe it was because Granny Em loved him and wanted the best for him.

He had no doubts that Leah would be good for him. If the situation with Ivy hadn't been enough to keep them apart, however, now Paul added another pull.

He knew Leah well enough to know she might go back to Gold Leaf, although he believed it wouldn't be what she wanted. Unlike

Ivy, Leah would try to do what was best for others, not herself. She might try to help her family, if she thought they needed her.

Paul had also just taken away the element that had brought Leah here in the first place. She wouldn't be forced into a marriage with Archibald Biles.

Luke's stomach turned at the very idea of Leah being married to someone like Archibald, but, then, he sickened at the thought of her marrying anyone else. Was this an indication of the truth in the words Granny had hurled at him tonight? Did God put those words in her mouth so Luke would hear?

Luke thought he'd been waiting for God to bring a resolution or show him what to do. Was this God's way of doing just that? Luke had expected something more decisive, something which would set things in motion, such as Zeb Brewer finding Ivy.

Luke suddenly remembered they hadn't held the family devotion tonight. He had been too upset to think of it, and he'd taken his Bible downstairs earlier. He decided to go down and get it. He needed to hear God's word right now.

He dressed and went down. To his surprise, Leah sat on the couch still fully dressed, and she held her Bible close to the candlelight, so she could read.

She looked up. "Couldn't you get to sleep either?"

"No, and I remembered we forgot to hold devotions, so I came back down to get my Bible."

"I remembered, too, and I came down so the light wouldn't disturb Patsy. She's already asleep."

"Would you like to read and pray together?"

"I'd like that very much."

"Why don't you continue reading aloud?"

She read in a clear voice. "'Unto thee O Lord, do I lift up my soul. O my God, I trust in thee: let me not be ashamed, let my enemies not triumph over me. Yes, let none that wait on thee be ashamed: let them be ashamed who transgress without cause. Show me thy ways, O Lord, thy tender mercies and thy loving kindness . . . ' "

She continued reading from Psalms. David had felt anguish, too, and he cried out for God's help. Luke would do the same. God helped those who loved Him. Luke would take comfort in that.

After a while, Leah stopped reading. "Would you pray for us?" she asked.

He did. He poured out his soul, as if it were just the Lord and him. He pleaded for help, direction, and divine intervention. When he raised his head, silent tears ran slowly down Leah's face.

"Don't cry." He tried to gently rub her tears away with his thumb. "Everything will be fine. God will work it out. You'll see."

"Your prayer . . . our devotion together moved me." She gave a weak smile.

"What are your thoughts about Paul's letter? Are you going to try to go back?" The words almost hung in his throat, but that question worried him, and he needed to know the answer.

"I don't think going back now would help anything. My returning without Ivy would most likely make Mama worse. Hester Sue and I are not close, and I don't think I could help by being there. I can write Paul what he can give her to calm her and not harm the baby, but Hester Sue has always been high-strung. It would be better if I could find Ivy and take her back. I could stay for a short visit and return here, if I haven't worn out my welcome."

He took her hand in his. It might affect him too much, but he needed her touch. "You could never do that." He wanted her with him always. Didn't she know that?

Her hand felt cold, so he got up and stoked the fire. "You know Granny may be right," he said when he came back to sit beside Leah. They both turned to face each other. "Maybe it's time for action. We've waited three months. I'll get things in order here and leave Monday morning with the cabbages for Wilkesboro. Hopefully, I can find Zeb, and he'll have some information. If not, I'll try to pick up a trail going south, myself. If that doesn't work, I'll head west toward Tennessee. If there's still no word, I'll travel north into Virginia. She has to have gone in one of those directions."

"I wish I could go, too, but I know that's not possible."

"I wish you could, too, but it certainly wouldn't be best."

"How long will you be gone?"

"As long as it takes to find something. I should've done this when she first left. I'll be more tenacious than someone else, because I have more at stake."

He noticed the forlorn look on her face. "I hate to leave you women here by yourselves, but I must. You three work together well and should be fine. You and Granny are a lot alike in that you're both strong, independent, capable women. Granny is just more outspoken and you're gentler. I love you both."

Leah looked startled. Her eyes went wide and her breath seemed labored. She stared at him with a confused look. Had he spoken too soon?

"It'll be all right, Leah." He softened his voice to soothe her. "We'll hold onto God's promises, and it'll be okay." She nodded.

Another thought entered his mind. "I didn't frighten you, did I? I mean, I hope you have feelings for me, too." All at once, he found himself unsure. What if he'd misread her, and she held no affection for him? What if she felt no attraction? He waited for what seemed forever, but it could only have been a few seconds.

"I have feelings," she said quietly. "I have deep feelings, too."

He breathed again. He would do as Granny had suggested. He would bring all of this to a conclusion, and he'd work his hardest to get the result he wanted. He felt better, and at peace, an indication of God's approval.

They both went upstairs. He wanted to kiss Leah with a fierceness that burned all through his body. Instead he took her hand and looked into her eyes. Cavaliers of old had kissed a lady's hand. It should be allowable. He raised her hand to his lips and kissed the back of it, as he watched her expression. She closed her eyes, and he felt a little quiver pass through her before he released her hand. There was an attraction here stronger than any he'd ever known. They would both have to be mindful of it, and not let it take control.

The next few days were a blur of activity. Luke might not get back for weeks, even months, and he wanted to leave the farm ready for winter.

Saturday would be Leah's birthday. He'd bought her a leather journal for her to write down her thoughts and experiences. He smiled as he thought of suggesting she keep one, because of the wonderful way she had with words. He fancied she might share at least parts of it with him someday, when things worked out for them. He'd think positively and say "when" and not "if."

Granny baked Leah a walnut cake. She even put a sugary glaze on top, something she didn't usually do, because of the cost and sometimes scarcity of sugar.

"This is a special day," Granny said, "and that girl needs to celebrate."

They held the celebration at dinner. Granny often liked to cook enough for dinner to eat leftovers for supper. As the weather cooled, however, she wouldn't do that as much. September would be cool enough to expect frost.

Granny had sent Leah out on some errands while she and Patsy set the table and put the food out. "Go get her for dinner," she told Luke.

Luke found her in the smokehouse. She'd come to the smoke-house to rub more salt into the fresh pork they'd butchered.

"Granny says to come on to dinner," he told her.

"I'll be praying for you the whole time you're gone," she told him. "Please take care of yourself and get back to us as soon as you can."

"I will, and I'll be praying for you, too. Stay as close as you can to the house. Just because the bears will hibernate and the snakes stay in the ground more in the winter doesn't mean there's no danger. There'll be mountain lions, bobcats, wild boar, wolves, and things like that, and they'll all be hungrier and looking for prey. There may also be men, and they can be the most dangerous of all."

Afraid that he'd frightened her, he took her hand in support as they walked to the house. Holding her hand felt so right, but it caused him to fill with longing. He gave her hand a quick squeeze and dropped it before they went inside.

Granny and Patsy began singing "Happy Birthday" as they entered the kitchen, and Luke joined in. Surprise showed on Leah's face.

"Oh my," Leah said. "I hadn't expected this."

"Well, sit down," Granny said. "We'll eat first, while it's hot, and you can open your presents afterwards."

The food tasted wonderful, and they all tried to keep the conversation light and carefree. Leah seemed impressed when Granny sliced the cake. "This is mouth-watering good," she told Granny.

Leah opened Patsy's gift first, a white apron Patsy had made her. "It's just what I need," Leah said. "I only brought two, and one of them is about worn out now. Thank you, Patsy." Leah reached over and gave Patsy a hug, and Patsy grinned from ear to ear.

She opened Luke's present next. "Oh, thank you," she said excitedly. "I'll keep it while you're gone and through the winter, when I'll have plenty of time to write in it. I remember us talking about a diary for me, and it's the perfect gift. I'm glad you remembered."

"I have you a new pen and ink to go with the journal. Granny didn't want to try wrapping it. You're also welcome to borrow any of my books you'd like to read while I'm gone. Go into my room and get one anytime you want."

She nodded, and he realized she was too filled with emotion to speak. She turned to open Granny's present.

"My, this is big. What can it be?"

"Well, it's not a horse," Granny said and got a faraway look in her eyes.

Leah untied the string at the top of the large sack and lifted out a beautiful patchwork quilt. It had an interlocking ring design cut from different colored solid and patterned scraps and an unbleached muslin background. Between the circles and in the center of the circles, Granny had quilted intricate designs with her stitches.

"It's called 'Double Wedding Ring,'" Granny said. "I thought you could put it away until you got married." She looked from Leah to Luke. He smiled to himself. Granny was something.

"I love it, but it's too much for a birthday present."

"Nonsense. Don't you know how much you mean to all of us?" Granny looked at Luke again.

"I pieced this top last winter, before you came. Oralee and Polly came over and helped me get it in the frame and start quilting on it in the spring. It took a long time for me to get that one quilted out."

"Thank you so much. Thank you all. This is the best birthday I've had in a long time."

"And may there be many more even happier ones," Luke said, as he raised his glass of water.

"Hear, hear," Granny affirmed as she and Patsy raised their glasses, too.

Luke first thought he'd leave Monday morning, but he didn't want to harvest the cabbage, pack them in the wagon, and have a flurry of last minute activities on Sunday, the Lord's Day. Instead, he would leave early Tuesday morning.

Even yet, Sunday turned out to be bittersweet. He wanted to be with Leah and explore these newly declared feelings, but they were being ripped apart. He also hesitated to really start courting until they knew about Ivy. He felt like a dandelion seed being blown by the wind, not knowing where he'd land.

"Write your replies to Father and Paul, and I'll post them in Wilkesboro," Luke told Leah. "I'll have Oralee's grandson pick up any mail for you when he goes to Boone and check on you from time to time. If you need anything, you let him know."

"Okay, but I think we're pretty well stocked. I can't see we'd need much else."

"Granny knows how to take care of the livestock and things. Since the new calf is a bull, I'm going to lead the old bull and the yearling's mother down the mountain and sell them. Everything else should be manageable for you."

After an early supper Sunday, Granny said, "Why don't you two go out and take a short walk together before the sun goes down? You don't have to go far, just out to the pasture or across to the meadow."

"Thank you, Granny," Luke told her and held out his hand to Leah. Leah grabbed her wool cape from a peg beside the larder door, and they started out.

They walked across the hint of a road to the meadow. The brightly colored fall leaves and the majestic mountains painted a lovely scene.

"Heaven could be just this pretty, and it would be all right with me," Leah said. Then she looked at him. "I hate to see you go, but I wish you a speedy and fruitful journey. May God guide you and keep you safe."

"I love you, Leah. No matter what happens, remember I love you with all my heart, and I'll always work to be with you, no matter how long it might take."

Puzzled, Leah looked at him. Did she think he was trying to tell her good-bye?

"I love you too, and I'll wait for you. No matter how long it takes, I promise to wait for you."

He took her in his arms and kissed her then, as he'd been wanting to do for a long time. Time became fluid, liquid, and he melted with it. The intensity of it all engulfed him and washed him to a place he'd never been before.

He pulled back to regain control of himself, but he still held her in his arms. She must have been affected similarly, because she held to him, as if she might not be able to stand at all, if he let her go. They stood there for a while, locked in each other's arms.

"I'm praying that everything will work out for us sooner, rather than later."

They let go of each other and walked back to the house. They'd said all that mattered.

They spent most of the day Monday harvesting the rest of the cabbage and packing them in the wagon. The wagon seat wouldn't be crowded this time with just Luke on it. Luke wished Leah could be jammed against him again as he traveled down the mountain.

Tuesday morning brought a rush of activity. Luke packed his things on his horse. He would tie him to the wagon and sell the wagon and mules when he got to Wilkesboro. The mules would be one less thing Leah would have to tend to, and Luke could buy others when they needed them.

He would have to take it easy with the cow and bull also tied to the wagon. He hoped he could sell them in Boone, so he could make better time down the mountain.

He'd given Leah and Granny a ton of instructions, but he knew they were equipped to handle things. Granny had lived here a long time, and Leah was strong, smart, and capable. Still, he worried he could be gone most of the winter, and anything could happen. He'd leave them in God's care and try not to worry.

Granny wanted to pack him a lot of food, but he told her to just get enough for lunch. He would be in Wilkesboro for supper and planned to overnight there. He could get hot food at the inn.

All too soon he sat in the wagon with all the good-byes said. He pulled off and looked back. Three women stood in a row waving, and he felt sure Granny and Leah had tears in their eyes.

Luke felt burdened on the way to Boone. He made a quick stop there, told the sheriff what he planned, and let the post office know the neighbors would be picking up their mail. He also managed to sell the bull and cow there.

The day turned out to be cold, overcast, and misty. It almost looked as if the mountains wept for him and Leah. They'd heard enough sad ballads ring out around them over the years. Did they know he and Leah would be another one? He scolded himself. Just because the day looked so gloomy didn't mean he needed to be.

The fog hung so thick in Deep Gap he could barely see the mules in front of him. He kept them going slowly, but he let them have the lead down the mountain. They would navigate the way better than he could in this pea soup. *Pea soup.* Would everything remind him of Leah?

About halfway down the mountain, he came out of the clouds and the sun burst forth. He drove into Wilkesboro early enough to deliver the cabbage and find the sheriff.

"I haven't seen hide nor hair of Zeb Brewer," the sheriff told Luke. "I'da thought he'd be back by now. Ivy's trail must have been hid good. Zeb's the best tracker I know."

Luke went to the post office before it closed. Leah told him she'd written to Paul and told him Ivy had run away, but she didn't say it'd been three months ago. She said she'd try to bring Ivy home as soon as they located her.

Finally, he took the wagon and mules to the log stable. He thought of joking with Leah and Ivy about the mules staying in a courthouse. Events sure had taken twists and turns since that day.

"I'll take the wagon and mules off your hands if you're wanting to sell," the stable owner told him.

"I'd have to have a least what I have in them," Luke told him. When he named the price, the man took it.

He went to the other inn in town. For some reason, he didn't want to stay in the same one he had stayed with Ivy and Leah. He feared the memories would keep him awake all night.

It still took Luke a long time to get to sleep, but, once he did, he slept soundly. He had just finished his breakfast when the sheriff came in looking for him.

"I thought you'd want to know. Zeb Brewer just got in late last night, but he's still sleeping. He looked pretty done in, so I let him sleep in the jail. He seemed glad to hear you were in town, so he won't have to ride up the mountain. He said he'd located Ivy."

Luke's heart skipped a beat, and he felt as if his blood drained from his head. "Where?"

"I don't really know any more. I expect you can ask him yourself soon enough."

"Not soon enough for me. I'll walk back with you and see if he's awake."

Zeb sat up when they walked in. "Well hey there, Luke. Glad to see you. Come in and set a spell. This here talk might take a while."

"What did you find? How's Ivy? Where is she?"

"Whoa, now. Hold your horses. One thang at a time. Let me just tell my story. I hauled off and headed toward Lenoir, like you said, but I didn't pick up no clues. I take it she was with Sam Whitley at that time, and they wuz a-layin' low. They didn't go near a town whar somebidy might ax around and pick up a scent. But, I had me this gut feelin' I wuz headed in the right dye-rection, and my gut's usely right. I mosied on south, axing at every place I come to. I wuz a-getting 'bout ready to call it quits, 'cause I'm gittin' too close to Charlotte to suit me. That place's just too big fer a country boy. I wuz a-talkin' to this feller just outside the city, when he ups and tells me iffin he wuz a-runnin' he'd go over the line into South Carolina. Well, that made sense to me, so off I go. I git to Rock Hill, and I git my first lead. Seems some folks thar recollected a good-lookin', young couple with blond hair trapsin' through on thar way to Charleston. I wuz shore hit wuz Ivy and Sam. But, the last person I talked to said the two had some fallin' out, and the man goes off and leaves the woman. Said he heard the man yell back she whined more'n his old hound dog. Best I can tell, he headed off, and left her high and dry."

"Was Ivy still there?"

"No she weren't. That's whar everthang got hard agin. I looked and looked and couldn't find her nowhars. She shore weren't in inny of the towns 'round thar. I kivered ever one of them. I wuz just 'bout to give plumb up and hightail hit back home, when I ups and comes to this here farm. The guy tells me he thanks somebidy might've took up in an old abandoned shack down the road a piece. Shore 'nuff, hit wuz Ivy."

"Where is she now?"

"She wouldn't come back with me. Said she wern't goin' nowhar with some man she didn't know. She wuz lookin' right bad. I brung her food to last her a spell and told her to clean herself up, and I'd brang you to git her."

"Besides being hungry and dirty, how was she?"

"Iffin you axing me 'bout her mind, I don't rightly know. She's doin' none too good, I'd say. Got right frantic when I tried to talk her into comin' back with me."

"Are you up to traveling again this morning?"

"I reckon so. Are we headin' south?"

"I want to go to my farm west of Boone and get Ivy's sister first. I'm thinking we might need Leah to help with Ivy."

"That thar might not be a bad idee."

"I'll even give you a warm bed tonight."

"I hain't in inny shape to lay down in no clean bed. Just a pallet on the floor will do me fine."

Luke left to go to the stable. He would need another horse and a side saddle for Leah.

CHAPTER FOURTEEN

Found

They'd just finished supper when Leah heard someone ride into the yard. She peeped out the larder door and saw a strange, grimy man dismount. She grabbed the muzzleloader she kept by the door. Luke needed to get her a better gun if he kept leaving them alone. She took a deep breath and walked out.

"Hold it right there, mister." She aimed the gun. "What do you want?"

"It's okay, Leah," Luke said, as he walked from the barn.

"Luke!" She set the rifle down and ran toward him. "I'm so glad to see you! You weren't gone long. Have you found Ivy?"

"Zeb found her, but let us get our horses stabled, and we'll be in and tell you everything. I hope supper's ready. I'm hungry."

"Granny Em fixed a squirrel stew. Let me go tell her to get it ready again. We've already eaten."

"That little gal's got a whole heap of gumption," Leah heard Zeb say as she walked away.

"That she does," Luke said and laughed, as if he were pleased.

Luke told them Zeb's story as he tried to eat. Zeb finished his meal much before Luke, since he said little.

"I might need you to see to Ivy, Leah."

"I'll be happy to go with you, but Ivy will listen to you better than she will me."

"We don't know what Ivy's been through," Luke told her. "I'm thinking she might need a woman to talk to."

"Oh, I see." Leah realized what Luke was saying. He was afraid Ivy had been dishonored. "Of course I'll go. Do we need to take Patsy, too?"

"I'd prefer Patsy stay here with Granny, but we'll take her if that's what you think best."

"What had you rather do?" Leah asked Patsy.

"I'd rather stay here. If I go down there, I'm afraid I might end up a slave again, no matter what those papers say. But, if you need me to go, Miss Leah, I'll go for you."

"What do you think, Granny Em?" Leah asked.

"I don't guess it would be proper for a young, unmarried woman to go off with two men, who weren't related, but we don't have to say anything about this part of it, do we?"

"Are you afraid to go with us, Leah?" Luke asked.

"Oh, no. I wouldn't be afraid to go anywhere with you, Luke. I trust you completely. I just don't want to do anything that would put us in a worse situation."

"The only consequence I could see coming out of this is you might have to marry me if we're found out, but that wouldn't be a bad thing in my eyes."

"Mine, either." She smiled and looked him straight in the eyes.

"Can you be ready to go after breakfast in the morning?"

"Yes, what will I need to take?"

"Pack a light bag for Ivy and one for you. I don't know if we'll be going to Salisbury or Anson County from South Carolina. It will depend on Ivy, but, since she ran away, I don't expect she'll want to come back here. We can buy you more clothes if need be, however."

"I'll go start packing now." She paused. "I am so glad you're back, and this didn't take you all winter."

"I am, too, but it's not over yet."

They mounted and rode off just after breakfast. Leah hated riding sidesaddle, but she knew she must. One of these days someone needed to invent pants or a skirt where a woman could ride astride, and it not be considered improper.

From Boone, they turned south toward Lenoir. This side of the mountain didn't seem as long, but it was still steep. At least the toll road seemed in pretty good shape.

They made Lenoir by midafternoon, and Luke decided to go on toward Hickory Tavern. He had a friend from college whose parents owned a farm near there. He'd visited them once before, and he felt sure they'd be able to stay the night.

Luke introduced everyone, but Leah barely heard, because she felt too exhausted from riding all day. She did remember Luke's friend was Joshua Everett and his wife, Margaret. Joshua's mother saw how tired Leah looked and whisked her off to freshen up for supper.

Leah did feel better once she washed her face and hands and changed to a clean dress. The meal was good, and Leah felt better after she ate. Zeb had refused to come to the table. He accepted a plate and took it out back to eat. He said he would bunk down in a clean barn stall.

"I don't know what this country is coming to," Leah heard Mr. Everett tell Luke. "I'm afraid we're headed to a great rift. I just hope it doesn't lead to war."

"Which side would you and Josh be on, if it did come to war?"

"I don't know. We've never owned slaves. We've always hired any extra work we needed doing, but we raise mainly corn, and it doesn't take the work some crops do. I'd have a hard time fighting against my neighbors, though. I just don't know. I hope it doesn't come to that."

Leah retired after supper. Luke stayed up to visit some more. She and Luke were both up early the next morning, but so were the others. Leah had donned her dress from yesterday. She would just ride all day, so there would be no sense in dirtying another one. Luke had milked with Joshua, and Leah helped Margaret strain the milk.

They ate a hearty breakfast, and Mrs. Everett even packed them a dinner. They were on their way again soon after breakfast.

"Are you all right?" Luke asked her.

"Yes, why?"

"You seemed awfully tired last night, and you haven't talked much or laughed since we left."

"You ought to try riding sidesaddle and see how you feel." She said it lightly, so it wouldn't sound as if she complained.

"Perhaps I should have bought a wagon."

"No, this is faster, and I want to get to Ivy as quickly as I can." He nodded.

They made it to Charlotte, but they pushed to get there by dark. They found rooms in an inn on the outskirts and ate supper.

"Zeb tells me Ivy isn't that far away, so, I'm sending Zeb out in the morning to purchase a wagon or carriage. They'll take one look at him and give him a better price than they would me."

Leah smiled. Even a hard wagon seat sounded good right now. She felt sore and stiff from being on the saddle so long, and her back ached like a toothache. Well, she didn't exactly know what a toothache felt like, but she'd heard Granny Em say that. They ate supper and went straight to bed.

"When Leah went to the dining room the next morning, Luke sat waiting for her. "Zeb got us a nice carriage that should be more comfortable. I've already loaded my things. Let's eat breakfast, and then we'll get yours."

Leah nodded. "I have everything already packed."

Zeb drove the carriage for them. The time went quickly since the carriage made it easier to carry on conversations with Luke.

They went straight to the little dilapidated shack where Ivy had been staying. Zeb stayed with the carriage, while Luke and Leah went in.

When Ivy opened the door, she didn't say a word. She left the door open and walked to the corner where a dirty, torn quilt lay on the floor. She sat down and hung her head. She wouldn't look at Luke or Leah.

Leah's heart went out to Ivy. Never in her wildest imagination did she consider she might find Ivy like this. The one-room shack still held the dust and dirt from years of abandonment, and Ivy hadn't tried to clean. It looked as if she'd washed herself and her clothes, but her clothes bore stains and her hair hung in tangled strands.

Luke stood on the other side of the room, close to the door he'd shut. He looked unsure of what he should do. Leah gave him a quick smile to let him know she wanted him to stay.

"Ivy," she said. Ivy didn't look up. Leah sat down on the quilt. "Ivy?" Still no response came. Leah reached over and pulled Ivy into her arms. Ivy didn't resist, but she started crying, and Leah just held her and rocked her back and forth. When she noticed Ivy's tears had subsided, Leah pulled back, but held Ivy's hands in hers. "It'll be okay, Ivy. We'll take care of things."

Ivy looked up then. She stared at Leah, and then she looked over at Luke. "I'm sorry." she said to him. "I'm so sorry."

Luke came closer, then. He pulled over a broken chair, set it close to Ivy and Leah, and sat down. "It's okay now," he told Ivy. "We've found you and everything is going to be all right."

"No it's not," Ivy said. "Nothing will ever be right again."

"Do you want to tell us what happened?" Leah asked. Ivy said nothing.

"We want to help, Ivy," Luke said. "You can't stay here with no way to get food and with winter coming on. We're going to have to get you to a safe, clean place."

"I'm not going back up the mountains," she said in a determined voice, the first emotion she'd shown, other than the tears. "I'm never going up the mountains again."

"You don't have to, Ivy. We'll take you any place you want to go, as long as it is a place where you'll be safe."

Ivy looked Luke in the face. "I have nowhere to go."

"You can go home to Gold Leaf, Ivy," Leah told her. "Paul wrote us a letter. He said Mama's not doing well. I think she's worried herself sick over you. Paul wants us to go home. He said we won't have to marry anyone we don't want."

Ivy shook her head almost vehemently. "I can't go home. Not now."

"I'll take you to Salisbury, then," Luke said. "You liked it there."

Ivy didn't say anything but hung her head. Leah didn't know if she was considering going to Salisbury or not.

"I'm going to have a baby," she finally said without looking up.

Leah sat back, stunned. She looked at Luke and he looked anxious, or was it hurt?

"Do you still want to marry me?" Luke asked. "Do you want me to give your baby a name?"

Leah wanted to cry out and tell him he shouldn't ask such a question. What about his promise to her? But, he'd only promised no matter what happened, he'd always love her, and he'd work for them to be together. He didn't promise he wouldn't take care of Ivy. She could see Luke's viewpoint. He'd taken Ivy from her home, and she'd been unhappy enough to run away. Luke felt partly responsible. He wanted to save Ivy from being totally ruined, and he must also be thinking of the innocent child.

"No," Ivy shook her head slowly this time. "We'd only make each other miserable. We're too different . . . worlds apart really. There's a better way." She looked at Leah. "You know herbs and remedies, Leah. I know you know some that will cause a miscarriage. I've heard you tell pregnant slaves you couldn't give them certain medicines for that very reason. Give them to me, Leah. Please help me. Can't you see it's the only way?"

Leah saw Luke recoil and pull back. Leah didn't move. She willed herself to use a calm, soft voice. "That's not the answer, Ivy. That will just bring more grief and heartache down the road. You know it's wrong. You don't want to take an innocent little baby's life . . . your baby. Think of what a beautiful child it will be."

"What then? I'll be an outcast. What kind of life is that to bring a child into?"

"We'll go to Dr. Moretz and keep your pregnancy a secret. When you deliver, Luke and I will take the child and bring it up as ours. You can go back to the plantation and Mama." She looked at Luke. She hoped she'd not spoken something he wanted no part of, but he nodded at her. *Dear Luke.*

"If you won't give me anything to take for it, I guess that's my only choice."

"Let's get you out of here, then." Leah rose and helped Ivy up.

Zeb drove them back toward Charlotte. Ivy leaned back and closed her eyes.

"I was unhappy at Luke's farm," Ivy finally said, "but I thought I would be shamed if I went home. When we traveled to Boone, I looked for someone who would take me away from it all. At the church service, a handsome young man began eyeing me. He had blond hair and blue eyes and looked more like me than Luke. He turned out to be more like me in other ways, too." She looked up and laughed an eerie laugh that held no humor or mirth.

"His name's Sam Whitley, and he's the preacher's son. I thought I would be safe with him. We went outside behind the church and talked during the service. I flirted merciless, and he kissed me until I was breathless. I told him how I felt, and he asked me to come away with him. He wanted to leave, too. He'd grown unhappy being the son of a preacher. He said people expected too much of him. He promised to take me to Charleston, a real city with plenty to see and do. He said he knew how to get us plenty of money to spend."

"I slipped out of the house that night, and he met me with horses. We skirted past Boone and headed south, but we stayed on the back roads and had little contact with anyone. The first night we stayed with friends Sam knew, and he was a perfect gentleman. Then we had to camp out. Sam said we should share bedrolls in order to stay warm and safe, and one thing led to another. I knew it was wrong, but I felt sure Sam would marry me.

"In Charlotte, Sam went to a man who'd been printing bank notes. He gave him a small bag of money, and the man gave Sam two large bags he'd printed. I asked Sam where he'd gotten the money to pay the man with, and he said from his father. I later learned he'd stolen it from the church offerings. That's when I began to question what we were doing.

"Sam said he intended to take the counterfeit money to Charleston to give us a start. I asked him what he was going to do in Charleston, and he said he hadn't decided, but he might gamble in order to switch some of the bogus money and buy a saloon or some type of business.

"I didn't want to be associated with a bar. That's not the life I'd imagined us having together. I began to question Sam more, and I began to see he had no desire to be part of decent society. He said he wanted to experience life and have a good time. We started arguing, and he called me vile names. He walked out on me in Rock Hill. I tried to find a temporary job to get some money, but the only things offered were jobs where I'd have been treated even worse than Sam had treated me. Because of the way some of the men looked at me, I became afraid, and I felt alone and helpless.

"I'd soon spent all the money I had, so I wandered away from town and stumbled on the abandoned shack. I became sick and despondent. I lost all sense of time, and I lost me for a while. That man you sent, the one who's driving the carriage, came. When I wouldn't go with him, he brought me enough food to last a couple of weeks and said he would bring Luke back."

She looked at them, and Leah reached over and patted her hand. "I'm so sorry all this has happened, Ivy, and I want you to know I still love you, and God loves you."

"I was so dumb and naïve. I thought most men were like Father or Luke. I just didn't know. If I could go back, I would marry Lawrence. I think he and I would have suited each other."

"How would you feel if Lawrence would marry you now?" Luke asked.

"No one but you would be willing to marry me now, and you'd only do so because you feel guilty about what happened." Ivy looked at Luke. "You shouldn't, you know. You told me what the farm would be like. In fact, it was actually much nicer than you said. I was set on going, but I didn't know I would feel so isolated there or hate it so much. Despite what you said, I expected a small plantation with servants. When it didn't turn out to be like that, I obsessed over leaving. I would have done whatever it took to get away. Sam treated me okay, until I started complaining. Things could have been much worse. He didn't beat me or abuse me. I think when we first left, he intended to marry me, but then I began to get on his nerves. As it turned out, he wasn't what

I wanted, and I wasn't what he expected. So, here I am, and to answer your question, if by some miracle Lawrence would have me, yes, I would marry him. I'd be on a plantation, and I'd be close to Mama."

They headed north, came to an inn, and got rooms for the night. They ate supper without much conversation and retired.

Ivy fell asleep quickly, but Leah had more difficulty. Luke must have had trouble, too, because she heard him moving around in the room next door.

She got up and quietly got dressed. She took her Bible from her bag, but there wasn't enough light to read, and she didn't want to wake Ivy. She went to the door and peeped into the hallway to find it empty. She walked the few steps to Luke's door and listened. When she heard movement again, she tapped lightly on his door.

"Is something wrong?" he asked, when he opened the door and saw her standing there. He hadn't undressed.

"No, I just couldn't sleep, and I heard you moving about, so I got up. Is there someplace I could read without disturbing Ivy?"

"Let's go downstairs. We'll see what we can find. Perhaps we can get a table in the dining room."

The dining room stood empty, but the fire still burned brightly in the fireplace, and a few of the tables had a lit candle. Luke led her to a table by the fireplace, which had a candle burning. "How's this?" he asked.

"Fine," she said and sat down in the chair he held out for her.

"I don't want to disturb your reading, but do you feel like talking?"

"Sure."

"I wanted to thank you for the way you handled things with Ivy today. I was so glad you were there. I don't know what I would've done if I'd been by myself. It shocked me when she said she was with child. I don't know why. I'd known it would be a possibility. When she asked you to help her get rid of it, I felt so disgusted that

I think I would have left the room if you hadn't been there. At first, the only solution I could think of was to marry Ivy myself. I was relieved when she turned me down. You were wonderful, Leah."

"When you asked Ivy if she still wanted to marry you, I was terrified. I wanted to scream at you not to do it. When she said it wouldn't work, I could breathe again."

"I'm sorry, Leah. I've got to remember whatever I do now affects you, too. It's not just me anymore. If I sacrifice, it will be sacrificing you, too."

"What would you have done if Ivy had wanted to marry you?"

"Died on the inside and lived in misery. You need to remember I promised to marry her, and it's essential for me to be a man of my word. It's crucial for you to be able to trust me. If I were the kind of man who would break his word once, then I would do so again, even with you."

"You'd have made an accomplished attorney. You're adept at arguing a case."

"You're good at understanding my arguments."

"You mentioned Lawrence today. What are you thinking in regards to him?"

Luke looked at her strangely. Was there a hint of jealousy in his eyes?

"I know Lawrence has been yearning for Ivy for a long time. I have reason to believe he may still want to marry her. He's a good man. He'll take care of her and would never hurt her."

"Are you sure you want to do this to him, and I'm not just talking about the baby. Ivy is not an easy person to live with. She can wear away a person, until they are threadbare. That seems to be what happened to Sam."

"Lawrence is not Sam. Why are you so against this, Leah? Do you still have feelings for Lawrence yourself?"

Leah looked at Luke in disbelief. She couldn't believe he had just asked her that.

"I've never had those kinds of feelings for Lawrence. You are the only man I've ever loved enough to marry, Luke."

Luke suddenly stood. "Well, I'm getting sleepier. What about you? Are you ready to go back up?

Leah nodded and got up. She hadn't read her Bible, but Luke seemed to be in a hurry to get away from her. They walked upstairs without a word.

"Goodnight," he said at her door, and walked down to his.

"Goodnight," Leah said as she opened the door and went in.

Something didn't feel right. Leah lay in bed and thought about the things Luke had said. Was he hoping Leah had feelings for Lawrence, because Luke still wanted to marry Ivy? It almost seemed like it. Did having the most beautiful wife on his arm mean so much to him? Had he been in love with Ivy from the very first and still wanted her, regardless of anything else. If that were true, why had he told Leah something different?

CHAPTER FIFTEEN

Doubts

Luke lay in bed emotionally exhausted, but sleep eluded him. First there'd been Ivy. She had run off with a man and spent several nights with him. Now he and Leah would have to help her through the consequences.

He shouldn't have offered to still marry Ivy, however. He'd recognized the terrible fix she was in and knew he'd once promised to marry her. Yet, once he'd made the offer, he'd regretted it. God wanted a couple to be totally committed to each other in marriage, and Luke wouldn't have been doing that. He was so glad she'd said no.

That Ivy wanted to get rid of her child had been the worst part of all. The very thought repulsed him.

Then there was Leah. Leah had handled the situation wonderfully. Luke would never have thought to hide Ivy away and raise the child for her. It was a viable solution, and one they could offer Ivy right away, because it didn't involve anyone else. How he loved Leah!

But he wasn't sure she loved him in the same way. He feared Leah might love Lawrence more. Hadn't she told Luke herself, if her family had wanted her to marry Lawrence instead of Archibald, she wouldn't have run away. Did Leah want a chance with Lawrence?

Lawrence had once told Luke he'd been in love with Ivy for a long time, but he'd kept it to himself and adored her from afar. What would Lawrence think of her running away with Luke, his best friend? Luke hoped he'd be able to explain it and that Lawrence would understand. Accepting a pregnant Ivy would be even harder, however. Would this complicated mess ever be worked out? He'd thought if he could just find Ivy, settle things, and get on with his life, things would be better. Now he'd found Ivy, but things were more complicated than ever.

Luke slept little that night. He tossed and turned and stayed awake more than he slept. He got up early and went to find Zeb. He thanked the man profusely for all his help, reimbursed him for the money he had used to buy food for Ivy, gave him the money they'd agreed upon, and added extra money for his faithful service. Zeb would head back toward the mountains, and Luke would take the carriage north-northeast to Salisbury.

When Luke went back inside, Leah and Ivy were up. They ate breakfast but said little. Ivy looked rested. She'd changed to a better dress, and Leah must have done her hair.

Luke looked at Leah. When she looked at him, he saw questions in her eyes, but he didn't want to open Pandora's box. The less said the better until he could be sure how she felt. He needed to pull back from Leah until he figured out how things really stood between them. He certainly didn't want to go rushing into things with Leah the way he had with Ivy. He needed to wait and see what happened. Leah seemed to like Lawrence, Lawrence liked Ivy, and Ivy didn't seem to like anyone very much, unless it was herself. As for Luke, he loved Leah, but that didn't mean she loved him. When she had said she did, she could have just been caught up in the moment. Hadn't she just repeated what he'd said each time?

214 SOWN IN DARK SOIL

Leah looked at Luke. *What could be wrong now?* She thought when Ivy refused his offer, they'd be able to start their own courtship and life together. Surely he didn't still love Ivy? Her heart missed a beat. *Perhaps he had been so hurt when Ivy ran away that he had turned to me in his pain.* Now with Ivy back and needing someone, maybe he no longer wanted Leah. Ivy had rejected Luke again, but wasn't it human nature to want what you can't have?

Leah thought that maybe she should have played hard to get, but she hated playing games. That's one reason she didn't like plantation life. Society there had become a series of games played to a specific set of rules. Leah preferred plain truth and honesty.

They finished breakfast almost in silence. When they went to the carriage, Zeb had already left, and Luke got up front to drive.

"I'll ride with you for a while," Leah told him. "We can talk and you can show me some points of interest along the way."

"No, you'll be more comfortable inside, and I have some things I need to sort through in my mind."

Leah crawled in the coach with Ivy. She tried not to be hurt by Luke's words, but she was. He didn't want to talk with her. He must be thinking about Ivy.

"Thank you for coming for me, Leah," Ivy said. "I know I haven't always treated you well, but I'd like for us to get closer. I'd like for us to act like the sisters we are."

"I'd like that, too, Ivy." *But, not if you take Luke from me.* Ivy wouldn't really be taking Luke from her though, would she? Luke had been Ivy's first.

The trip to Salisbury seemed to take forever. Leah couldn't read in the bumpy carriage, so she watched the scenery move by. She longed for Luke to come back to her. This wall he'd built between them pressed in upon her and made it hard to breathe. She felt the sharp pain of rejection.

Ivy turned sick, and Leah banged on the carriage with her fist to get Luke to stop. As soon as he pulled the carriage over, Leah helped Ivy out, and her breakfast came up.

Luke jumped down and looked concerned. "Maybe you'd feel better if you rode up front with me," Luke said to Ivy. "It may sway, but I don't think the ride is quite as bumpy up there, and you'll definitely get more fresh air." Luke gently helped Ivy into the seat beside him. Leah quickly got back in the carriage. She already felt tears trickling from her eyes. Luke didn't say a word to her. He got into the driver's seat, beside Ivy, and they continued down the road.

Leah's tears burst forth then. She sobbed until her breath would hardly come. No one would hear her in the noisy carriage. Yet, her frustrations and hurt didn't leave her but seemed to grow stronger. She ached inside and out.

Luke had asked the innkeeper to pack them a dinner. They stopped to eat it beside a stream where Luke could water the horses. Leah wouldn't look Luke in the eye, because she feared tears would come pouring down again.

Luke and Ivy sat in the grass and ate. Leah grabbed an apple and walked slowly about as she ate it. She wasn't hungry anyway. Luke didn't say anything to her, but she could see him talking with Ivy.

When they got back in the carriage, Ivy felt better and got inside the coach with Leah. She looked at Leah carefully.

"You don't look like you feel well, either," she said.

"I don't feel my best."

"Well, maybe when we get to Salisbury, you'll feel better. Dr. Moretz will see to you."

The morning had been long, but the afternoon stretched on forever. They finally made it to Salisbury about dusk, but, when Luke stopped the carriage, they weren't at the Moretz house. They were at another inn.

"I'm going to check us in here for tonight," he told them. "I think it's better Frances doesn't know you're here. I'll go talk with Father and be back. I'll order your supper brought to your room."

Supper looked good, but Leah had no appetite. Ivy ate most of hers. Afterwards, Leah took out her Bible and read.

She read in Psalms, where she'd always found the most comfort, but they helped little this time. She prayed and poured her heart out to God. Her silent tears flowed as she prayed, not only from the hurt and pain, but also from the emotion of feeling God's presence envelope her. She would focus on God and His love and make that enough. "But, I'm going to need Your help," she whispered. "I don't have the strength to forget about Luke on my own."

"Leah, what's wrong?" Ivy asked when Leah raised her head. Her voice held real concern.

"It was just a moving prayer," Leah told her.

"You're close to God, aren't you? I mean you have that personal relationship I've heard some preachers mention."

"He's my strength."

"I want that in my life, too. I need some changes and direction. Do you think God can forgive what I've done?"

Nothing Ivy could have said would have shocked Leah more. "There's nothing we can do that God won't forgive. He has that much love and mercy."

"What do I need to do?"

Leah turned to John 3:16, 14:6, and other verses, which explained salvation, and she helped Ivy with the prayer to ask Christ into her life. There were tears in Ivy's eyes when Leah looked up, and Leah hugged her. At least one good thing had come from this mess.

Luke brought Dr. Moretz back with him. The older man hugged both the girls. "It's so good to see you again," he said, but he looked at Leah.

"Luke tells me one plan is for Ivy to have the baby in secret and give it up for adoption, maybe to Luke and Leah," Dr. Moretz said after they sat down.

"Yes, that's what I agreed to," Ivy confirmed.

"I haven't told you the specifics of this, Ivy," Luke said, "but I plan to go see Lawrence. I want to ask if he's willing to marry you before the baby is born. This might actually be the best answer of all, because you'd get to keep your baby, but I need your permission to tell Lawrence the full story. I know him very well, and I'm sure he will always keep your secret, no matter what he decides. I know he's always cared deeply for you, and I think he should be given this option." Luke said this to Ivy, but he kept glancing at Leah.

Ivy considered what Luke said for a minute. "Yes, but make Lawrence promise to never tell a soul before you say anything to him about me."

"I shall."

"What do you think about this second plan, Leah?" It was the first time Luke had spoken directly to her all day, and it surprised her. She thought for a minute, too.

"I think this might be the best for Ivy. Lawrence is a decent man, and he'll be good to her. If he's willing to claim Ivy's baby as his own, he'll be a good father, too. Ivy will be getting back to the lifestyle she prefers, and she'll be close to Mama."

"You have no reservations, then?" Luke asked.

"No," Leah replied. "Any I've had in the past have just been wiped away. Ivy has just accepted Christ as her Savior, and I'm sure she will make a better wife." Let Luke make of it what he would. If being unequally yoked with Ivy had been the biggest stumbling block to him marrying her, then Leah didn't want to feel guilty for withholding the news. She wanted Luke, but not by deception.

"That's wonderful!" Luke exclaimed.

"It's good news, indeed," Dr. Moretz agreed.

"Father has something he wants to show you," Luke told them. "When I met and married Frances, she lived with her mother in a small house here in Salisbury. Her mother has since died, and I've been renting the house. The tenant just vacated it, and I think it would be a good place for you to stay while you're in town. I'll hire a chaperone, who will also serve as housekeeper and maid, and a gardener, who'll also drive you. I know just the closed-mouth people to ask. I think it'll be better if Frances knows nothing about all this. I don't want her to even know you are in town. She's been wanting to visit her sister in Charlotte, so I think I might send her and the children on that visit. What do you ladies think about moving to the house?

"It sounds like just the thing," Ivy said.

"Yes, it's a perfect solution," Leah agreed.

"Let me show it to you, then."

The house was made of tan stones with black shutters. It had a long kitchen area with a fireplace at one end and the dining table at the other. The sitting room seemed small but adequate. The upstairs held three tiny bedrooms, and there was even a cute little garden area enclosed in a fence out back.

"It's lovely," Leah said, and it was, but Leah suddenly longed for the mountain farm and Granny Em.

If Lawrence would marry Ivy quickly, Leah would enjoy her visit here. If the time stretched into months of waiting for Ivy to deliver the baby and waiting until the baby was old enough to travel, Leah wouldn't like it. The mountain farm felt every bit as much like home as Gold Leaf ever had.

The two men took Ivy and Leah back to the inn and made plans for them to move into the little house as soon as Dr. Moretz could procure the staff. Dr. Moretz kissed Ivy and Leah on the cheek and said good night. Luke didn't seem as withdrawn, but he still watched Leah with uncertainty.

———————

Luke planned to leave for Anson County as soon as he could. He didn't know how long he'd be gone, but he hoped he could talk with Lawrence, and they could both return quickly.

"Luke, if I've done something wrong, I wish you'd just tell me what it is," Leah said at the breakfast table. She sounded a little like Granny Em coming directly to the point.

He sat up straighter. "You haven't done anything wrong. I'm sorry if I gave you that impression."

"You have been treating her rather coldly," Ivy said. "I've noticed it, too."

Luke felt the reprimand and it shamed him. "Go down the street with me for a short walk," he told Leah.

"Gladly."

"I'll just go up and lie down," Ivy said. "I only had toast and tea this morning, but my stomach still feels unsettled."

"I'll be up shortly to check on you," Leah told her.

Luke tucked Leah's hand into his arm as they began their walk, and he felt his blood rushing. Even his ears were pounding.

"I'm sorry," he began. "I know I haven't been myself lately. I guess I've been more tired than I'd realized, and trying to get everything worked out for Ivy has consumed me."

"I can understand that, Luke, but before you would talk with me about your worries. I miss that. I miss the closeness we've shared." She stopped talking, because the tears had begun to well up in her eyes.

"When did I become such a crybaby?" she shook her head, as tears silently ran down her cheeks. She seemed disgusted with herself, although she tried to smile.

"I'm sorry, Leah. I've been worried, not only because of Ivy's situation, but because I've been so afraid things might not work out for us. I've feared losing you. I didn't mean to hurt you. That's the last thing I'd ever want to do. "

"You do have that power over me, Luke. I've bared my heart to you and laid it at your feet. It's exposed now and easily hurt."

"Oh, Leah, I do love you." In that moment, he had no doubts. "Please bear with me. With all that's happened lately, I get confused. Sometimes I don't know what to think. Please be patient with me."

"As long as everything is right with us, I can bear anything. I can't tolerate a wall between us or for you to pull away from me." Now the tears flowed again.

"No, no, darling," Luke took his thumb and rubbed her tears away. "I've been so stupid. I was afraid I'd get hurt, and I didn't want to move too fast this time. I wanted you to be sure of your feelings, too. I see how wrong I've been. Please forgive me."

"Of course, but we need to trust each other. You should know I would never hurt you."

He knew she was right, but how could he be sure? He'd thought that of Ivy at first and look what happened.

"Thank you for the walk." Her smile still seemed tentative, but he didn't know what else to say and remain honest.

Luke rode toward Anson County on horseback. He felt sure he could make it to Lawrence's today if he rode steadily, since he'd started early.

He thought about Leah. He'd been miserable, too, when he pushed her from him. He needed her love as much as he needed food and water.

He felt better about her now, but he still couldn't entirely eradicate all the doubt. He knew Lawrence would make any woman a devoted husband. He could see Leah with someone like Lawrence better than he could Ivy. God help him, but he was still afraid of losing Leah.

Luke rode up to Lawrence's exhausted. Darkness had already fallen.

"Is something wrong?" he asked Luke. "You looked worried."

"There is a problem," Luke told him, "but I'm tired and hungry. "If I can get some food and a bed, I'll feel more like talking in the morning. It's a long story."

"Right away," Lawrence said and led Luke toward the kitchen.

Luke slept better than he expected. He woke up and found breakfast on the sideboard in the dining room. He couldn't tell if Lawrence had already eaten or not, but he helped himself and ate alone.

He finished eating and walked toward the stables when Lawrence came riding in. "Do you want to get your horse and join me?" he asked Luke.

"Sure, let's ride down to the river."

They rode at a good pace. Septembers were warm here, but not as hot as June had been. Luke tried to schedule his visits, so he never came in July or August. He didn't know how these flatlanders stood such heat.

They came to the river, which ran low this time of year. It would swell in the spring. They dismounted and tied the horses.

"We should have brought our fishing poles," Lawrence said, "but we'll do that another day. How long can you stay?"

"Not long at all." They strolled up to the bank of the river and sat on a log they sometimes used for fishing. Lawrence sat quietly to give Luke time to collect his thoughts and begin when he was ready. That was one of the things he liked about Lawrence. He had patience.

Luke waited for a moment, then took a deep breath. "How do you feel about Ivy?" he began. "Are you still in love with her?"

"You know I am. I would do anything I could for her. Rumor has it she ran off with you, and Leah went to help. All three of you did disappear at the same time."

"There's some truth in that," Luke said, "but I'm interested in Leah." That was true, and Luke wanted to ease Lawrence into this. He knew Lawrence would be hurt by Luke's betrayal, so he would wait and tell him about it after he told everything else.

"First I need you to promise you will never tell another soul what I am about to share with you."

"Okay, if you think that's necessary, I promise."

"Ivy didn't like the mountains at all. I offered to bring her home, but she didn't want that. She ended up running away with a preacher's son. She thought she could trust him, but he used her and then abandoned her. She later found out she was with child."

Lawrence turned as white as a sheet, and Luke thought he might pass out. Instead he got up, turned, and walked away. Luke understood he needed a moment alone and let him go. When Lawrence finally turned and came back toward Luke, Luke got up and met him.

"You said you would do anything for her, Lawrence. Will you marry her quickly and claim the baby as your own?"

Lawrence walked off again, but he didn't go far this time. He stopped and stood for several minutes, then turned and walked the few steps back. "Is Ivy agreeable to this?"

"She is, and there's another good piece of news. Ivy has just accepted Christ as her Savior. She's just started her walk of faith, and she'll need patience and guidance, but I think you'll see a kinder, gentler Ivy. You're the right man for her, Lawrence. You're patient and steady."

"I still don't understand why she went off alone with a man. Didn't she know what would happen?"

"I don't think she did. She said she'd been naïve. She's always been protected and pampered, and that's what she expected."

"Did this man force her?"

"No. He maneuvered her and overcame her emotions."

"Does Ivy love him?"

"No. I think she may have been infatuated with him at first, but she definitely doesn't love him now."

"I want to talk with Ivy first, but I'll consider marrying her."

"Good enough. Can we leave tomorrow? The quicker we get this settled, the better for everyone."

"Is she showing yet?"

"No, I can't see any difference in her, so I'm certain no one will notice."

"We'll plan to leave tomorrow, then. Is she with your father?"

"She and Leah will probably be in a rental house of his. We didn't want Frances to get wind of this."

"Okay, then." Lawrence started to walk off.

"There's a couple more things."

Lawrence turned around.

"I need to tell you I planned to marry Ivy when we left here. I knew she didn't want to marry anyone else, and we both thought we were in love. I didn't know you were the one her family had planned for her to marry until later."

"What happened between you two?" Hurt flashed across Lawrence's face.

"Reality set in. Ivy wasn't who I thought she was, and she hated the farm and everything about the mountains. She even had problems with my Cherokee blood. We grew apart quickly. I'm sorry, Lawrence."

"And now it's you and Leah?"

"I sure hope so, but I need to ask you a favor. Talk to Leah and find out if she's really in love with you. I've got to know how serious she is about you, and if she'd rather marry you or me."

Lawrence looked at him as if Luke had suddenly grown horns. "Let me get this straight. You want me to marry Ivy but find out if Leah cares more about me than she does you?"

"That's right."

"Not for any reason. First of all, I can answer that right now. Leah respects me, but she does not love me and never has. You have no business marrying Leah if you don't trust her, but I know Leah. She's one of the most honest people I've ever known. I don't know what you're thinking, Luke. Maybe you aren't. It's just not like you to try to be underhanded. You'd better ponder this and decide what your feelings really are. If you feel you had to ask this of me, maybe you don't really love Leah. Now let's go to the house and make preparations to leave."

That night Luke thought about what Lawrence had said, and he knew his friend made some valid points. Luke had absolutely no reason to think Leah shouldn't be trusted. When he and she were talking, really talking together, he had no doubts. He believed what she told him. Perhaps what had happened between him and Ivy had affected him more than he'd realized.

He needed to trust Leah completely. They wouldn't have a chance of building a strong marriage if he didn't. He expected her to trust him, and she had more reason not to than he did. After all, he'd once been engaged to Ivy.

The one thing Lawrence had gotten totally wrong was Luke's love for Leah. That Luke had never doubted. He'd only doubted Leah's for him.

He remembered Shakespeare's *Othello*, where tragic events were set in place, all because Othello didn't fully trust Desdemona and because of his jealousy. All the while, Desdemona truly loved Othello. Luke vowed to not let his love for Leah end in tragedy from his own uncertainties, insecurities, and stupidity.

CHAPTER SIXTEEN

Pairings

Luke and Lawrence left very early the next morning and got
to Salisbury by evening. They went to the Moretz house first,
and Lawrence took his things to a spare bedroom. He would stay
here, like Luke, but he wouldn't mention Leah and Ivy around
the house. Frances and the children had left to visit her sister in
Charlotte, but the housekeeper and maid were still around.

Dr. Moretz invited them to supper. "The girls have moved," he
whispered, "but I'm not sure how prepared they'd be for supper
guests. I'll let you two go after supper, so you can have more private conversations, and I'll come over later."

Leah acted the perfect hostess. She introduced Mrs. Price as
their companion and housekeeper. She invited them into the sitting room and asked if they'd had supper. She offered them tea or
coffee, but they refused. Lawrence seemed eager to talk with Ivy
alone, and he took her to the garden.

Luke had watched Leah's reaction to Lawrence. She acted cor-
dial, but nothing more. If she had any feelings at all for him, she
gave no indication, and Luke felt sure he would be able to tell. He
felt ashamed of himself for even looking for something.

Luke and Leah sat on the sofa. Mrs. Price went up to her room
but said she would return in a few minutes. Luke got the feeling

she was giving them some privacy but letting them know she would be around.

"As you can see, I brought Lawrence back as quickly as I could." He smiled at her.

She smiled, too. "I see that. Has he agreed to marry Ivy?"

"No. He wanted to talk with her first, but I think it's likely."

"When that happens, what do you want me to do, Luke?"

"What do you mean?"

"Do you want me to go back to Gold Leaf when Ivy and Lawrence go, or do you want me to go back to the mountains with you?"

Luke sat in stunned silence for a moment. "What do you want to do?"

"I asked you first, and you shouldn't answer a question with a question. It's a bad habit of yours."

"I hoped you'd go back with me. I'd never considered you might want to go back to the plantation."

Leah breathed a sigh of relief. "I don't. I love the mountains and the farm. I'd much rather go back there, but will there be just the two of us traveling alone?"

"I haven't thought that far ahead. I'll talk to Father and see what he suggests. I noticed you said you loved the farm, but you didn't say you loved me." He wanted to say it teasingly, but it came out more serious.

"Oh, Luke, are you so unsure of me? You must know I love you with all of my heart."

"You didn't sound so sure of me, either when you asked if I wanted you to go back with me."

"I guess these feelings we have are new to us both, and we need time to adjust. We felt reluctant to share our feelings until things were settled with Ivy. I know the love I feel is so strong it almost scares me at times."

"I'll be glad when we can be together always, and I can *show* you how much I love you," Luke regretted saying it as soon as it was out of his mouth. He knew he had overstepped the bounds of propriety. He and Leah weren't even engaged yet.

Leah blushed, but looked him in the eye and said softly, "So will I."

Lawrence and Ivy returned, and they both looked elated. "We want to wed, as soon as everything can be arranged," Lawrence said.

"Congratulations!" Luke stood and shook his hand.

Dr. Moretz came, and they began to plan. Ivy wanted a small church wedding. She wanted a new dress, but Mrs. Price knew of a shop where some of the dresses were partially made and could be completed in a day or two. She planned to take Ivy and Leah tomorrow. Luke would be best man and Leah the maid of honor. There would be no other attendants. Dr. Moretz would give her away. Dr. Moretz said he'd take care of most of the arrangements, including procuring the church and pastor and inviting a few select guests. There would be enough prominent citizens to make it public, so it didn't seem like a quiet, hurried-up affair.

"Some people at home might talk," Lawrence told Ivy, "but they'll never be able to prove anything, and we'll handle it together."

Ivy nodded and smiled at him.

That night Ivy wanted to have a talk with Leah. It reminded Leah of the time Ivy had come to her to talk her into accompanying her and Luke to the mountains. Had that only been about four months ago? So much had happened, it seemed much longer.

"I'm so excited that I need to talk to someone. Lawrence was so wonderful when we talked. Do you know he's loved me for a long time, and I never guessed?"

"I don't think you gave him a chance to tell you. We ran off when Mama started talking of Lawrence courting you."

"We did, didn't we? How silly of me. Do you know Lawrence offered to not touch me as a husband until after the baby comes. He said that would give me a chance to get to know him better, but I told him I thought that would make our relationship more difficult. I think it's better to start off like we want it to be. After all, Dr. Moretz checked me out, and everything's fine."

"You do seem happy, Ivy, and I'm happy for you."

"I am, and I intend to be a good wife. Lawrence knows my feelings for him are new and just developing, but he said he'd treat me so well that I'll have to fall in love with him. I know love doesn't work that way, but I think we'll become a loving and devoted couple."

"I think so, too. Lawrence is a special man, and you're very lucky."

"I know it, and Luke is that kind of man for you. I expect you two will be getting married before long."

"He hasn't asked me yet."

"He will. Just don't expect me to come if you get married in the mountains. I plan to spend the rest of my life on level ground."

They got an early start the next morning. Leah enjoyed the dress shop more than she thought she would. This shop specialized in wedding and ball gowns.

Ivy chose a gorgeous white gown that gave her skin a healthy glow. It had a high neck with lots of lace. Rows of the same lace formed horizontal panels in the skirt, and each row down the dress got wider. Leah had never seen a more beautiful gown, and it suited Ivy as if it had been designed just for her.

The dress looked nearly finished. The dressmaker just needed Ivy to put it on in order to mark the final seams. It even had a lovely veil to go with it.

Ivy insisted Leah get a dress, too, and Leah knew she needed one. She hadn't packed anything suitable for a wedding. She hadn't realized there'd be one.

"Don't worry about it," Ivy said. "Lawrence is well-off, and he told me to get whatever I wanted, and he'd pay for everything."

Ivy helped her choose a lovely deep purple dress. The color suited Leah well. The style was simpler than Ivy's, but the fabric's shimmer made up for the lack of yards of lace.

Leah remembered the ivory dress and slippers she had taken to the farm. Since Ivy had decided to wear white, however, this purple one would be much better. Leah could wear her ivory one as her own wedding dress, and she hoped that day would come soon.

She did use some of her own money to buy an ivory veil to go with her dress in the mountains. She hoped she wasn't making a mistake by getting it before Luke actually proposed, but she decided to think positively. She hoped Luke would want to marry before winter.

Mrs. Price had turned out to be a jewel. Leah didn't know where Dr. Moretz had found her, but she knew how to get what they needed. She was a pretty woman in her mid-forties. Although she'd probably never been a beauty, she had a confidence about her and such a pleasant, cheerful attitude that it made her an excellent companion.

Ivy's wedding took place on Wednesday. The September day started off cool but turned comfortably warm. Luke had been given the job of getting Lawrence to the church—not hard, because Lawrence definitely seemed eager.

The men got to the church forty minutes early. As the service started, Lawrence and the pastor came into the sanctuary from the front side, where they would wait for the rest of the wedding party. Luke would lead Leah down the aisle, first, and Dr. Moretz and Ivy would follow.

When Leah came into the vestibule to take Luke's arm, she took his breath away. He had never seen her so dressed up, and she looked spectacular. He gladly escorted her down the aisle.

Luke noticed Lawrence's expression as Ivy came down the aisle, and he seemed mesmerized, too. Luke looked at her. She did make a pretty bride, but he looked across at Leah, who would outshine anyone. He couldn't wait to see her in a wedding dress. If she wore what she had on now, it would be fine with him.

The ceremony didn't take long. Afterwards, Dr. Moretz had arranged for a traveling photographer to come to the church and make an image of the wedding party.

Luke also had the photographer make one of Leah and him, as well. He really didn't need anything to remember this day by, however. The way Leah looked today would forever be etched in his memory.

Ivy chose not to hold a reception, and Dr. Moretz had helped Lawrence arrange for a special cottage where they would spend the night. Lawrence and Ivy went back to the little house to get Ivy's things first. They planned to head for Lawrence's plantation tomorrow morning. Leah and Luke wouldn't see them again.

Leah hugged Ivy. "I love you, Sis."

"I love you, too. Let's write each other."

When he took her back to the cottage, Luke said to Leah, "Come walk with me in the garden."

"The wedding was lovely," she told him as they strolled down a path.

"You're lovely," he replied. "You were the most beautiful woman I've ever seen at the church today."

"You must mean besides the bride."

"I meant what I said. That dress made your eyes look even greener. Your hair gleamed like my chestnut's coat in the sun, and your skin looked like sweetened cream. You took my breath away."

"You're the tall, dark, and handsome one. You're every girl's dream."

"I don't think so. I wasn't Ivy's. My Indian blood really doesn't bother you, does it?"

"No, I think the Cherokee are an admirable people, and you should be proud. Besides, maybe you were meant for me, not Ivy." She gave him a playful smile.

He couldn't help but laugh. "You know I think you're right about that."

He led her to a garden bench, sat her down, and got down on one knee in front of her. "Leah, would you do me the great honor of becoming my wife and make me the happiest man on earth?" He held out the emerald ring surrounded by diamonds.

Leah's eyes grew wide, and he heard her suck in her breath. He held his.

"Oh, yes, Luke. Yes, yes, yes."

He breathed again. He pushed the ring on her finger, and it fit perfectly.

"The ring is beautiful."

"It was my mother's. My father gave it to her as a gift, not for their engagement, but. I wanted you to have a ring for ours. I hope we can be married soon, before winter, but I wanted you to have a ring right now."

He pulled her to him and kissed her then. He lost himself in the kiss, and he knew without a doubt she loved him, too. He would never doubt her again.

"Would you prefer to marry quickly here, the way Ivy and Lawrence did, or get married after we get to the farm?"

"I'd prefer to get married in the mountains. I want Granny Em to be there," Leah replied.

"I hoped you'd say that, although I can see some advantages to getting married right away."

Leah laughed when she realized his meaning. Being married to this man was going to be fun.

"I would like to leave Friday or Saturday. Father's going to go back with us. He's already made plans to close his practice for a month. A younger doctor in town is going to take over his patients while he's gone."

"That's great. Maybe we can marry while he's there."

"That's what I'm hoping. He's looking forward to seeing Granny Em, too. They don't get together often."

"I'm looking forward to getting back to the farm."

"I'm glad to hear you say that. If you need to make any purchases for the wedding, while you're here, go ahead and charge them to me."

"That's okay. I have everything I need."

Luke wasn't sure if she was referring to purchases or him. He hoped the latter.

"Will there be room for me to take some fabric back, since it's cheaper here, too?" Leah asked almost as an afterthought.

"There's room for anything you want," he told her. "Do you need some money?"

"No, I have my own."

He wasn't sure if he liked that. He wanted to be the one providing for her. Yet, maybe he should view it as a compliment to him. This independent and self-sufficient woman didn't really need a husband to take care of her, yet she still chose to marry him.

Luke's father couldn't contain his delight when they told him about the engagement. "I thought you were smart enough to latch on to Leah," he said. "I know you well, and I've never met anyone more right for you. I think you two will be as happy as your mother and I were."

They started back early Friday morning. Father planned to go north to Salem and spend the night with Aunt Gracie. Luke figured his horses would go at a faster pace than the mules had, and he wanted to try to make Wilkesboro from Salem. This way, they wouldn't have to camp along the way.

Luke had sold the carriage for more than he'd paid for it and bought an almost new, covered farm wagon, which was even smaller and lighter than the last one. He'd bought two Belgian draft horses to pull it. He'd gotten a real bargain on them, for no one in the area seemed to want the pair. The farmers preferred the slower-pulling Suffolks for plowing, and the town folks didn't want a draft horse at all.

The Belgians would be suited to pulling the mountain, and, since he wasn't carrying much back, the pair should make it okay. He and his father could take turns riding their horses up the mountain, and they could even hook up their two horses to the wagon to help out, if need be, but he didn't think that would be necessary.

"What a beautiful pair of Belgians," Leah said as she came out of the cottage.

"How in the world do you know about draft horses?" his father asked her.

"I've ceased to be surprised at the extent of Leah's knowledge," Luke told him. "She has as good an education as mine and better in some areas, although I went to college for a year and studied college texts afterwards."

"I've decided to rent this house from Dr. Moretz," Mrs. Price told Luke and Leah before they pulled out. "Whenever you come to Salisbury, you are welcome to stay here or at least visit me."

Leah and Mrs. Price hugged good-bye. "If you ever need a place in the mountains, you come," Leah told her. "I could always make room for a friend like you."

"I'm going to miss you," Mrs. Price said. "You've become like a daughter to me."

"I adopted her as a daughter the first time I met her, too," his father said.

Luke knew Leah needed to hear some praise. She'd never had much of that, since her life had been lived in the shadow of the attention Ivy always drew. He felt terrible that he'd treated her somewhat like that at first, too. He'd been courteous to her at the dinner at Gold Leaf, but he'd barely noticed her that night. Only later, when they'd talked, did he realize they shared many of the same values. That's when she had begun to get his attention.

Leah also amazed him by how easily she could move among high society and still be perfectly at home in Oralee's primitive log cabin. She seemed to love the mountains as much as he did, and Luke felt truly blessed.

CHAPTER SEVENTEEN

Robbed

The overnight stay in Salem went much too fast. Luke had been a young boy the last time he saw his aunt, and she looked older than he expected. She welcomed them warmly, however, and hated to see them leave early the next morning.

They made good time. The Belgians handled better than the mules had, and they set a better pace.

They started out with all three of them in the wagon. Then, Luke and his father took turns riding their horse in front of the wagon, while the other one drove. They only stopped to eat the lunch Gracie had packed for them and water the horses.

"Eat well," Luke said. "It may be late before we reach Wilkesboro."

"There's enough left here that we can eat a snack," Leah said.

———

The ride to Wilkesboro didn't seem as far as the one from Charlotte to Salisbury had been, but it may have been farther. Luke had been out of sorts on the first one, and now he seemed happy and attentive. Leah still had a difficult time believing this amazing man had asked her to marry him. Granny Em would be just as pleased as Dr. Moretz, and Leah couldn't wait to tell her.

All three of them were travel weary when they got to Wilkesboro, and it had grown so dark Leah wondered how Luke could see to drive. The days were getting shorter now. Leah could also tell the air had become cooler here than it'd been in Salisbury. Luke pulled up to the inn and let them out before he went to stable the horses and wagon. Dr. Moretz got them two rooms. He and Luke would share one, and Leah would have one by herself. They took their things to the rooms and went to the dining area to order supper. Everything had been taken but vegetable soup with bread and cheese, so they ordered three.

Luke came in and joined them. "The stable owner acted very impressed with my horses. He offered me twice as much as I paid for them, but I want to keep them."

"You'll need them, since you sold the mules," Leah agreed.

"Your mother, you, and I stayed here on our trip back to the mountains when you were just two," Dr. Moretz said to Luke. "We were filled with happiness then. I'm so pleased you and Leah have found that with each other."

"Granny Em has promised to tell me the family history when we are housebound this winter," Leah said. "I can't wait to hear it. I understand Luke's mother was related to one of the braves who took Granny Em captive."

"It's quite a tale, but a long one." Dr. Moretz nodded. "Well, I'm tired. Are you two ready to call it a night?"

"Yes, I want to leave by daylight," Luke said, "so let's get to bed and get some rest."

Leah heard Luke knocking on her door to wake her before she realized she'd been asleep. She'd slept soundly.

She got dressed, packed, and they ate a breakfast of eggs, sausage, grits, and biscuits. Luke drank coffee, and Leah and Dr. Moretz had tea.

"I've already picked up our wagon and horses and brought them around," Luke told them. "The stable owner said a man offered to buy the Belgians, but he told him I didn't want to sell. There's a lot of interest in those horses."

They started off as soon as the sky had lightened enough to see. Leah pulled her shawl around her. Although she sat between Luke and Dr. Moretz, the morning air felt cold.

After leaving the town, they came around a curve to find three men on horseback blocking the road. Luke started to reach for his rifle, when one of the men drew his gun. "I wouldn't do that if I were you, mister," he said. By then the other two had their rifles pointed.

"Keep your hands in sight and get down. The woman, too." Leah's heart started racing. Was this going to be a repeat of the incident at Deep Gap?

"Now, start walking toward Wilkesboro. We need the team and wagon more than you do right now."

"If you're going to take the Belgians and wagon," Luke said. "Leave us the two saddle horses."

"That makes sense, boss," the youngest man said. "We don't need the extra horses to feed."

"We could sell them," the third man said.

"We don't have time for that," the boss replied. "Besides, I've found if you only take what you need, there's less chance of tripping up and getting caught. Get the saddle horses for them, Sam."

"Let them get them themselves," the third man said.

"You haven't got the brain of a sparrow," the boss told him. "I told Sam to untie the horses, because there could be a weapon back there somewhere."

Sam untied the horses and brought them over. When Leah saw his blond hair sticking out from beneath his hat and looked into his blue eyes, something clicked.

"Don't try to follow us, now," the boss said. "That'll be a sure-fire way to get shot."

"I plan to head back to town," Luke told him.

"Did you see the younger man, the good-looking one?" Leah asked when the men had left.

Luke gave her a piercing look. "What are you doing noticing how good-looking some other man is?"

Leah could have laughed, if Luke wasn't so serious and upset. "They called him 'Sam.' I think he may be Sam Whitley. He fits the description Ivy gave. And, Luke Moretz, no man on earth is as good-looking as you. You're good on the inside, too, and that's even more important."

Dr. Moretz did laugh at his son, and Luke gave a sheepish grin. "I'm going to ride quickly into Wilkesboro and get the sheriff," Luke said. "I'll tell him about Sam Whitley. Father, would you let Leah ride with you and go back to the inn? Go ahead and get two rooms. It looks like we are going to be delayed."

"All right, but are you sure you won't get jealous of me riding double with your fiancée?"

"I can see I'm not going to live that one down anytime soon," Luke said, as he galloped off.

Leah's dress pulled up above the ankle when Dr. Moretz put her on his horse and climbed up behind her. It wasn't seemly, but it couldn't be helped. Granny Em would say, "Desperate times call for desperate measures."

They had traveled most of the way to Wilkesboro when the sheriff, two deputies, and Luke rode up. The sheriff must have loaned Luke a rifle, since his had been in the wagon. He slowed and called out, "I'm going with them."

When she and Dr. Moretz got to the inn, they got two rooms again. She hoped the sheriff recovered the wagon and horses. All their things were in it. She sat down and prayed for a quick end to this, and that everyone would be safe.

"Do you want to try to catch a church service?" Dr. Moretz asked.

Leah looked down at her wrinkled everyday dress. The Lord would understand, whether or not anyone else did. "Yes, I think that would be good. Just let me wash my face and hands."

They went to the Presbyterian Church. Leah remembered it from the first time they came to Wilkesboro. The pastor had seemed friendly and invited them to come anytime.

The small church had already filled. Dr. Moretz slipped into an empty space in the pew on the left side, and Leah found one on the right.

The pastor spoke on putting trust in the Lord for all things. Leah looked over at Dr. Moretz, and he smiled. They needed to hear this today. Leah made an effort not to let her mind wander to worry about Luke. Instead, she concentrated on what Reverend Pharr said.

"That's what I needed," she told Dr. Moretz at the end of the service. "I'm so glad we came."

A couple of the better dressed women walked by Leah without speaking, but most of the women welcomed her. When she told them what had happened, they were understanding and said they would pray for the situation.

She and the doctor walked back to the inn and immediately went to dinner. The meal was good, and Leah felt more at peace after attending church. Dr. Moretz prayed for Luke's speedy and safe return when he asked the blessing, and Leah kept praying her own silent prayers.

"I wish I had something to read," Dr. Moretz said, when they'd finished.

"I know," Leah said. "Even my Bible was in the wagon. I hope they're able to recover everything."

"I wonder why they needed the wagon and team so badly. Most thieves would want to be on horseback."

"They must be hauling something heavy," Leah said. "Maybe they've stolen some gold or something."

Suppertime came, and Luke still had not returned. Leah went down with Dr. Moretz, but she ate little. What if something happened to Luke? What if he didn't come back? No, she shouldn't think such thoughts. She would pray him back unscathed.

By bedtime, Leah could do little but pace the floor. "Aren't you worried?" she asked the doctor.

"I'm concerned, but my getting upset won't help Luke. My medical bag is in the wagon, so I don't have anything to give you to help you sleep."

"I don't want the effects that drugs would have anyway."

"At least lie down and rest, even if you can't sleep," he told her. "Say your prayers, and that's bound to help."

Leah did as Dr. Moretz suggested. She prayed and prayed.

Suddenly she awoke to sounds coming from the hallway and Dr. Moretz's room. She must have finally dozed. She'd stayed in her dress, so she went to see what was happening.

Luke sat in a chair with his shirt torn and his arm bloody. The deputy handed the doctor his medical bag. She rushed to Luke's side.

"I'd better get back and check on the sheriff," the deputy said." We left him at the jail, since he'd been shot in the hand, and sent for Doctor Calloway."

"Thank you," Luke said to the deputy.

"How bad is it?" Leah asked as she gingerly started removing the bloody handkerchief.

"It's just grazed," Luke said, but he winced at her slightest touch.

She got the handkerchief off, poured some water into the basin, and began cleaning around the wound. It might be just grazed, but the bullet had taken a hunk out. At least it wasn't still in there. She looked up and saw Dr. Moretz standing watching her. She backed off to give him room.

"No, that's okay," he told her. "You're doing a good job. I could use your help in my practice. You remind me of my wife, and she was an excellent assistant."

The doctor came forward and applied a tincture. "Where did you learn your doctoring skills, Leah?"

"I've read all the books I could find and listened to the slaves who knew medicinal herbs. Most of the time, I took care of the slaves on the plantation. I've had some experience."

"I can tell."

"She's gentler than you, too," Luke said to his father.

Leah had just finished Luke's bandage when Dr. Moretz said, "I'm going down to the kitchen and see if I can find him anything to eat. He doesn't seem to have lost too much blood, and the arm should heal nicely. It'll be sore and painful for a while, though." Dr. Moretz left the door open as he went out.

"Oh, Luke, I've been so worried. I've prayed and prayed."

"Come here," he said and patted the knee on his good side.

She didn't question him, but sat in his lap and put her head on his good shoulder. He hugged her tightly with one arm. He kissed her lightly on the cheek. "I needed this," he said.

She didn't get a chance to tell him she did, too, because they heard Dr. Moretz on the stairs, and she jumped up. She was sitting in the other chair when he came in.

"I didn't realize it's as late as it is," the doctor said. "They're going to start serving breakfast before too long. What do you say we go down? The hot water is ready for tea."

"I'm ready," Luke said. "I haven't had anything to eat in almost twenty-four hours, and I'm famished."

"Do you feel like telling us what happened, son?" Dr. Moretz asked when they'd sat down for breakfast. "I'm guessing you got the team and wagon back."

"Yes, the wagon and team are at the stable, so we can leave in the morning."

"We'll see how you feel first," Dr. Moretz said, "but tell us what happened."

"They left a clear trail. It must have rained recently, and the Belgians' hoof-prints, along with the wheel marks, stood out. We followed the trail to a cabin out in the wilds to the southwest. The sheriff sneaked down to see what was going on and found five men, who had a printing press they needed to move. They had a heavy-duty wagon and a team of six, but I'm sure they would've never got the heavy press very far up the mountain with those. We later discovered they planned to take it somewhere in the Stony Fork area, east of Boone. They didn't really need our wagon, just the horses to go with theirs."

"I guess they used the printing press to counterfeit bank notes," Leah said.

"That's right," Luke said. "Since we were outnumbered, we decided to wait for an opportunity to jump them, and we ended up waiting for them to go to sleep. They left a guard out, but we thought he'd fallen asleep, too, so we went down. He must have been a light sleeper, because he woke up when we got near. He started shooting and woke the others. We were in a shootout but managed to rush them, anyway. I think some of them were confused and shot their own men. No one was killed, but some were wounded. I started using the barrel of my rifle, so a couple of them will wake up in jail with an awful headache. I got shot right before it all came to an end. The full moon gave some light, and the deputy found some lanterns, so we came back, although we had to go slowly in the dim light."

"Do you want me to give you something for pain?" Dr. Moretz asked.

"Yes, when I go upstairs. I'm tiring fast, and I'd like to get a nap."

They went upstairs, and Dr. Moretz went to help Luke into bed. He knocked on Leah's door a few minutes later.

"I thought you might want to walk to the stable with me and help me get our travel bags."

"Sure. I'd be glad to."

They brought the bags back to the inn, and Leah freshened up. Then, she read her Bible and said prayers thanking God Luke wasn't hurt worse.

Luke got up and ate lunch with them. He looked better, but his arm seemed to bother him.

"I want to go by the jail and see how things are going," Luke said after they finished eating.

"I'll go with you." Dr. Moretz looked at Leah.

"That's fine," Leah said. "I'll just go up and take a nap. I didn't sleep long last night, and I'd like to be fresh in the morning, in case we leave early."

Luke led the way to the jail. The deputy leaned back in a chair just outside the door and appeared asleep. He woke up when they came up and said the sheriff had gone home.

"How are things?" Luke asked.

"As well as can be expected, I guess. The sheriff will have to take it easy, until his hand heals, but at least they got his left one. None of the prisoners are bad off. It didn't take long to patch them up."

"What are you going to do about the printing press?" Luke asked. "The sheriff's going to see if he can get a crew to go get it. He thinks it might be good to have for evidence. It's partially disassembled, anyway. It won't be as hard to get here as it would have been to take it up the mountain."

"Speaking of Boone, is one of the prisoners a young man by the name of Sam Whitley?"

"Yes, he is. He wanted us to send his father word of where he is. He said his father's a preacher. Do you know him?"

"Not really. I've heard of him, and I went to one of his father's services in Boone."

"Do you want to talk with him?"

"I don't think that would be wise, son," Father said. "There might be repercussions. He could make things rough on the new bride and groom as they start their family."

"You're right." Luke knew what his father didn't want to say. He turned to the deputy. "We plan to leave in the morning. Thank the sheriff for me."

"I'll do that. You helped us catch them before they started the counterfeiting around here, so you helped us, too." They shook hands.

Luke went back to the inn, took some more pain medicine, and went to bed. He woke up for supper. His arm throbbed with intense pain, but he wanted to hold off taking any more pain medication. He needed to stay up so he could sleep some tonight. After missing sleep last night, he had his schedule all mixed up.

"If you want to go shopping, I'll give you some money," he told Leah. "Staying in the inn all the time must be boring."

"No, I don't need anything. I have my Bible to read now."

"You really do have a jewel, here," his father said. "Imagine a woman who turns down shopping. Your mother was the only other one I knew who'd do such a thing."

"I know. She's a rare one," Luke agreed with a smile.

After supper, they got together in the men's room and had a family devotion. Luke had missed doing this. He endured his aching arm as long as he could, but once the devotion was over he finally took something for pain and went to sleep.

Luke had a rough night. Without the pain medication, he didn't think he would have slept at all. He hoped resuming the trip wouldn't make things worse, but he felt a strong need to get home. They ate breakfast and left at daybreak.

His father insisted he drive instead of Luke. "Using your arm too much could break open the wound and start it bleeding again."

So, Luke sat on one side of Leah as they started off with his father on her other side. Luke would ride his chestnut a little later, but he needed to be near Leah for now. Finally, when the wagon ride became rougher, he got off to ride his horse.

"You go ride, too," Leah told his father. "I can drive the team for a while."

"You can handle a team of horses?" Luke asked. He didn't know why that surprised him. What couldn't she do?

"I can." Her eyes sparkled with amusement. "Can't any good farmer's wife?"

Leah drove until they started up the steeper incline. Then, she got out of the wagon and Father drove.

"Should I walk or ride?" Leah asked. "If I ride it won't be side saddle, and too much of my limbs might show, but we're family, aren't we?" She waited for his answer.

"Sure, can you mount by yourself?"

"I can try, but it would be easier in pants instead of a dress."

"Have you ever worn pants before?" Luke asked her. He knew she had an independent spirit about her.

"No. I haven't dared, but I've wanted to."

She tried to swing up into the saddle, but her skirts got in the way, and she fell back to the ground. She did manage to land on her feet.

"Wait there," his father said. "Let me help you. We don't need any broken bones on top of everything else." He helped her into the saddle, and then resumed his place on the wagon seat.

Luke and Leah rode ahead, so they wouldn't be behind the dust from the wagon. It felt good to have her riding beside him. He might have to think about getting her a horse of her own come spring.

He glanced over and saw her dress showing about twelve inches of leg and ankle. He looked away, but she must have noticed, because she said, "If anyone comes along, I'll slide off and dismount."

"That's probably a good idea, since you're so pretty."

"I never knew you were such a flatterer. You must have some Irish ancestor, who kissed the Blarney Stone."

"No. It's the absolute truth, Leah Morgan. Besides, my ancestry is about all German on Father's side."

"Ah, now go on with you, Lukie, me boy," she said in an exaggerated Irish accent. "Methinks I heard tell of an Irish grandfather on ye mutter's side, I have.

"Now, I see who's full of the Irish ancestors."

"I think Morgan may be more Welsh," she said, "but I'm not sure about Mother's family."

"But, probably no American Indian?"

"No, but my children will have some. Does that count?"

Luke put back his head and laughed. "You're quite the debater and tease all wrapped into one delightful package."

"You two seem to be having way too much fun up there," his father called out. They rode in comfortable silence for a while. Soon they topped the mountain and came to Deep Gap.

"The team pulled the wagon just fine without me getting down," his father said.

"I thought they might," Luke replied.

Dr. Moretz got out of the wagon, helped Leah dismount, and got on his horse.

Luke tied his chestnut to the back of the wagon and got in beside her. "You drive us to Boone," he told her. "I'll drive from there until we get to the steeper part on the mountain, and Father can take us on in home."

"I can't wait to see Granny Em and Patsy."

"I'm eager to get back, too."

This time, they only stopped in Boone long enough for Luke and Leah to change positions. Luke saw Reverend Whitley riding quickly east, and he wondered if he had headed to Wilkesboro to see about Sam.

"You know, you were right," he told Leah. "The blond man who helped steal our horses and wagon was Sam Whitley."

"I thought so. Did you see him when you went to the jail?"

"No, I considered it, but I decided it would be better if he didn't know about Ivy or where she's living now."

"You don't think he has a right to know about the baby?"

"I think he forfeited that right when he left Ivy stranded. Anything could have happened to her. Besides, I think he's in quite a bit of trouble now. Do you think I should have told him?"

"I don't know, but I trust your judgment. You have a strong sense of duty and responsibility. When Ivy ran away, most men would have washed their hands of her, but you didn't. I can see how Sam might cause innumerable problems for Ivy and Lawrence. I think you probably did what's best. If God wants Sam to know, the story will surface."

"I didn't lie about it. I just didn't see Sam. I didn't have long to consider it, and Father thought not telling Sam would be best."

Luke's arm was throbbing, but he found talking to Leah helped keep his mind off it. He would make it home, and then he would take some pain medicine and go to bed.

He drove to the place where they turned to go up the mountain to home, and then his father took over. Luke would ride his chestnut the rest of the way.

CHAPTER EIGHTEEN

Sickness

Dusk had painted everything in hues of gray by the time they got to the farm. Smoke waved from the chimney in greeting, and Luke looked forward to a warm house, supper, and bed.

He and Leah took their things and went inside. Father would take care of the team. They could unload the rest of the wagon tomorrow.

They entered the house, but no one was around. That seemed strange.

"Granny," he called.

"Mister Luke!" Patsy came running from Granny's room. "Oh, Miss Leah! I am so glad you're here. It's Granny Em. She's terrible sick. I didn't know what to do, except keep her comfortable and try to get her to eat and drink something. Maybe you can do more."

They went into the bedroom. Granny lay in the bed with her eyes closed. She obviously had a fever. Luke picked up her hand, and it felt like fire.

"Granny," Luke said. "Wake up, Granny, I'm home."

"Is that you, Luke?" Her voice came out in a whisper so weak he could barely hear her. "Where's Leah?"

"I'm right here," Leah came up and felt her forehead. "We need to get this fever down." She turned to Luke. "Go see if you can hurry your father."

Luke hurried to the barn. His father had just finished putting the horses into the pasture.

"Hurry," Luke told him. "Granny is bad sick with a high fever."

His father grabbed his medical bag from the wagon and ran with Luke to the house. When they went into the bedroom, Leah wasn't there.

"This temperature's too high. Let's get some cold water compresses."

Leah came in the room with a bowl of cold water and cloth. "You're a wonder," his father said, as she began to apply a cold cloth to Granny's forehead.

"You go on to bed, Patsy," Leah said. "You look completely worn out. We'll watch Granny Em tonight."

Luke could tell by his father's worried expression that he was thinking about Luke's mother. She had run a high fever like this before she died.

"Clifton, is that you, or am I dreaming?" a weak voice asked from the bed. Granny's teeth had started to chatter.

"It's me, Mama. I'm here."

"I must be really bad off if you're here."

"I came for Luke and Leah's wedding."

Luke couldn't tell if she heard or not, because she'd drifted off again. He bowed his head and prayed for Granny. Father and Leah were better at caring for her than he, but he could pray.

Leah brought in a cup of water, propped Granny's head up with pillows, and helped Dr. Moretz give her some medicine. Granny didn't open her eyes through the whole process.

"Luke, you look about as bad as Patsy did." Leah told him. "Go up and get some sleep. I'll stay with Granny through the night, and you can sit with her some tomorrow."

"I'll get you some pain medicine," Father said. "I know your arm must be hurting."

"You both go get some rest," Leah said. "I can handle this tonight. I know when I should give her more medicine, and I'll keep

252 SOWN IN DARK SOIL

using the cold compresses. You'll be needed more tomorrow. I'll call you immediately if there's a change for the worse."

"I don't think I could sleep now," Dr. Moretz said.

"Take something for sleep then," Leah said.

"I don't want to take something that might knock me out in case I'm needed with Mama."

"I can brew you some tea, if you'd like."

"Leah's tea for sleep helped me before," Luke said.

"I'll give it a try, then."

Luke went to bed. As exhausted as he felt, once the medicine took effect and his arm eased somewhat, he should sleep. He knew Leah would take good care of Granny.

Luke rose to the smells of coffee and something frying. He went down, and Leah stood before the fire making buckwheat pancakes. "How's Granny?"

"About the same, but she's not taking as many chills. I'm going to try to get some broth in her today. Patsy's with her now."

"I'll relieve Patsy to come help you."

Luke went to Granny's room, but he left the door open so the heat would filter in, and he could see more of what was happening in the rest of the house. He felt Granny, and she still felt hot to the touch.

A few minutes later, Leah stuck her head in the bedroom door. "Come eat some pancakes while they're hot. I'll send Patsy back in here, while I finish cooking the pancakes. She's already eaten."

"Come sit down and eat with me," Luke told her as he took a seat at the table.

"Okay, for a bit." She sat down, and Luke reached across the table and took her hand to say the blessing. When he finished, Leah smiled at him. She looked tired after being up all night.

"Your tea worked," Father said to Leah, when he came down. "I slept much better than I expected."

"I told you," Luke said.

"How's Mama?"

"I can't tell much difference," Leah said, "but the chills don't seem as severe."

"Well, at least she's doing a little better. And these pancakes are delicious. I could get used to staying here."

"I wish you would," Leah told him. "We love having you here."

"You go on up and take a nap," Luke said to Leah. "Father and I'll watch after Granny."

"Let me start dinner, Miss Leah," Patsy said when they entered Granny's room. "You need to sleep some."

Leah gave Patsy instructions and headed upstairs. Luke noticed she moved slowly, almost as if her feet were too heavy to lift.

Luke got his Bible and went back to Granny's room. He planned to read and pray while he sat with her.

"I'll go unload the wagon, if you'll tell me where you want everything," Father said.

"Leave the things Leah bought where they're easy for her to get. There's not much else, and I think you can tell what should be left in the barn and what should be brought to the larder."

Leah came down as they were sitting down to dinner. Patsy had made a pork stew with meat and vegetables.

"Did you get any sleep?" Luke asked Leah.

"I did. I feel better."

"I'll take Granny Em some broth. I had Patsy save some from the pork, and I'll feed it to her."

"I'm going up and take a nap," Father said. "It'll be my turn to sit up with Mama tonight, but first, I want to check Luke's arm and change the bandage. It looked fine yesterday morning, but I want to keep a check on it."

Luke sat down in a chair and his father took off the bandage. Leah came and looked, too.

"What do you think?" Father said to Leah.

"There seems to be some redness just forming at the edge of the wound. I think we should begin something for infection, just to be on the safe side."

Dr. Moretz nodded. "I think you're right. Can you make a poultice? I find Granny's remedies often work better than mine."

"I'll make a tincture from purple coneflower root. I like to use a tincture instead of a poultice when possible. Boiling the herbs down to make them concentrated and adding a little alcohol seems to help more on an infected wound than just applying the herb. I'll also make a tonic of coneflower root and garlic. I'll add a little honey, so it won't taste quite as bad. His breath may not be good, but this should help with the infection, too." Leah said.

"That sounds good. I'll just leave this bandage off, while he's sitting here, and, when you get the tincture, we'll use it and put a clean bandage on."

In about an hour, Leah came back with the tincture and tonic. Luke drank the tonic first. It didn't taste good, but he'd taken worse medicines. Leah applied the tincture, while his father held his arm out and watched

"This is going to hurt some," she told him.

She put a bowl under his left arm and poured the medicine around, and then she took a soft cloth dampened in the tincture and wiped it. It stung when it hit the open wound. His father wrapped a clean bandage around it.

"I hope we caught this in time," Father said. "Infections are so hard to get rid of and spread so quickly."

"What happens if it gets worse?" Luke asked, but when he saw his father's face, he knew. Amputation. He'd lose his arm.

"Let's don't think about that now," Father said. "Leah seems to know what she's doing. We'll have faith this will work."

"And pray for that," Leah added.

Leah helped Luke's father milk after supper. They refused to let Luke do anything but sit with Granny.

Leah had continued to spoon some kind of meat broth into Granny. They also gave her sips of water whenever she seemed to rouse a little.

Leah put the tincture on Luke's arm three times a day and changed the bandage. She still had him drink the tonic four times a day. He couldn't tell if his arm had gotten better, but it didn't look any worse.

Luke decided to only take the pain medication at night now. He didn't want to become too dependent on it, and he knew it contained opium.

Tuesday night his father sat up with Granny. "You need your rest, too," he told Luke. "It'll help your body heal faster."

Wednesday morning Granny Em looked better. "She seems to still have some fever," his father told them, "but the chills are gone, and she seems a little cooler."

"You can just quit talking about me like I'm not even here." Granny looked at Father. "I'll be just fine, since I got my family looking after me." She looked at Leah. "This girl will make me well, if anyone can." Her voice still sounded weak, but it had a little more volume.

"Do you think you might eat some soft scrambled egg?" Leah asked Granny.

"I don't have much of an appetite, but I'll try. Bring me some of that apple cider, too. I am thirsty, and apples are supposed to have some healing properties."

After they'd all eaten breakfast, Leah checked Luke's arm. "Look, I can't see any redness now," she told his father.

"It does look better," his father agreed.

"I'm going to continue with the tincture, until the open wound heals over better, but I'm only going to give him the tonic this morning and tonight. If the arm looks good tomorrow morning, we will stop the tonic altogether."

Luke took Leah's hand. "Thank you, sweetheart."

She bent over and kissed his forehead. "I'm as happy as anyone," she said. "I've been worried. I'm glad to see Granny Em's making improvement, too."

"You could have handled all this just fine without a doctor," Father told her.

Patsy sat with Granny Wednesday night. "It's my turn," she said. "If we all take a turn, it won't be so hard on any one of us."

The wound on Luke's arm began to scab over and seemed to be healing fine. He quit taking any medicine and left the bandage off at night. Leah had changed his sheets to make sure they had no dirt or grime to irritate the wound, which he thought unnecessary, but he didn't say anything.

Leah sat up with Granny Thursday night, and Luke did it Friday. Granny complained, but Leah won that argument. "You need to keep taking your medicine until you have no more fever," she told Granny, "and someone needs to get it for you." At least Granny could drink it by herself now.

"You need to hurry and get well so Leah and I can be married before the temperature gets too cold," Luke told her. "I don't want to wait for spring."

"I'm trying my best," she answered. "I'm wanting that day to come as much as you."

"I doubt that, Granny." He laughed. "I doubt that very much."

"Well, it's the best news I've had in a long time. God truly blessed us when He sent Leah our way," she continued. "That mess with Ivy sure was troublesome, but it was worth it to find Leah."

"You're right there," Luke agreed.

Granny began sitting up in bed and eating what the others ate. She remained too weak to come to the table, but she tried her best to eat something.

By Monday, it had been a week since they'd come home. Granny had been able to stop taking any medicine. Her ague, or whatever it was, had left, but she still felt weak and tired.

Granny told Leah to make her a tonic to build her up and to be sure to put some ginseng in it. Leah complied. Luke didn't know if it really helped or not, but Granny thought so, and, since she began to eat better, her strength returned.

Luke and his father did many of the chores around the farm together, since the doctor didn't need to sit with Granny. Luke loved having his father's help and companionship.

With Granny still having to take it easy, Leah did most of the cooking and household chores. Patsy helped, but Leah could cook better than Patsy.

"You couldn't have found a better woman than Leah," his father told him one day when they were working outside. "She's a fantastic cook and keeps a clean house. She can doctor and she's a pleasure to be around and talk with. I'm pleased for you, son. I pray you two have a long, happy life together."

Luke knew his father must be thinking of Mother. "I'm happy, too. Marrying her is almost too good to be true. I think all the trouble we had at first with Ivy has made it even more special now things are working out for us."

CHAPTER NINETEEN

The Wedding

Granny seemed to be improving daily, and, by the first of October, Leah began wedding preparations. She pulled out the ivory gown, and she and Patsy got it ready. The ivory veil went perfectly.

Luke didn't know if he'd be able to talk one of the Boone preachers into coming up the mountain or not, but he discovered an itinerant circuit rider would be in the area until the end of October. He got in contact with him, and they set the wedding for Saturday.

Leah wanted to hold the ceremony in the pretty meadow across the road, but she wasn't sure of the weather. Some mornings had heavy frosts now. Saturday could be cold, or even rainy, icy, snowy, or any combination.

Luke said they could take some of the furniture to the barn, rearrange the seating, and hold the wedding in the house if they had to. He had sent out word to invite everyone around. They didn't know how many people to expect, but Granny said most of the neighbors would turn out for weddings or funerals.

They planned the ceremony for two o'clock. That way they'd have time to make a decision on which place would be best. Maybe the day would warm up some by then, too.

She and Luke decided not to have any attendants. As her surrogate father, Dr. Moretz would give her away.

"I'll be the happiest man ever to give a bride away," he joked, "because I'm giving her to my son, and she's becoming my daughter." He suddenly turned serious. "You know, Luke, your mother would have loved her as much as we do. She would've been so proud of you both." Luke just nodded.

Patsy and Leah cooked about all day Friday. Granny helped from time to time, but she would have to stop and rest along. They fixed small biscuits to stuff with ham and sausage tomorrow morning. They baked cakes, sweet breads, small apple fritters, and persimmon pudding cut into small squares. Patsy said she would slice fresh carrots, apples, and get out some pickles right before the ceremony.

"I can do that," Granny said. "You need to be fixing Leah's hair and helping her get ready. I need to do what I can, or I'll never get my full strength back."

A few clouds rolled in Friday, but the wind wasn't blowing for a change, and it felt chilly but not cold.

"Put on some warm clothes and come for a walk with me," Luke told Leah. "I asked Granny and Father, and they said for us to go ahead. Things have been so hectic lately with the health issues and preparing for our wedding that you and I haven't had time to talk or to be alone."

Leah put on a wool dress and got her heavy cloak. One thing she'd learned is that it could be nice and sunny one minute here and turn completely different the next. Luke took her hand, and they walked toward the woods.

"There's some trails back here I used to hunt, but I'm guessing the Cherokee used them years ago. I thought we would hike some of them. Are you up to a long mountain trek?"

"If it's with you, I am up to anything."

He looked at her for several seconds. "I'd planned to wait until we were on the mountaintop to bring up this conversation, but now seems to be a good time, since you've given me an opening." They began to walk slowly along the trail. Luke still held her hand. "Are you worried or frightened about tomorrow night?" He watched for her reaction.

She took her time to form her answer and didn't look at him. "I guess it's natural to have uncertainties about the unknown, so I can't honestly say I am not apprehensive, but I trust you completely, Luke. I trust you to guide our relationship, and I trust you to be patient with me and my lack of knowledge about intimate things." She felt him squeeze her hand. She looked at him then and said, "Why do you ask? Are you worried?"

"Well, I knew you didn't have a mother here, and I didn't know if you'd say anything to Granny or not. I didn't want you be worried or upset thinking about things. I'm very glad you don't know what to expect. I know everything will be just fine. You'll see. Our love will be enough. Do you remember the kiss we had in the meadow before I left to find Ivy. I imagine we'll both become so wrapped up in each other, passion will take over, and we won't have to think; we'll just react to each other."

She smiled at him then. "Thank you, Luke." His honest concern gave her a warm feeling, like sweet, hot cider on a cold day, only better. "Even with Mama near, I could never talk to her like this."

"That's one of the many special things about you, Leah. I love the way we can talk about anything. There's no subject off limits to us. My mother and father seemed to have had that kind of relationship, too, but I wondered if I'd ever find it. The Bible talks about two people becoming as one. That's exactly what will happen to us tomorrow. We'll become one."

"Does your arm still bother you?"

"No. I'm able to do anything I need to now." The mischievous look he gave her led her to guess he wasn't thinking about the farm work.

They picked up their pace then. As they gradually climbed, the walk warmed them, and Leah took off her heavy cloak and carried it. They talked of hopes and dreams and the future. On this day, it all looked bright and promising.

"What about children?" Luke asked.

"I'd like to have at least three," she told him, "and five would be fine. In fact, I'll take as many as you and God see fit."

Luke laughed then, a happy, contented laugh. "You are a delight, Leah Morgan, soon to be Moretz. You won't even have to change your last initial, will you?"

"No, all my monogrammed accessories will still work just fine." He'd know she just teased, because she didn't have monogrammed accessories.

"So that's why you agreed to marry me? I wondered how a simple, mixed-breed mountaineer like me ended up with a woman as fine as you." His eyes danced with merriment.

"The only thing I've found bad about you is you tease merciless and then shoot that devilish grin of yours. Shame on you, Luke Moretz. There's nothing simple about you. I'm proud of your Cherokee heritage, and I love the mountains. I wouldn't want to live anywhere else, and I love one mountaineer to distraction."

He pulled her to the top of the shorter mountain they had just hiked up. They stood in silence looking out at the other mountains and the valley below. The view seemed to celebrate with her.

After several minutes, when their breaths had calmed from the climb, he took her in his arms and kissed her. She felt like warm yeast dough in his arms. She became soft and pliable, but she began to rise to heights unknown.

After a while, he stopped, but she didn't want him to. She wanted to live the rest of her life in that kiss.

"See, darling," he said, "tomorrow night will hold no problems for us. We'll just start where we left off here."

She nodded. The way she felt right now, she knew he was right.

Saturday morning brought dense fog that covered everything. Leah couldn't even see the barn from the larder door.

"I'm supposed to be the one wearing a veil today, not Mother Nature," she said to Granny Em.

"Have faith, Little One," Granny said. "How many times have you seen the morning start out foggy up here, only to have the fog burn off in an hour or two?"

"Do we need to start moving the furniture out to the barn?" Luke asked after he came in from milking.

"Give it to midmorning first," Granny said. "I've got me a feeling this is going to be a pretty day."

"You can put a lot of stock in Mama's feelings," Dr. Moretz said.

"Leah, come here a minute please," Granny Em called about ten o'clock.

"What do you need, Granny Em?"

"I want to show you something." She led Leah to the window. The bright sunshine glistened like diamonds as it tried to dry the wet grass and leaves. "Didn't I tell you now?"

"You were right, and I'm glad." She gently hugged the older woman. "You're a wonder, Granny Em."

"You're pretty wonderful yourself, girl. You've made my grandson as happy as I've ever seen him in his whole life."

Leah smiled. She knew Granny Em said exactly what she thought. She'd also grown to love this little woman. They were closer than she'd ever been with her own mother.

"Let's eat us a bite, and it'll soon be time for you to get all dressed up."

Patsy wore a dress that had been Ivy's. The burnt orange brocade had been trimmed in tan lace, and it looked great with her dark complexion.

"I've never worn hoops or a dress this nice before," Patsy said. "I feel like I'm trying to be something I'm not."

"You have as much right as the next woman to wear pretty clothes," Leah told her. "I'm glad you have some of Ivy's things to wear. You worked many years for them, if you ask me."

Patsy helped Leah put up her hair, get dressed, and attach the veil. "You look radiant, like a dream princess," Patsy said, when she stepped back to get a better look.

Leah looked down. Her gown was probably a little out of date, but she liked it even better than the one Ivy had chosen. It made her feel special.

The ceremony would be short, so most people would stand. Dr. Moretz took Granny Em out and seated her on a big granite rock. Leah watched from the window. Dr. Moretz stood and stared at the rock for a moment. His face seemed far away and filled with memories, as if he'd taken a step back in time. Then, he looked up, turned, and walked back to Leah.

Granny Em had dressed in her finest, and she suddenly looked ten years younger. Much of her strength had returned, and she'd soon be her old self again.

Luke had gone out to stand with the preacher on the little knoll at the start of the meadow. When Leah looked out the window, she saw more people than she'd expected. There looked to be forty or fifty. Granny had been right again.

The meadow would have looked more decorated for a wedding in the spring with all its flowers, but this would do. The grass still showed some green, and the fall leaves blazed their colors on the trees. Even those past their peak still clung tenaciously to branches. They reminded Leah of the rugged mountain spirit of these people, who refused to be beaten down.

Luke had either had some musicians come or else some brought their instruments and played spontaneously. Leah could hear a banjo, fiddle, and mandolin blending together in mountain music.

The instruments began playing "Love Divine, All Loves Excelling."

"That's our cue," Dr. Moretz said, "Are you ready, my dear?"

"I am, but who planned the music?"

"Your soon-to-be husband."

They walked out the front, across the road, and into the meadow. Leah kept her eyes on Luke the whole time, and he watched her. He looked every inch of royalty in his dark, formal suit and stark, white shirt.

As she got closer, she saw Luke's gaze had locked on her, as if he didn't know her, as if she'd cast a spell on him. She smiled at him; he blinked and smiled back.

She felt, rather than saw the people move closer, so they could hear. Dr. Moretz did his part in the ceremony and left her standing beside Luke.

The preacher read verses from 1 Corinthians 13. He told them to follow those verses and put Christ in the center of their marriage and family life, and they would live together in happiness. He asked them the questions and they made their promises to each other and to God. The preacher pronounced them husband and wife, and, when Luke kissed her, time stood still. "Ladies and gentlemen, I now present to you Mr. and Mrs. Luke Moretz."

Claps and shouts erupted, and she took Luke's arm, as they walked to the house while the musicians continued to play.

Almost everyone came to the house and helped themselves to the refreshments. Most stood around and talked, but the older ones sat.

Leah only knew Oralee and Polly, but Luke and Granny Em seemed to know everyone. Oralee walked with a cane, but she seemed stronger than when they'd visited.

"Youngin', y'all told me Luke weren't a-courtin' yuh none. Then, yuh ups and get hitched. What's goin' on?

"I guess things changed."

"Well, I guess thangs did." She gave a laugh. "Y'all make a right handsome couple. I'll give yuh that, and this here weddin's a real good time. I thank you fer the invite."

"I'm glad you could come."

"This here's the purtiest weddin' I ever did see," Leah heard a teenage girl tell her mother. "I want my weddin' to be jist like it."

A heavy-set, middle-aged woman came up to Leah. "Honey, your weddin' was so romantic," she said. "You and Luke Moretz make every other couple in this county look like nothin' but the dregs."

"There's the beauty," another woman said. "You knowed you broke the hearts of every sangle woman on the mountain when you captured Luke, don't you?"

Luke tried to fulfill his job as host, but he never left her for long. He introduced her to everyone, but she couldn't remember their names or who they were.

Luke came up to her and whispered, "The musicians want to play one more song and they want us to dance. Is that all right with you?"

"Yes, that's fine." She would like to dance with Luke, since they'd never done so.

They played "Barbara Allen," an old ballad the settlers had brought with them from Scotland or England so long ago it would be hard to trace its exact origin. A young woman began to sing it in a clear, sweet voice, a folk voice from the ages, one which spoke of clans, family, and heritage.

Luke took her in his arms and they waltzed to the music. She followed him as if she'd become his extension.

Ivy had been the dancer in the family, but Leah had gone to many balls and cotillions. She'd never lacked for dance partners, but she had never danced like this. It felt as if she and Luke were bound together by invisible cords, and when one moved the other followed in perfect precision and harmony. All the while, they never took their eyes from each other.

Leah felt Luke's respect, admiration, and love wrap around her. Those were the unseen cords binding them. She prayed it would always be so.

Gradually people began to leave, because they had farm chores to do before dark.

Finally, only the five of them were left. "Well, Clifton and I are going out and milk," Granny Em said. "I never thought I'd look forward to getting to milk, but after this time of being sick, I am."

"I'm going to clean up the kitchen and put away some things," Patsy said.

"Leah and I'll put everything back like it was," Luke said.

"You will do no such thing," Patsy said with her hands on her hips.

Luke gave her a disarming smile. "It's early yet, and Leah and I want to spend some time with our family."

"Well, don't do anything you don't want to," Patsy relinquished.

"Smooth talking charmer," Leah whispered to him.

"Temptress," he whispered back.

"When?"

"All day."

"To whom?"

"To me." He gave her that roguish grin of his, and she laughed.

They had just finished moving the furniture around when Luke's father and Granny Em came back with the milk.

"This was a wonderful day," the doctor said as he sat down. "I'm so glad I was able to be here."

"We are, too," Luke said.

"I'm sure glad you two are finally married," Granny Em said as she came in and sat down. "Things kept happening to keep you apart, and I began to wonder if this day would ever get here."

"It does seem like it took a long time to get everything worked out, but, when you think about it, it really didn't. It's only been about five months since I brought Leah up the mountain."

"Well, now that you're married, maybe nothing more will happen to keep you separated."

"Dr. Moretz, could I get you to help me?" Patsy asked.

Leah wondered what Patsy planned. She didn't have to wait long to find out.

Patsy and the doctor came slowly down the stairs, carrying the small trundle bed.

"What are you doing?" Leah asked.

"Granny said I could stay in her room for the next two nights," Patsy said.

"That way you can have this end of the upstairs to yourself."

Leah blushed, and the doctor made matters worse by offering to sleep on a pallet in front of the fireplace.

"No," Luke answered for her. "Stay where you are at the other end of the hall. If you moved to the living room, you'd be right under our bedroom."

That made things even worse! She felt her face getting hot.

"I need some water," Leah said, and went to the larder. In a minute Luke followed her.

"I am sorry, Leah," he said. "I've really tried to make everything right for you today. The last thing I want is for you to be embarrassed."

"I know, and today has been wonderful."

"Do you wish we could've had a church wedding?"

"We did. The meadow is God's creation, and I felt Him there today. I liked our wedding better than Ivy's."

"I did, too, and you were a much prettier bride. I couldn't believe it when you came walking toward me. You were like a vision, and I've never seen anyone as beautiful."

"Thank you for the music, too. What a pleasant surprise!"

"I've tried to think of what you'd appreciate. The musicians wanted to play things like 'Turkey in the Straw,' but I chose the hymns, because I thought you'd like them better."

"I did, but I also enjoyed our dance."

"'Enjoy' is such an understatement for how I felt when we danced." He pulled her into his arms, hugged her tightly, and kissed her forehead. "Why don't you go up to our bedroom and get ready. I'll be up in about fifteen minutes."

"Okay."

He took her in his arms again and tenderly, longingly kissed her mouth. He opened the larder door for her. "I'll wait for you to get upstairs before I go in."

She nodded. She hoped her legs would support her up the steps after that kiss.

She went into the sitting room. "I came to tell you all good night," she said to them as she turned to go upstairs.

"Good night," they all said, but she didn't look back.

She went to Luke's bedroom, but she realized she'd have to go to her room and get her nightgown. Just as she started to turn, she noticed her best nightgown spread across the foot of the bed. She looked and many of her things had been brought in. Patsy. She must have done all this earlier.

Leah quickly got ready and crawled into bed. She left two candles burning for Luke.

CHAPTER TWENTY

Letters

Leah woke up to find Luke looking at her. "Good morning, wife," he said with a loving smile.

"Good morning, husband." *Husband.* Would she ever get used to it? She would, because Luke was going to be easy to get used to.

"How do you feel?"

"Wonderfully content. I love you so much, Luke."

"Not half as much as I love you. You're more than I ever dreamed possible. I know God must have planned you just for me."

"Are you ready to get up and have breakfast?"

"If I must, but I'd rather stay here with you."

They went down to find Granny setting the food on the table and the others seated. "You timed that just right," she said.

"You can take your time, Luke," Granny said. "Clifton and I did all the morning chores. It's cold out there this morning, too."

They ate a leisurely breakfast. Afterwards, they gathered for their worship.

"Play some hymns on your fiddle," Leah told Luke. "I love to hear you play."

"Either you've gotten better, or I've forgotten how good you were," Dr. Moretz told Luke.

"Maybe I just have someone in my life who inspires me now," Luke replied.

A fierce wind came up. It roared around the house and caused the fire to sputter and crack. "This sounds like a good day to stay inside," she told them.

"Luke's been telling me what a good chess player you are, Leah," Dr. Moretz said. "How about a match?"

"You don't want to do that," Luke warned.

Dr. Moretz took much longer with his moves than Leah.

Luke sat and watched. "Do you want to play me a game of checkers, on the side?" Luke asked Leah during one of his father's particularly long moves.

"Sure."

"Are you trying to make me feel like I'm not much of an opponent?" the doctor asked.

She defeated Dr. Moretz about the same time she and Luke came to a draw in checkers.

"I thought Luke had been exaggerating," Dr. Moretz said, "but maybe he only told half the truth. How often do you two draw in checkers or stalemate in chess?"

"Often, but I don't mind being tied with Leah." Luke enjoyed teasing her with innuendos and double meanings.

"Do you win sometimes?"

"Of course he does," Leah said.

"I do, but we tie more. I think the two of us are pretty evenly matched." He looked at Leah with a twinkle in his eye.

"He gets his teasing naturally," Granny Em said. "His grandfather was even worse, but that's one of the things I loved about him."

When they sat down to supper, Leah looked out the window to see snow falling. The flakes looked small, and the wind sent them dancing. She excitedly pointed it out.

"That's just blow snow," Granny Em said. "It won't amount to much."

"I'm glad this didn't happen yesterday," Luke said.

"I think your wedding would have been special no matter what," Patsy said.

"You're right," Luke agreed. "I guess I'd better brave the cold and go milk, though."

"Let me help you," Dr. Moretz said. "I think I'm still a mountain man at heart. I love it here and feel more at peace."

With being married to Frances, Leah could see why. Dr. Moretz deserved someone who'd love him and treat him special.

"I wonder if Luke and I wouldn't have been better off if we'd both moved back here after Sarah died. At the time, I thought the farm would be more painful as I saw the places Sarah and I had met and fell in love. Now, they make me happier and bring back lovely memories."

"Well, you had your medical practice in Salisbury," Granny Em said. "As much as I've wished it could be otherwise, you were called to be a doctor, not a farmer."

"That's true," he agreed.

Monday morning showed little sign of Sunday's foul weather. The ground had a white tint, as if glazed with frost, but the sky had cleared.

Leah and Patsy moved the rest of Leah's things to Luke's room, but, when they did, storage became tight. She left some summer things and bedding in her trunks.

By the time winter hit in full force, she feared they would need the extra covering. Their bedroom sat over the sitting room so some of the heat from the fireplace rose, but none of the bedrooms had heat. It would be terribly cold when the fireplace died down in the winter. She smiled to herself. At least she had Luke to keep her warm.

Luke and Dr. Moretz moved the wardrobe from Ivy's room into Luke's for her. It matched the one he had, and Luke said he would have another one made for Ivy's room.

"Are we well off?" she asked him. Papa had always shared his ledgers with her.

"Not wealthy by any stretch of the imagination, but we have enough. Father insists on giving Granny extra, and she puts it into the farm account. There are plenty of families here who have no cash. They barter for what they can and raise or make do for the rest. Why do you ask? Most wives leave money matters to their husbands."

"Papa always discussed plantation business with me, and I often helped him with his accounts."

"I should have known you'd not be like most wives."

"Do you want me to be? Maybe I could get Frances to train me to be more like her."

Luke looked taken aback, even alarmed. She tried to stifle her laugh, but when he looked her in the eye, he must have seen a mischievous twinkle, because he burst out laughing.

"I see you can give as good as you get. No, I truly wouldn't change a thing about you. I want us to share everything with no secrets." He went to his desk, picked up an account book, and handed it to her. "You're welcome to examine anything in this room or on the farm. I'll look forward to us making decisions together, and I'm actually glad you're interested in such things."

After supper, Raymond, Oralee's grandson, rode up. He carried a letter in his hand.

"I went to Boone this smornin', and this'd just come to the post office. I said I'd brang hit out. With you bein' newly wed and all, I didn't know when you'd git in."

"I appreciate that," Luke said, as he took the letter. "Come in and visit for a spell."

"No, I best be gettin' on. Thar's evenin' chores to be done."

Luke handed the letter to Leah. "This is for you."

It was from Ivy. Leah took it to the sitting room, sat down, and began to read:

Dear Sister,

If I could only express how happy I am! Lawrence treats me as if I'm the most precious thing he's ever known. I fell in love with him quickly, and I love him more every day. I didn't know what love really was before Lawrence.

His mother has been welcoming. Learning my duties won't be hard, since Mama taught me much of this at Gold Leaf.

The family held a ball for Lawrence and me when we first arrived. Lawrence bought me a new dress, and I had it made in such a way it concealed my thickening middle. Lawrence dances divinely. Of course, the ball was to announce our marriage. If there were any rumors flying, I didn't hear them. Archibald Biles didn't come.

I'm over being sick in the mornings, and that's much better. I'm showing now, but I've been able to hide it so far. Perhaps I'll stay small enough it'll look more like the baby comes early. Hester Sue's baby and mine might be close to the same age.

Mama is not doing well. She overreacted when she saw me. She clutched me and refused to let go. Paul and Hester Sue had to pry her hands away. She cried and cried when I left even though I assured her I was staying close and could see her often. She has let herself go, too. She appears disheveled and almost wild.

I want to thank you for helping me accept Christ's forgiveness. I think that has done as much to turn my life around as anything. Lawrence and I read, study the Bible, and pray together every night. Strange how I've spent so many Sundays in church but never really learned much at all.

Well, enough about me. I want to know all about you. How was your trip back? Has Luke proposed to you, yet? Is it already getting cold up there? Write and let me know everything. I think of you often.

Love,

Ivy

She looked up to find Luke watching her. "By the look on your face, I'm guessing it's good news."

"All except the part about Mama." She handed him the letter. "No secrets," she said, when she saw the question on his face.

"I'm glad for them," Luke said, when he finished reading. "It sounds as if they're very happy. I think we finally got the correct couples paired up. Ivy is better for Lawrence and you're better for me."

As they got dressed Tuesday morning, Luke said, "As much as I hate to, I need to get back to doing more work before the thick of winter gets here. I guess the honeymoon is over."

"I beg to differ," Leah said. "I don't think the honeymoon will ever be over for us. I think we will live years together in a perpetual honeymoon."

"I like the way you think, but I believe what you call my roguish nature is rubbing off on you."

"Oh no, it was there all the time, but, like any proper lady, I didn't let it out."

"Are you saying I bring out the worst in you?" he teased.

"I guess that depends on what you think's bad. I certainly thought you were the most handsome man I'd ever seen. My feelings got all jumbled and confused when you touched me, and our marriage brought out a passion in me I didn't know I had."

"I wouldn't call any of those the least bit bad. It's what I longed for in a wife. The better I get to know you, the more I like what I see, but I'm still having a hard time believing you're really my wife. You seem too good to be true."

"That's okay. I'm willing to spend the rest of my life proving to you how real I am."

"Enticer," he whispered right before he kissed her.

Luke and Dr. Moretz spent most of the day cutting wood. Surely they had enough already, but Luke seemed afraid, with an early onset of winter and the possibility of a late spring, they might come up short.

"I enjoy getting out and working around the farm," Dr. Moretz said at supper. "I miss doing the physical labor. There's a special fulfillment to seeing what you accomplish mount up."

"I've enjoyed your company and your help," Luke said. "We work well together. Anytime you need a break and want to come, you know we'd love to have you. Granny is happier with you here, too."

"I really should have packed up and moved us back up here when your mother died. I think you and I would've both been happier if I had. But I guess that's water under the bridge now. We must deal with things the way they are, not what might have been."

"Water under the bridge can end up washing you too far downstream," Granny Em said. "Are you so unhappy now, Clifton?"

"No, I'm not unhappy. I'm just not as happy as I could be. I look at Luke and Leah, and I'm reminded of how it can be. I had that with Sarah. I guess it's too much to expect such a love twice in one's life, but I'm glad Luke's found it. I'm happy because of his happiness."

"I think the three Moretz men have been blessed with the love of three outstanding women." Granny Em chuckled as she realized she had included herself in that. "What more could you ask for?"

"Maybe to have yours by your side always," Dr. Moretz sighed.

"I know what you mean, Clifton. I had Edgar much longer than you did Sarah, but I miss him something terrible. Yet, I thank God for what we had."

"I understand completely, Mama. I thank God for Sarah, too. I always have."

Dr. Moretz decided to return home the third week in October. "I've left my practice long enough," he said. "I've really enjoyed being here, but I need to get back before my patients forget all about me."

Luke decided to ride to Boone with him. They left on horseback early Wednesday morning. Luke said he planned to be home well before dark.

Granny Em spent most of the day trying to teach Leah some complicated weaving patterns and Patsy the basics. Leah caught on quickly, because she understood the warp, weft, and how to weave a solid color.

"If I had to wear only clothes made from what I wove," Patsy said. "I'm afraid I would be scantily clad." They laughed.

Leah heard a horse. Luke was back, and she ran out to meet him, but stopped short. Luke and Dr. Moretz were both back. Something must be wrong. She went out to see.

"Hello, darling," Luke said. He pulled her to him and held her tightly, as if he released her, she might blow away.

"What's wrong? Why is Dr. Moretz still with you?"

"I'll see to the horses, Luke," the doctor said. "You go on in. I'll be in shortly."

"Come on," Luke said. "I'll tell you inside."

"You had a letter from Paul at the post office," he began. "I hope you don't mind, but I opened it. After Paul put the seal on it, he'd added a note to the back that said, 'Let me know if you can't come immediately.' Father and I wanted to see what was wrong. Read it and then we'll talk."

"It's fine you read the letter," Leah said as she began to read.

Dear Leah,

I hate to inform you that your mother passed away. Ivy is taking it very hard, and we need you to come home.

Ivy found some shocking information when she was helping your mother sort through some of her things. I think Myra had managed to hide it all these years, but she's not been thinking straight, since Ivy left, and she didn't conceal it this time.

There were some letters and a diary to prove Ivy is only your half-sister and is no blood relation to me. She had a different father. It seems Myra was in love with a man named Patrick

Ivey. Her parents didn't approve of him, so Patrick wanted them to move to Missouri. Knowing Myra had been used to a more lavish lifestyle, he went out first to secure a livelihood and place for them. He planned to return for Myra within a year. Neither knew when he left she was with child. After she realized she was expecting, news filtered back through Patrick's family that he had been killed in an accident. Myra became desperate and frantic. She latched onto Father, who was lonely and grieving himself. I don't think he knew any of this. I'm sure he didn't at first, anyway. Ivy was born and presented as his, but Myra named her "Ivy" after her father.

Ivy is devastated. The news of her parentage was shocking enough, but now she blames herself for her mother's death. She thinks her discovery killed the woman.

The doctor says Ivy is in danger of losing her baby and perhaps her own life. Lawrence is beside himself with worry and adds his pleas for you to come with all haste. Your sister is not eating and looks deathly ill. We'll be expecting you soon.

Love,

Paul

"Oh, my," Leah said, as she looked at Luke. She saw his concern for her, and it was her undoing. The tears came. Luke didn't say a word. He just moved closer, scooped her into his arms, and let her cry on his shoulder.

When the tears finally stopped, she pulled back. "What am I going to do?" She wanted Luke to tell her what to do. She didn't feel capable of figuring it out herself.

Luke quickly read the letter again. "What do you want to do?" Why did he like to answer her questions with a question?

"I don't know. I feel I need to go to Ivy, but I don't want to leave here again. It would be hard to leave Granny and Patsy alone for the winter. What if Granny got sick again?"

"That's why I came back," Dr. Moretz said. "I thought you could return with me, and Luke could stay here at the farm."

She looked at Luke again. *No!* She didn't want to leave Luke. The thought terrified her, and she knew Luke could see it in her eyes.

"Luke," was all she could get out. "Oh, Luke." She grabbed for him and used his shoulder again. She knew she had soaked his shirt with her tears, but they wouldn't stop.

"Come on, darling." Luke pulled her up, and, with his arm around her, he led her upstairs. "We need some privacy to figure this out," Luke told his family.

He put Leah on the bed and lay beside her to hold her in his arms. "Let's just talk."

"You know I don't want us to be apart," he began, and she nodded. "It will be hard on both of us, but I really think our love is strong enough to withstand a separation. We need to look at what God would want us to do. What do you think that is, Leah?"

"We are supposed to love and care for one another."

"That's what I thought. Do you think you might help Ivy, if you went to her?"

Leah nodded.

"I think so, too. Besides being Ivy's sister and giving her support, you have a gift for healing. But, I think the decision must be yours. It's your family."

"I know I need to go, but it's not what I want. My desire is to stay here with you."

"I felt some of the same things when I needed to find Ivy before I felt free to pursue you. I felt it was the right thing to find Ivy first, but I wanted to stay here and marry you then."

"It seems something with Ivy continues to draw us apart. Will it never stop? Will we never be able to live and love without interference?"

"Oh, sweetheart, I pray so. What's your decision?"

"I guess I have to go. I couldn't forgive myself if something happened to Ivy or her baby, and I hadn't tried to help."

He nodded. "Are you hungry? Do you want some supper?"

"No, I don't feel like eating."

"Neither do I. I'll go down and tell father what we're doing. You two will leave in the morning. Get ready for bed, while I'm out, and I'll be right back. We'll at least have tonight."

Morning came way too soon, and Leah found herself mounted sidesaddle on Luke's chestnut riding away from the farm away from Luke.

She only had room to take her travel bag, but that would be okay. There should be plenty of dresses in her closet at Gold Leaf.

She thought she'd cried out all her tears on Luke's shoulder the night before, and she promised herself she wouldn't shed more, but, when Luke gave her the last kiss good-bye, the floodgates opened.

"Remember how much I love you," Luke said as he lifted her into the saddle. She thought she saw tears in his eyes, too, but she couldn't be sure, because everything blurred through hers.

"I love you, too," she whispered. "More than you'd ever believe."

"We'll ride to Wilkesboro," Dr. Moretz told her. "If you need me to get a carriage there, I can, but, if you can make it to Salisbury, we'll go by my house and get one."

"I can make it to Salisbury," she said. "I rode sidesaddle for two days, when we went to get Ivy in South Carolina, and I can again." She felt so uncomfortable about leaving Luke that she probably wouldn't notice the discomfort of the sidesaddle.

The actual physical pain she felt throughout her body surprised her. The intense, dull ache began in her core and radiated out to every part. She'd always been competent and independent. She'd never dreamed she could need someone as much as she needed Luke.

At least this would only be a temporary separation, and they should be together again soon. She would cling to that.

They didn't stop in Boone, but went on to Deep Gap. Leah felt as if she might be wearing down the mountain she had gone up and down it so much in the past months.

She tried to eat supper, but the food got stuck in her throat. The doctor ordered her some broth. "At least drink it," he said. "We can't have you getting sick, too." She managed most of it.

She went to her room and got out her Bible. She read from Psalms, but they failed to encourage her this time. She wondered if Luke would be reading his Bible now for the family devotion.

She undressed and crawled into bed. She said her prayers and then lay, meditating and opening her mind to God. *Lo, I am with you, always, even unto the end of the world.*

They made it to Salisbury late Friday. Leah felt stiff and achy, but she didn't complain. That was the least of her problems.

She went straight to bed. If she could only fall into an oblivious sleep, but sleep rarely came. She lay and thought of Luke. She could close her eyes and see his face as clearly as if he stood before her, but, if she reached out to touch him, her hand met only air.

Tomorrow she would see Gold Leaf and Paul for the first time, since she'd left, but there would be no Papa and no Mama there.

Tomorrow she could begin to help Ivy. The sooner she helped her sister recover, the sooner she could get back to Luke.

She dozed some, but mainly she lay awake in the dark. Despite her melancholy, she felt God with her, being her support and comfort. She held to His promise that He would never leave her. If it hadn't been for that, she would have turned around and gone back up the mountain. But she knew those thoughts stemmed from her selfishness, and she would not give in to them.

Luke lay awake in a cold, lonely bed and stared into the dark. He did more work than ever, but he just went through the motions. He hoped he'd be tired enough by the end of the day, that he could fall asleep, but sleep eluded him. How was it possible to be so strongly bonded to someone that you were only a fragment of yourself without them? Never in his wildest imagination had he thought he would miss Leah so much. He had even encouraged her to go, and now he feared she would be gone through the winter, as she waited for Ivy's baby to come.

He could close his eyes and imagine her in his arms, but such thoughts only made the pain more intense. His whole body ached for his wife. He needed her as much as he needed food, water, or air. Why had he let her ride away? *And thou shalt do that which is right and good in the sight of the Lord: that it may be well with thee.*

CHAPTER TWENTY-ONE

Ivy

Dr. Moretz brought his driver for the carriage. He stopped by the cottage on the way out of town Saturday, and Mrs. Price appeared carrying a bag. "I thought it would look better for you to have a lady companion," he said, "and you might need a friend after I have to leave. If you don't want her to stay, I can bring her back with me."

Leah smiled warmly at Mrs. Price, who hugged Leah. "I've been lonely since you left," Mrs. Price said.

As they rode, Mrs. Price asked her questions about the plantation and her family. She discovered Luke and Leah were married, and she asked questions about the wedding. Leah would have thought talking about the wedding would be painful, but it wasn't. Leah found herself reliving all the details of that happy day, and it made her feel better.

"Your face is aglow with happiness when you talk of Luke." Mrs. Price smiled at Leah. "I can tell you're very happy. I'm so pleased for you."

"It was hard for me to leave him to come here."

Mrs. Price patted her hand. "I'm sure it was, dear. When Mr. Price died, grief tore at me. Eventually, I realized if I wanted to honor him and our marriage, I needed to be positive and happy. I reveled in the many good years we'd had, and I lived well for him and the Lord. When I changed my attitude, my days became brighter. After all, our greatest love should be for the Lord, and our mates should be second."

Leah thought about what Mrs. Price said. She could wallow in her misery, but it wouldn't put Luke beside her. She would try to focus on good things and cherish the time she'd had with Luke. She would see herself as blessed because, unlike when Mrs. Price and Dr. Moretz were separated from their spouses, she would get to see her loved one again soon. As much as she loved Luke, she realized she did love the Lord more, although Luke might be a close second. She smiled to herself and felt better.

Leah wanted to go straight to Ivy, but she was afraid it would be an affront to Paul. After all, Gold Leaf had been her home.

They pulled up to her old home just as the sun began its descent. The sun hit the windowpanes at an angle to make them turn opaque and golden.

"It's beautiful!" Mrs. Price exclaimed.

"I knew we could count on you, Leah," Paul said. "Hester Sue is resting. Bertha will show you to your rooms. You'll be in your old one, of course."

Leah turned to find herself smothered in an expanse of brown skin. "Miss Leah, Miss Leah, is dat really you?

Leah gave Bertha a hug and kissed her cheek. "It's Mrs. now."

"Lawsey me, he betta be treatin' my baby right."

"He does. You may have seen him, Bertha. He was here for dinner right before Ivy and I left. Luke Moretz."

"Dat handsome devil. I shore do remembers him."

Bertha led them up. Leah had her old room, Mrs. Price had Ivy's old room, and Dr. Moretz was in a guest room.

"If you'll be okay here by yourself," Leah said to Mrs. Price, "Dr. Moretz and I'll go see Ivy."

"Of course, dear. These old bones don't travel like they used to. I'll be glad to rest a while."

When Leah and Dr. Moretz entered Lawrence's house, Mrs. Nance came immediately. "I'm so glad you're here, Leah. Ivy's not doing well at all, and if something happens to her, I fear what will happen to Lawrence. He won't leave her side. He won't eat, and he can't sleep."

When Leah entered Ivy's room, her sister lay in the bed with her eyes closed. Lawrence sat by her bed, holding her hand and watching her. Someone had brushed Ivy's hair, and she looked clean and neat, but Lawrence was unshaven, disheveled, and dirty. He looked as if he'd pulled a drunk, but Leah knew better.

"Lawrence, I'm here."

He looked up then. "Thank the Lord."

Ivy opened her eyes. When she saw Leah, she began to cry.

"Leave us alone for a little while," Leah asked.

"Come with me," Dr. Moretz told Lawrence. "You can tell me about Ivy's illness, and I'll try to help her. I've had some experience in cases like hers." He led the distraught man out.

Leah leaned over and hugged Ivy. "I love you, Ivy. Why are you like this? You've lost weight and look so frail."

"Oh, Leah, I killed Mama."

"What nonsense. You did no such thing."

"She only lived two days after I found the letters and the diary. I'm not even your full sister, and now I'm about to do the same thing as Mama. I'm giving birth to a baby that's not Lawrence's."

"Ivy, you and Paul wrote me how crazed Mama had been behaving. She wasn't herself before you got here. I know without a doubt it thrilled her to see you. You were all she's ever cared about. She would be most disappointed in how you're acting now.

And, unlike Mama, we told Lawrence the truth before he agreed to marry you."

"You just don't understand."

"You're the one who's not thinking straight, Ivy. You're trying to punish yourself for a number of things, but you shouldn't. It's not our job to deal out punishment, even to ourselves. Are you trying to punish your innocent baby, too?"

"No, of course not."

"Once you asked me to give you something to take it from you, is that what you're doing now—trying to get rid of it."

"No! No! I'm not like that now. I've accepted God's mercy, and I'm different."

"Well, show it. Even if it's not intentional, that's exactly what you're doing. When you don't eat, it doesn't get nourished. If you die, it dies, and most likely Lawrence, too. Have you even looked at your husband lately? He looks horrible. He's miserable with worry for you. Hasn't there been enough death at our doorstep? Must we also bury you, your baby, and Lawrence?"

Ivy seemed too stunned to cry. Leah knew she had shocked her sister, but something had to jolt her out of this stupor.

"Come on, Ivy. Let's fight for this baby, and, regardless of what happens, let's get you well. Do you remember how happy you were when you wrote me? Your newfound love flowed in every word. Lawrence is still here, and he still loves you. Do you have any idea how rare that is? Fight for it; keep it. He's in your life right now. Don't desert him."

Ivy took a deep breath. "Tell me what to do, and I'll do it."

"First, I want you to tell your husband to go shave and clean up. Then, Dr. Moretz is here, and I want him to examine you. In the meantime, I'll get the kitchen to fix you something to eat, and I want you to eat it all, even if you have to force it down your throat." Leah said it sternly, but she smiled at Ivy and kissed her cheek.

Leah sent Lawrence in first. "He'll be out in a minute or two, and you can go in and examine her. I'm going to order her something to eat, and I'll be right back."

"Make it something light, like an egg and toast." Dr. Moretz said.

Leah told the cook what she needed, and the slave said she would send it right up. Leah met Mrs. Nance in the hall.

"How did it go?" she asked.

"I think we've made progress. Dr. Moretz is with Ivy now. She's ready to try to eat, and Lawrence has gone to clean up."

"Bless you, Leah. God surely sent you to us."

Dr. Moretz had almost finished when she entered the bedroom. Lawrence must have moved at record speed, or his man did, because he came back, and he looked much more presentable.

"It doesn't look as bad as I feared," Dr. Moretz said. "She is spotting, but it's slight. I'm thinking we may be able to get it stopped. She does need to eat and stop being so anxious and distraught. I want her to stay in bed, but she needs to become interested in what's happening and the things around her. Do you think you can do that, Ivy?"

"I think so. Leah being here helps."

"I'll be back in the morning to check on you, Ivy," the doctor said. "I'll walk down and wait on you, Leah. Take your time."

"I'll be down soon. Could I talk with you in private, Lawrence?"

"Certainly." He led her to a small sitting room.

"How good are you at being with Ivy and controlling yourself?" she asked him.

He looked at her as if she had gone crazy. She guessed this was her day to shock everyone.

"I can do whatever I need to for Ivy's wellbeing."

"That's what I thought." Leah remembered Ivy telling her Lawrence had offered to give her time to love him before they became intimate.

"I think Ivy needs you to get her through this time. I don't want her withdrawing into herself again, so I'd like to keep her from distressing over bad things. I want you to lie down beside her tonight in your clothes. Pull her into your arms and just hold her, nothing more. You can kiss her forehead or cheek, but nothing passionate. Talk to her and get her to talk to you. Can you do this?"

"I can."

They went back to Ivy's room. Someone had brought up a tray with a scrambled egg, a piece of toast, and some tea. Ivy had eaten about half of it.

"I'm going back to Gold Leaf now," she told Ivy, "but I'll be back in the morning. I want you to eat all the egg and at least half the toast. I expect you to be feeling better in the morning."

"Thank you for coming, Leah. It seems that you're always having to rescue me. How is Luke?"

"Fine, I hope. We were married about two weeks ago. Get some rest tonight, and I'll tell you all about it tomorrow."

"You seemed to be pretty bossy up there," Dr. Moretz teased as they drove back to Gold Leaf.

"Yes, but I think the situation warranted it. At least things started taking a turn for the better. Ivy has snapped out of some of her hopelessness and she's eating, and Lawrence has cleaned up and has something he can do to help."

"I think you've decided to push things along quickly, so you can get back to Luke."

"That sounds like a great plan to me," Leah said with a twinkle in her eye. Dr. Moretz put back his head and laughed, just like Luke did.

In the morning, Ivy did look better, and so did Lawrence. He smiled at Leah when she came in, and Leah knew things had gone well.

"While Leah is here, I'm going to take care of some business I've neglected," Lawrence told Ivy. "I'll be back and eat dinner with you." He kissed Ivy's cheek and left.

Dr. Moretz examined her. "Well, there's some new spotting, but it doesn't seem to be any worse. Her color is a little better."

"I ate a boiled egg and half a biscuit for breakfast," Ivy said.

"Good. I'm going to leave Leah to visit with you. I'll be back in a couple of hours."

"Oh, Leah, last night was wonderful," Ivy said when the doctor had left. "Lawrence acted so tender and sweet. He said Dr. Moretz had told him not to get too intimate with me until after the baby is born, since I'm having trouble, so he lay beside me and held me in his arms, and we talked well into the night. I fell asleep in his arms, and, when I woke up, he was there beside me, just watching me. You were right. Our love is too precious to waste. I'll be all right, as long as I have Lawrence."

"I know just how you feel, because I feel the same way about Luke."

"You promised to tell me all about your wedding, so let's hear it."

Leah began by telling Ivy about the robbery and Luke getting shot. Then they got back to the farm to find Granny Em sick. She told her every detail about the meadow wedding and how special Luke had tried to make everything for her.

She attempted to tell Ivy how much she loved Luke and how he seemed as much a part of her as her own heart. She thought Ivy might begin to understand what words couldn't explain, since she and Lawrence were in love, too.

"Your wedding sounds so romantic, it almost makes me wish I'd been there, and you know how I feel about going back to the mountains." They both chuckled.

290 SOWN IN DARK SOIL

"It's so good to hear you laugh."

"It's good to feel like laughing again."

By Wednesday, Ivy had stopped spotting. "You can get up and sit in a chair beside the bed for an hour at a time mornings and afternoons," Dr. Moretz told her. "If there's the least bit of spotting, I want you back in bed for good."

Leah met Lawrence in the hall as she was leaving. "Thank you so much for everything," he said. "How did you know what Ivy needed from me right now?"

"I just went by what I'd want from Luke in the same situation."

"Luke's a lucky man," he said.

Thursday on the way to Lawrence's, Dr. Moretz told Leah, "I'm going to have to return to Salisbury tomorrow. I've got to get back to my practice, or I'm going to end up a pauper. I think Ivy is over the worst of it. You can return with me if you want."

"I'm not sure. Ivy might need me, if she were to lose the baby. Let me talk with her, and I'll let you know this afternoon."

"If you stay, you'll probably have to remain here until after the baby's born. Are you willing to be gone several more months?" He made a good point, but she still wanted to talk to Ivy.

"Of course you must go," Ivy said. "By what you've told me, I know you sacrificed to leave Luke in the first place. I'll be all right, Leah. Even if something happens to the baby, and I don't think it will, I'll cling to Lawrence. I know he'll be there for me. I'll depend on Lawrence and trust in God. Everything will be fine. Go make your own babies."

"Ivy!"

They both laughed.

Leah had two more things she needed to do before she left. She said her good-byes to Ivy and Lawrence a little early Thursday and returned to Gold Leaf.

She went immediately to the stable. "Jasper, Jasper," she called. The old slave came out of a stall. "My, oh my, if it ain't Miss Leah in de flesh. Come here." He held out his arms, and Leah ran to them. She felt like a little girl again and almost expected Papa to ride in at any minute.

"I's missed yuh somein awful. I heard you be back, but I 'spected you'd forgot all 'bout ol' Jasper."

"You know better than that. Would you take me out to Papa's grave?"

"Yuh knows I'd carry ya anywheres yuh wants go."

Leah stood just looking at the gravesite. Papa's grave had been placed on the right side of Paul's mother, and Mama's newer grave was on the other side of him.

"I miss you, Papa. I love you, but I found a real good man. I'm happy, just like you always wanted."

Jasper waited beside the carriage. The old slave had always been there for her. He was as special as they came.

Leah said her good-byes to Jasper again. She told him she loved him and left him with tears in his eyes.

The doctor, Mrs. Price, and Leah left early Friday morning. Leah knew her face must be glowing with excitement. She couldn't wait to get home.

"I feel like you made the trip for nothing," Leah told Mrs. Price.

"Nonsense, dear," she said. "If things had taken a turn for the worst, and you'd had to stay longer, you'd have needed me. I'm glad you didn't have to stay, but it's been good for me to get out. This has been like a vacation for me."

The dear lady always seemed so cheerful and positive. Leah told herself she needed to be like that, even when bad things happened.

How to get Leah back to the farm became their new problem. Dr. Moretz would accompany her if need be, but he really needed to stay in Salisbury. He'd been away for a month.

Dr. Moretz mentioned the problem in the carriage. "I wish I knew of someone we could trust who's planning to go to Watauga and you could accompany them," he told Leah.

"I know just the thing," Mrs. Price said. "My brother's a minister. His wife is from Sugar Grove, and they're heading out to Mountain City, Tennessee, on Monday or Tuesday. He's accepted a church there, because his wife wants to be closer to home. Leah should be just fine with them."

Leah would have preferred to go back quickly, but this would have to do. At least she would be traveling toward Luke.

"Now you must stay with me," Mrs. Price said. "It will be like old times in the little house."

Leah did. They spent a leisurely day Saturday resting and reading. Dr. Moretz joined them before supper and stayed until almost dark. He planned to pick them both up for church the next day. They would go to the church where Mrs. Price's brother would be a guest speaker.

A cold rain with a little sleet mixed in fell Sunday morning. "I hope you don't hit weather problems up the mountain," Dr. Moretz said, worried. "Winter seems to have set in early this year."

The Picklers looked to be a middle-aged couple, and they had a bundle of energy. Their twelve-year-old son, Timothy, looked older than his age. He was as tall as Leah and taller when he wore his hat.

"I'm so pleased to have you come with us," Mrs. Pickler said. "It'll be good to have some female company."

Mr. Pickler preached about the Good Samaritan. He talked about going out of our way and beyond what man expects to help others. Mrs. Price reached over and patted Leah's hand, as if she were telling Leah this is what she'd done. Mrs. Price didn't know how reluctantly Leah had come down the mountain to help Ivy.

After the service, Mr. Pickler told Leah they would leave at daylight tomorrow, if the weather cleared. Otherwise, they would wait until Tuesday. Leah prayed for clearing.

Dr. Moretz ate dinner with them. By the time they'd finished eating, the rain had stopped, but it had grown very windy.

"Don't worry, dear," the always positive Mrs. Price said. "The wind is just blowing the clouds away and drying out the ground."

"I wanted to suggest a drive, but not in this wind," Dr. Moretz said.

"Shall we play some chess or checkers, since we're stuck inside?" Mrs. Price asked.

"Leah beats me too soundly," Dr. Moretz declared. "I don't think I'm up to that today. It humbles me too much."

"I don't feel like playing anyway," Leah told them. "You two play, and I'll sit with you and read."

They spent a peaceful afternoon talking, laughing, and sitting in comfortable silence. Leah spent some time praying for good weather, at least until she got back to the farm. Dr. Moretz won the game of chess without much problem.

"That's more like it," he laughed. "Leah's bad for a man's ego."

"I don't know. I haven't seemed to deflate Luke's ego."

"No, you build his up, because he knows he's won your heart." Luke had certainly done that.

The air felt nippy Monday morning, but the sun smiled brightly. Mrs. Price had been right.

The heavy covered wagon pulled in front of the cottage at first light. It held many of the Pickler's household goods, since they were moving permanently, and they'd packed the wagon tightly. Leah hoped they would make it up the mountain with all this, but they had an eight-mule team.

Dr. Moretz rode up to see her off, and he led Luke's chestnut. Leah petted the horse, and he acted as if he were glad to see her. Perhaps he knew she would take him back to Luke.

She hugged and kissed the doctor and Mrs. Price. "I love you," they both called as the wagon pulled out. "Have a safe trip."

They started off with the three adults on the front seat, and Timothy wedged into a small slot in the back. Timothy had begged to ride the chestnut, but his father had told him to wait until they got out of town, and then it would be up to Leah.

"As you can see, I only have the sidesaddle with me," she told the lad.

"I can ride bareback," Timothy said. "I've ridden that way many a time."

"I didn't know we were rearing such a little savage," his father said.

The word "savage' didn't sit well with Leah, but she didn't say anything. She hoped the trip didn't turn unpleasant. She really didn't know these people.

"I'll probably ride the horse some," Leah told Timothy, "but you can ride him some, also." That seemed to satisfy the boy.

"I have a saddle in the wagon," Mr. Pickler whispered to Leah, "but it would be even more trouble to keep switching saddles, and the boy will do fine bareback. Maybe he won't be so glued to the horse this way."

CHAPTER TWENTY-TWO

Home

As Leah expected, they traveled slowly with the heavy load. They spent Monday night at a farm near Yadkinville with a family the Picklers knew.

The Picklers had a bedroom together. Leah had a tiny room, but it had a bed, and she had some privacy. It would be fine for one night.

They left early the next day. They should make it to Wilkesboro by nightfall, and Leah couldn't wait.

Leah found herself riding about half of the time, and Timothy rode the other half. Timothy fed, watered, and took care of the horse, and that helped. This arrangement also meant no one had to ride in the crowded back of the wagon.

Mrs. Pickler turned out to be a friendly woman who liked to talk. "You must be happy to be getting back to your husband, especially after being married for such a short time," the older woman said.

Leah nodded. "Yes, I am."

They stayed with another farm family to the west of Wilkesboro. It seemed strange to ride through the town without stopping, but at least they would be closer to their destination when they started off tomorrow.

The morning came with dense clouds that made the day seem dark and dreary. A cold wind cut through the travelers and whipped at their clothing, as if it wanted to snatch a piece to warm itself. Leah hoped the wind wouldn't bring worse weather. They started up the mountain at a crawl. The mules strained to pull their heavy load, and Mr. Pickler kept his whip crackling above their heads to urge them on. At least he didn't lash their hides. Leah and Mrs. Pickler walked, and Timothy rode the chestnut bareback.

"Not now," Mr. Pickler said as he stopped the team on the incline, set the brake, and got down. Leah looked and saw a loose strap dangling and knew something had broken or come loose.

"Timothy," Mr. Pickler said, "gather some rocks and scotch the back wheels, and, since we've stopped, let Mrs. Moretz ride her horse."

Mr. Pickler bent over to assess the problem. "It's just loose." He paused. "I can fix it easily enough."

While Mr. Pickler took care of the problem, Timothy did as his father asked. He put Leah's saddle on the chestnut before climbing onto the wagon seat.

Mr. Pickler had just finished with the repair and moved to straighten up when the mule in front of him startled and kicked with both legs. The preacher fell to the road and didn't move. Leah hadn't mounted yet, because Timothy usually helped her. She quickly tied the chestnut to a wheel and rushed to check the injured man.

Blood oozed from his head just above his left ear, and his left arm appeared broken just above the elbow. Mrs. Pickler sobbed loudly and sounded almost hysterical.

"Find me two sticks or something I can use for splints," Leah told the distraught woman. "I'll also need long strips of cloth to wrap his arm and a compress for his head."

Mrs. Pickler came back with her hands full of the requested items. She'd stopped crying as she tried to help.

"You clean around his head wound as I set this arm," Leah told her. As Mrs. Pickler washed the wound, Leah saw the gash wasn't deep, so it should stop bleeding soon. She had Mrs. Pickler hold a clean, damp, cold cloth over the head injury and apply pressure, while Leah tied the splints in place and wrapped the upper arm in the bandages. She also wrapped a cord around his arm and body to strap it tightly, so it wouldn't dangle. She could fix him a sling when he recovered some. By the time Leah had finished, the gash had already stopped bleeding.

Leah worried more about his head injury. Since he was unconscious, she couldn't tell how serious it might be. There could be internal bleeding, and she wished Dr. Moretz were here.

Timothy hurried to his father's side. "What can I do to help?"

"I'll need your help to try to get him in the wagon," Leah told him. "Can we get him in the wagon? Is there room to lay him down back there?"

"I'll make room," Mrs. Pickler said. The woman threw several things out of the wagon and rearranged some others.

Leah took the injured side. She locked her hands underneath Mr. Picker's armpit, being careful not to disturb the broken arm. She told Mrs. Pickler to do the same on the other side. She sent Timothy to the back of the wagon.

Mr. Pickler wasn't a big man, but the dead weight made it extremely difficult to handle him. They somehow managed to drag the unconscious man to the back of the wagon.

Timothy reached down and grabbed the back of his father's shirt and coat and helped as the woman pulled upward. They managed to get the man pulled and pushed onto the back flap. Timothy then pulled him on in while Leah and Mrs. Pickler picked up his feet and legs to help.

"It's a good thing you are a hefty, strong lad," Leah told Timothy. "Now, can you drive the team?"

"Yes, ma'am."

They made it up the mountain to Deep Gap with Mrs. Pickler walking, Leah riding, and Timothy driving the wagon. Leah had him stop so she could check on Mr. Pickler when they'd finished the climb. There seemed no change, but at least his head had not started bleeding again.

Leah turned to Mrs. Pickler. "What are your plans?"

"We'll take him to my brother's house in Sugar Grove. You can spend the night with us, and someone will escort you home tomorrow. I'm not sure how much room there'll be at the house, but we can make do for one night."

"We'll see," Leah said. It would be late afternoon by the time they got to Boone, and she was worried about darkness falling before she got to the farm, but she really wanted to go on home. She yearned to spend the night in her husband's arms.

Just before they reached Boone, Mr. Pickler began to gain consciousness. They stopped the wagon. He seemed addled, but he recognized them.

"Just stay where you are," Leah told him when he tried to rise. "You'll need to take it easy for a while."

"I'll see that he does."

"Timothy, could I buy a set of your clothes, including your hat?"

"Yes, ma'am."

"You'll do no such thing," Mrs. Pickler said, taken aback.

"Mrs. Pickler, please understand. I really need to get back home, and I don't want to impose on your brother. I can dress as a teenage boy, and no one will know the difference. I'm sure I won't even meet anyone on the way up. Put yourself in my place, and you'll understand."

"Well, it's most unconventional, and I'm sure Dr. Moretz would never allow it."

"I'm not so sure about that. He knows me well and knows I can be independent and self-sufficient."

"I still don't like it, but you are a grown, married woman. I can't stop you, but we'll give you the clothes. If it wasn't for you, we'd more than likely still be stranded on the mountain, and my husband might be dead now. Give her your heaviest coat, too, Timothy. Your lighter one will do you no farther than we have to go."

"Get her the saddle from the front of the wagon, too," Mr. Pickler told them. "She won't want to draw attention by using a sidesaddle."

Leah hid behind the wagon and changed clothes. She tied a wool scarf around her head and hat. She knew the men did that in cold, windy weather, and it helped hide her hair, although she'd tucked most of it beneath the hat.

Timothy had changed saddles for her and tied on her travel bag. She mounted like a man in pants for the first time, and no one needed to help her. She guessed she had finally gotten her wish.

She waved good-bye and hurried on her way. She needed to at least make it up the mountain before dark. She hoped it would be a clear night with a full moon, but that didn't look likely. The wind had blown in thick clouds, which threatened precipitation.

She didn't have to go far down King Street or into the center of town. She entered the east side, and turned south. Some men stared at her, trying to figure out who she was, but most of them gave a friendly wave. She waved back. She'd found a pair of Timothy's leather gloves in his coat pocket, and she put them on over her knitted ones. Layers would help on a day like this.

The horse made better time than the wagon had, and Leah kept him at a canter. When she made the turn to head up the mountain, she had no idea what time it might be. The farther the horse climbed up the mountain, the colder it became. Even with her heavy clothing and several layers, her feet, legs, hands, and face felt frozen. She let the horse take the mountain at the pace he wanted.

As they got over the steepest incline, snow began to fall. The flakes began as what Granny Em called 'blow snow,' but they soon became as large as the neck feathers on a chicken. As darkness began to fall and the blizzard intensified, Leah couldn't see the road or where she was going.

She gave the chestnut its lead and prayed the horse knew where to go. At least he trotted forward, as if he had a destination in mind.

Leah saw the glow from the candles and fireplace before she could see the house. She slid out of the saddle in the side yard, and led the chestnut. There was also a glow coming from the barn. Surely Luke wasn't in the barn after dark on a night like tonight. From the dim glow, Leah saw a four-legged shadow slowly head toward the barn. The chestnut must have seen it, too, because he pulled back and whinnied in alarm.

Some creature lurked about the barn. Knowing Luke always kept a rifle by the larder door, Leah ran and retrieved the gun. She turned to see Luke head toward her. She could barely make him out through the heavy snow, but the animal had him within its sight. Leah aimed the rifle. She suddenly felt weak and shaky as she considered how close the animal crouched to Luke. What if she missed and hit Luke by accident? She clutched the rifle tighter and tried to dispel such thoughts. She needed to fire soon, or the beast would be on top of him, and then she wouldn't be able to do any more than watch his death. *Lord, help my hand be steady and my aim be true.*

———————————————

Luke had been in the barn trying to help a cow birth a calf. It would be hard to get the baby through the winter, unless it turned out to be a hardy little thing. He heard a horse whinny, and he went out to see what was going on. He saw a small figure of a man, but he couldn't see who it was through the night and snow, especially with the wind whipping the snow in his eyes.

The man raised a rifle and aimed. Luke stopped. Who would be out on a night like this, and why was he about to shoot Luke? Luke started to call out, when a shot exploded, and his heart stopped for a split second. He heard a thud and looked to see a mountain lion on the ground not ten feet from him.

He looked up and saw Granny Em open the larder door and look out. He started to thank the man for saving him, only to see what now looked to be a teenage lad running straight at him. This was crazy. He almost started to turn and run himself, but the lad ran so fast, his hat and scarf fell off, and long hair flowed out.

Leah? Had he imagined her so many times he was seeing her now in this boy? The racing figure hit him with such force, he had to spread his legs to steady himself and keep from falling. Arms went around him. "Luke, oh Luke," a familiar voice cried.

How many times had he heard that voice call to him at night, only to feel for her, and she wasn't there? He wrapped his arms around her, and hugged her tightly. He didn't know why she came dressed as a boy in the middle of a snowstorm after dark. She'd even saved him from a mountain lion, but here she was, unharmed. He thanked God she was in his arms where she belonged. He could find out about all the rest later. He put his lips on hers and felt her passionate response. His wife was home!

Author's Note

All my main characters in *Sown in Dark Soil* are imaginary. The towns and some of the most minor characters are real, however. Reverend Pharr really served at the Wilkesboro Presbyterian Church, and Dameron did build it and the town's Episcopal Church. Faculty and students from the Valle Crucis Seminary also walked to Wilkesboro for its dedication. The Siamese twins, Eng and Chang Bunker, lived in Wilkes County, as well as Tom Dula (pronounced "Dooley"), whose hanging for murder after the Civil War became controversial. Sheriff Horton is mentioned and was the sheriff in Watauga County. I've researched as thoroughly as I could and have tried to make the novel as realistic as possible. I hope you enjoyed the effort.

For more information about
Janice Cole Hopkins
&
Sown in Dark Soil
please visit:

www.JaniceColeHopkins.com
wandrnlady@aol.com
@J_C_Hopkins
www.facebook.com/JaniceColeHopkins

For more information about
AMBASSADOR INTERNATIONAL
please visit:

www.ambassador-international.com
@AmbassadorIntl
www.facebook.com/AmbassadorIntl

Made in United States
North Haven, CT
10 March 2023

33878289R00166